"You taste like champagne," she murmured, leaning her head back and looking up at him from within the circle of his arms.

He laughed huskily. She could feel the suggestion of movement in his chest, even in the taut muscles of his stomach. "Let me guess," he said. "Krug Collection 1973?"

Jane nodded. Then she wet her lips with her tongue and drew in a deep breath. "What do I taste like?" She'd never asked a man that kind of leading question before.

"Like no one else," he told her.

She laughed. It was a gigolo's line. She didn't believe him, but she wanted to.

"You taste of sweetness and sadness, innocence and seduction," Jake said, lowering his head and kissing her again.

It wasn't the kiss of an inexperienced man. There was no hesitation on his part, no lack of self-confidence. His lips were neither too hard nor too soft, not too gentle or too demanding. They were, however, unabashedly curious about her, blatantly interested, sexually hungry.

It wasn't the kiss of a man on the make. He didn't grind his lips against hers. He didn't try to thrust his tongue into her mouth and halfway down her throat. There was no indication that it was an act. He wasn't pretending passion.

The passion was real.

The
PARADISE
MAN

SUZANNE
SIMMONS

St. Martin's Paperbacks

THE PARADISE MAN

Copyright © 1997 by Suzanne Simmons Guntrum.

All rights reserved. No part of this book may be used or reproduced in any manner whatsoever without written permission except in the case of brief quotations embodied in critical articles or reviews. For information address St. Martin's Press, 175 Fifth Avenue, New York, NY 10010.

ISBN: 0-312-95633-9

Printed in the United States of America

St. Martin's Paperbacks edition/August 1997

St. Martin's Paperbacks are published by St. Martin's Press, 175 Fifth Avenue, New York, NY 10010.

10 9 8 7 6 5 4 3 2 1

This one is for Jennifer Enderlin:
editor, friend, kindred spirit.

"I lived on . . . full of sea dreams and in anticipation of strange islands and adventures."

—Robert Louis Stevenson, *Treasure Island*

chapter*One*

Old money.

She reeked of it.

Nothing ostentatious, of course. The understated designer dress with a silk scarf casually draped over one shoulder. French. Very soignée. Very expensive. Italian shoes; probably Ferragamo. Handbag, American; definitely Ghurka. Just the right touch of gold at her ears, her throat, her wrist. A subtle perfume that wafted past his nostrils: light, airy, elusive, with a hint of sandalwood. It was an unfamiliar fragrance; no doubt a private blend.

Yup, old money. *Very* old money. And a lot of it, if his was any guess.

Jake Hollister leaned back against the railing of the island ferry, crossed one tanned forearm over the other and watched the young woman from behind dark aviator sunglasses.

She was tall, lithe yet shapely. Her hair was barely visible beneath the wide-brimmed hat—also French, also designer—but the glimpse he caught revealed it to be light brown and softly wavy.

Her features were obscured by the hat and the oversize sunglasses she was wearing. Her neck was long, slender, ballerinalike. Her legs seemed to go on forever, and her ankles were fine-boned. She made him think of a thoroughbred racehorse.

Every now and then her voice carried to him: It was low, a little husky, educated, a cultured blend of the East Coast and Europe. He was willing to wager that she'd spent a year at the Sorbonne, perhaps even longer at Oxford or Cambridge.

What in the hell was a woman like *that* doing on a ferry bound for Paradise?

Jake rubbed the three-day beard on his chin. To get the right answer, you first had to ask the right question. Maybe he should be asking: What in the hell was *he* doing on a ferry bound for Paradise?

But Jake Hollister already knew the answer to that question. He had arrived on Paradise nearly a year ago for a few weeks of R and R. He'd stayed for two reasons. In a late-night poker game he had won the deed to the only bar on the island. And, shortly after his arrival, he had become convinced he knew where to look for the Spanish galleon, the *Bella Doña*, and her legendary cargo of gold and silver, pearls and emeralds. The ship and her mother lode had been lost in a hurricane on the way back to Europe from South America in 1692. There were those who believed the *Bella Doña* and her rich cargo were strewn across miles of ocean floor.

Jake believed otherwise.

He wasn't the only one who suspected the *Bella Doña* may have run aground on a sandbar and sunk somewhere in the chain of tiny islands that surrounded Paradise. That theory—and a number of others—had been bouncing around this part of the world for more than three centuries. Most well-organized and well-funded searches for the wreckage, however, were currently concentrated in the waters off Puerto Rico, or even as far north as Hispaniola.

Paradise still got the occasional treasure hunter or tourist, despite the fact the island wasn't the usual *turista* stop. It had been overlooked by the cruise lines in favor of St. Thomas and St. Kitts and the numerous other saints from the Yucatán Peninsula to Barbados, up and down the nearly two thousand miles and literally hundreds of islands loosely referred to as the Caribbean.

So how had the lady ended up here?

Jake shrugged his shoulders, unfolded his arms, and stuffed his hands into the pockets of his jeans. For all he knew, she and her friends had been making the rounds of the chic night spots in Miami or San Juan—clubs with names like Amnesia, Jumbo, and Bang, where the drinking and the dancing went on until four or five every morning—and had somehow wandered off the beaten path.

Maybe they were lost.

Jake shrugged his shoulders again. Or maybe they were just slumming.

He studied the couple with her: A man and a woman who looked enough alike to be brother and sister. He was tall, blond, and wore an expression of polite ennui. She was tall, blonde, and beautiful. They were dressed to the nines. Maybe even the tens. The woman wore diamonds. A little overdone, in Jake's opinion, for midafternoon in the tropics. The rock on her right hand alone was worth more than the average citizen on Paradise earned in a year.

Jake couldn't imagine what these three would want on the island. There was no shopping, no fashionable hotels, no elegant eateries. There was only one small, ramshackle town: Purgatory. One bar: the Mangy Moose. One hotel: the Four Sisters Inn. Hell, there were only *three* sisters! There was some fabulous scenery, but you had to be willing to trek through tropical jungle and forested mountains to see it.

The blond Adonis was talking; pontificating was more like it. Jake heard the word "saddle," then "Giddens." He assumed the conversation was about W&H Giddens of London, "Saddlers to the Queen." The man looked like the type who played polo. He was, from all appearances, wealthy, aristocratic, athletic. While he was talking to the classy dame, his female counterpart removed her dark glasses, turned her head, and glanced at Jake. A seductive smile parted scarlet lips to reveal perfectly straight, perfectly white teeth.

Jake Hollister—John Spencer Hollister III—wasn't a conceited man, but he knew when a woman was flirting with him. Besides, the blonde's approach was pretty direct. He figured it wasn't the first time for her. She certainly wasn't the first woman he'd run into in the past year who had decided that he might be fun—read, a change of pace—from the usual, well-dressed, civilized male.

So far, Jake had declined all offers.

He ran his hand back and forth along the stubble on his jawline. Whatever the attraction, he was pretty sure it *wasn't* sartorial. He was dressed in his island uniform: faded jeans, faded denim shirt with the sleeves rolled up to the elbows, well-worn hiking boots. Sometimes he traded the denim shirt for a T-shirt and the boots for sandals.

Not that jeans and a T-shirt had always been his style. He used to have a closet full of tailored suits, another of fine, white Egyptian cotton shirts, and yet another of nothing but handmade Italian leather shoes. He'd run with the wolves, swum with the sharks, and dressed with the best-dressed in the world of Big Business.

He'd made his first million by thirty. The second had quickly followed on the heels of the first, and it had snowballed from there. Somewhere along the way, the money had ceased to interest Jake as money. It had become a way to keep score. It had been a game and he'd played·it well: with a cool head and a cold heart, with ruthless intent and always, always to win. When he'd been a wheeler-dealer he had been the best. Now he was a beach bum. He was equally good at that.

"*Senor*, would you like to buy *cigarrillos*? Chewing gum? Choc-o-late? Water lemon?" came a singsong voice at his elbow.

Jake turned. A tiny woman of indeterminate years was standing beside him. He could see the varied ethnic background of the island written on her features: they were a unique blend of Spanish, Anglo, Chinese, and Caribe.

"I'll take one of the candy bars," he finally said, digging for loose change.

The island woman nodded her head several times in rapid succession and pointed to the bamboo tray hanging by a pair of men's suspenders around her neck. "Hershey or Almond Joy?"

"Hershey." Jake nudged the sunglasses up the bridge of his nose. "*¿Cuanto es?*" he inquired. Then he repeated in English: "How much?"

"Three dollars, American," came the answer.

Three dollars for a Hershey bar? She was robbing him blind. Nevertheless, Jake peeled off the bills and handed them over. It was, after all, only money.

He unwrapped the candy bar, popped the first piece of

already melting chocolate into his mouth and watched as the native woman moved on to the nearby trio.

"*Senorita*, would you like to buy *cigarrillos*? Chewing gum? Choc-o-late? Water lemon?"

"What is water lemon?" the young woman inquired in that distinctly cultured voice of hers.

A large, egg-shaped berry was held up for her inspection. "Water lemon. Also called *pasion fruta*."

"Passion fruit, you say." The sophisticated man laughed in the back of his throat.

"It is not that kind of passion, *senor*," the diminutive woman informed him. "Passion fruit is so named because its flower bears the marks of the crucifixion of our Lord, Jesus Christ."

"In that case, I'll pass," he said, quickly losing interest.

The native woman lingered. "For you, *senorita*," she volunteered, turning to the woman in the hat, apparently trying to see through the barrier of tinted lenses and failing, "I will toss the teeth."

The beautiful blonde interrupted. "Toss *what* teeth?"

"These teeth." One small, brown hand disappeared into a tunic pocket and emerged a moment later with half a dozen elongated, yellowed teeth.

The blonde wrinkled up her nose. "I hate to think where they've been." Still, she inquired, with a kind of grotesque fascination, "What kind of teeth are they?"

"Shark. Mako. Very old." The tiny woman looked back at the slender creature in the haute couture design. "I will tell your fortune, *senorita*, if you will permit me."

"No doubt for a price," interjected their male companion.

"Tell mine, first," insisted his sister.

The fortune-teller turned her attention to the second young woman. With a sigh, she agreed. "If you wish, *senora*."

"It's *senorita*," came the swift rebuttal.

"Perdón, senorita."

The local woman shook the handful of shark's teeth as if they were dice, first by her left ear, then by her right. She closed her eyes and chanted something in a language Jake didn't recognize. He had to admit she put on quite a show.

"Do I need to do anything?" queried her customer.

"Hold out your hand, if you please," came the reply. The shark's teeth were tossed into the outstretched palm. "Do not move *por el momento*." The random arrangement of teeth was studied for perhaps ten or fifteen seconds. Then the woman raised her eyes. "You have a *secreto*, do you not, *senorita*?"

"Everyone has secrets," the blonde said dismissively, her scarlet lips pressed together.

The fortune-teller continued with her prophecy. "All is not what it seems to be."

"Bunch of mumbo jumbo," muttered the man.

" 'A virtuous woman is a crown to her husband,' " was the next piece of sage advice given.

The beautiful blonde put her head back and, shaking her long hair from side to side, laughed lightly. "It seems I must find myself a husband, then."

The clairvoyant concluded with: " 'As a jewel of gold in a swine's snout, so is a fair woman who is without discretion.' "

The man muttered impatiently under his breath, "Damned native nonsense."

"Actually it's not native nonsense," the elegant woman spoke up. "It's Proverbs."

"Whatever it is, it's your turn," her female traveling companion pointed out.

The island seeress went through the identical procedure again. However, this time she took longer to read the shark's teeth. At last she proclaimed: "You seek something. No. You seek some*one*. A man." Wise, aged eyes stared up into a youthful face obscured by a wide-brimmed hat and dark glasses. "You will find him, *senorita*."

"But . . ."

"But there is danger. For it is said, 'Come not between the dragon and its wrath.' " The shark's teeth were gathered up and disappeared once more into a pocket.

"Why don't you give the old lady something for her trouble, Tony," his sibling suggested.

"I don't believe in encouraging this kind of tourist scam, Megs," Tony protested, dropping a single dollar bill onto the bamboo tray.

The third member of their party discreetly pressed a folded bill into the woman's hand. Jake didn't see the denomination, but he was certain it was a damn sight more than Tony had given her. "A little something from me as well," was given by way of an explanation.

"*Muchas gracias, senorita,*" the fortune-teller murmured gratefully before she moved on.

The polo player picked up the conversation where he'd left off a few minutes before. "As I was saying, I played a few chukkers while we were in Newport last summer. Megs and I were visiting friends we'd made in Portofino several years ago. Perhaps you know the Clarkes."

"I'm afraid I don't."

The man tried again. "We also spent some time with Marilyn Washborne."

"I've heard the name, of course, but I don't know Mrs.

Washborne personally." Then the young woman added, "My former college roommate has a house in Newport."

"I wonder if Megs and I have met her."

There was a slight hesitation in the cultured voice. "Her name is Torey Storm."

"We were introduced to Victoria Storm," the sister chimed in. "She has that big house by the shore." Scarlet nails drummed rhythmically against scarlet lips. "What's it called? Storm . . . something."

"Storm Point."

"That's it. Storm Point. We went to a party there one evening. Remember, Tony?" The blonde turned from the woman to her brother and back again. "Your friend has a stunning house."

"Yes, she does."

"Tony and I adored Newport," gushed Megs. "Do you get there often?"

"I haven't been to Newport in three or four years," came the admission.

Jake found himself tuning out their conversation and simply watching the young woman in the hat. Her back was to him now. His gaze dropped from her head to her shoulders to her narrow waist, from her waist to her slightly flared hips, and from there down her long, long legs.

Jake Hollister was a sucker for long legs. He always had been. In fact, when he was a younger man they had been his downfall. He'd get caught up in the girl's legs and forget to notice whether there was anything inside the head . . . or the heart.

"The greatest griefs are those we cause ourselves," wrote Sophocles over two thousand years ago.

It was still true today.

Jake blew out his breath expressively. His penchant—

perhaps weakness was a better word—for long legs and high-class women had caused him no end of grief. He had encountered one too many females in his time who were cold, calculating, and pampered. Experience had taught him that class, like beauty, was often only skin deep.

He'd seen this woman's type before. The type born with a silver spoon in her mouth, the kind who spent her life amid luxury the average human being couldn't begin to imagine, the kind who wore a sign around her neck that read: LOOK, BUT DON'T TOUCH.

Crack!

Jake's thoughts were interrupted by a flash of lightning. It was quickly followed by a rumble of thunder and the threat of dark, angry clouds. The wind came up out of nowhere. The blue sea turned gray. Right on schedule, the skies opened, and it began to rain.

Maybe twenty years ago the thatched roof of the red wooden ferry had kept the rain out but not now. Tiny streams soon wended their way through the palm branches. Rainwater plopped, drop by drop, onto the polo player's shoulder.

He brushed at it with his hand and complained to his sister. "I'm getting bloody wet, Megs. Let's go downstairs."

She patted his arm. "If you wish, Tony." Turning to their companion, the blonde inquired: "Won't you come with us?"

"I think I'll stay up here," she said, politely declining their invitation. "I'd like to have a view of the island as we come into shore."

Once she was alone the woman removed her sunglasses—Jake had looped his over his shirt pocket when it had begun to rain—and slipped them into her handbag.

Then she walked to the edge of the ferry, leaned against the railing, and gazed out at the tropical storm.

The rain was coming down in earnest. Jake was willing to bet it wouldn't be more than a minute, two tops, before she changed her mind and joined her friends on the deck below. Instead, to his amazement, the woman reached up, swept off the designer hat and lifted her face toward the sky.

She didn't seem to notice or care that her expensive leather shoes were getting wet. Nor that the rain was soaking the front of her dress and plastering it to her body. Jake could clearly see the outline of her breasts and nipples. His mouth had gone dry and he found himself wiping his palms on the legs of his faded jeans.

For some reason—Jake had a pretty good idea what that reason was; he'd been celibate for more than a year—she made him think of a painting by Sir Edward Poynter that he'd once seen in a London museum: *The Cave of the Storm Nymphs*. It was a classic Victorian view, innocent yet erotic, of young nubile nudes luxuriating in an island cave, swathes of rich silks and brocades spilling from half-open trunks, gold coins and gemstones strewn at their bare feet, ropes of precious pearls draped over alabaster skin, the dark, stormy sea in the background, the mast of a sinking galleon visible above crashing waves that were about to sweep all asunder for the last time.

The Sirens' call.

Jake had heard it. For treasure. For adventure. The unknown. Success. Wealth. Sex.

Damned if he wasn't hearing it now!

As if on cue, the young woman turned and looked directly at him. He had to say something. He opened his mouth. "It rains around here every afternoon at this time. of year."

"It usually snows every afternoon in Buffalo at this time of year," she replied.

"You're from Buffalo?"

"Originally."

"And now?"

The lady hesitated. "Sometimes New York. Sometimes London. Sometimes Paris."

It seemed he had been right. "You're a long way from home," he commented.

"Yes, I am," she agreed. "And you?"

Jake fell silent for a moment. He finally said to her, "I'm a long way from home too."

Then, as quickly as the storm had appeared, it vanished. The lightning and thunder ceased. The rain stopped. The dark clouds rolled on. The sea grew calm, and the sun came out. The ferry chugged around the tip of the smaller outer island and into Preacher's Bay.

Paradise lay straight ahead.

Jake squinted against the blinding sunlight reflected off crystal-clear water and pristine white beaches. He'd seen it a dozen times before, but it still made him pause: lush palm trees and occasional bursts of color provided by bougainvillea and hibiscus, the picturesque wooden dock, the clanging of the bell telling the locals that the ferry was pulling into Purgatory, the tiny town nestled around the waterfront, the great Victorian house on the hill overlooking the bay, the mountains in the distance. Not mountains by Colorado Rockies standards but certainly mountains by Paradise standards.

The crowning touch was the rainbow—that miraculous arc of color between sun and mist—that suddenly formed over the island. He could hear the sharp intake of breath from the young woman. Or maybe he only saw it, pale breasts moving against damp silk.

"Welcome to Paradise," he said with a touch of irony.

"It is paradise," she murmured aloud.

Yup, Jake thought to himself as he eventually disembarked, the sun high overhead, the bay as blue as summer wisteria, it was just another goddamned perfect day in Paradise.

chapter *Two*

"*T*axi?"

The workman on the dock paused halfway through the job of unloading her luggage from the island ferry, straightened, squinted into the bright Caribbean sun, took a red bandana from his pocket, and mopped his brow. Then he wiped the handkerchief back and forth along his nape, stuffed it back into his pants' pocket, and repeated, gold tooth glinting in his mouth, "Taxi?"

Jane Bennett searched her vocabulary for the Spanish equivalent. "*Coche de alquiler.*"

"*Coche de* what?"

The man obviously spoke little if any Spanish. Jane tried again in English. "Could you please tell me where I can get a taxi cab, Mister . . . ?"

"The name is Tommy. Tommy Bahama," he informed her.

Jane opened her handbag, took out her sunglasses and slipped them on. In that case: "Could you please tell me where I can get a taxi cab, Mr. Bahama?"

Her luggage—five matching pieces of Ghurka's dis-

tinctive leather-trimmed herringbone design—was lined
up in front of her. "No."

She was taken aback. "Why not?"

He didn't waste any time on an explanation. "No
taxis."

"I can see there aren't any along the dock." Although
she had assumed there would be at least one or two driv-
ers for hire waiting to meet the afternoon ferry.

"No taxis on Paradise," he announced.

Jane Bennett reached the end of her patience. It was
one thing to have to put up with Megs and Tony St. Cyr
on the ferry ride from the Virgin Islands. She was used
to dealing with difficult and demanding people, she reminded herself, although she usually tried to draw the
line at *boring* people. It was quite another thing to be
informed that there was no transportation on the island.

"How do the locals get around Paradise?" she asked,
exasperated.

The workman mopped his face again. "Mostly on
foot."

There wasn't any way she could walk *and* carry five
pieces of luggage. "And . . . ?"

He went on. "Sometimes by bicycle. Sometimes by
donkey."

A bicycle she might manage sans suitcases, but Jane
Bennett had no intentions, under any circumstances, of
riding on the back of a donkey.

Tommy Bahama's expression was devoid of curiosity.
"Where are you going?"

"I have a reservation at the Four Sisters Inn."

There was a short pause. "In that case, the boss will
drive you in his Jeep."

At last they were getting somewhere. With a genuine

sense of relief, Jane inquired: "Where can I find the boss?"

"At the Mangy Moose."

"And where is the Mangy Moose?"

The man pointed down the nearly deserted street. There was a solitary figure pushing a handcart piled high with coconuts, two young children playing in the sand beneath a clump of palm trees, and a scraggy dog sniffing its way from door to door. "Just past the general store. You can't miss it," he claimed.

"Thank you." Jane dug into her handbag again and took out a ten-dollar bill.

Before she could ask for any further assistance with her luggage, Tommy Bahama plucked the money from her fingertips, mumbled, "Thanks, lady," and something about unloading the boss's supplies, and promptly vanished.

Jane Bennett—Cordelia Jane Bennett according to her birth certificate and the passport securely tucked among her travel documents—stood on the weathered dock, in the midday sun, surrounded by her belongings. She was a thousand miles from nowhere, not a taxi in sight and none expected.

She adjusted the brim of her wide-brimmed hat, rearranged the silk scarf draped around her neck—it concealed the somewhat wrinkled condition of the front of her dress—and permitted herself a small sigh. "Now what in the world am I supposed to do?"

"Lost?" came a deep, masculine voice from behind her.

Jane turned. It was the man who had spoken to her on the ferry; the one who apparently didn't stand close enough to his razor. She'd seen his type before, of course: the type who was all brawn and no brains; the kind who spent his life drifting from one beach to the next, one blonde to the next; the kind who used his rugged good looks and muscular physique to attract every female in the vicinity.

There were men like him, *males* like him—some were no more than mere boys—from Manhattan Beach to Palm Beach, from Cancun to the Côte d'Azur. They went by many names. Beach bum. Gigolo. Fancy man.

"Not lost," she finally answered. "Stranded."

He took a step toward her. "What happened to your friends?"

"You mean the St. Cyrs?"

Broad shoulders were raised and lowered in an almost imperceptible movement. "The polo player and his sister."

"Megs and Tony St. Cyr." Jane was tempted to set the record straight: the St. Cyrs were not her friends. But it really wasn't any of this man's business. *She* wasn't any of his business. "They were met by their host and driven off in a vintage Rolls Royce."

"They're staying at the Hacienda." It was a statement of fact, not a question.

"Yes."

"You aren't?"

"I'm not."

"Where are you headed?"

"The Mangy Moose."

He raised his hand and pointed in the same direction that the dock worker had. "The Mangy Moose is just beyond Maxwell's General Store. You can't miss it."

"So I've been told." Jane took in a slow, resigned breath. This man was the most likely candidate for the job she needed done. In fact, with the disappearance of Tommy Bahama, he became the only candidate. She had to ask him. She had no choice. She must simply think of it as the means to an end. "I'd appreciate some help with my bags." Quickly adding: "I'll pay you."

The handsome beach bum stared at her from behind his dark aviator sunglasses. "Will you?"

Jane felt the heat of embarrassment rise up her neck and spread onto her cheeks. She swallowed with a degree of difficulty. "Yes."

One dark eyebrow was arched in a sardonic fashion. "How much?"

The tip of her tongue was suddenly tied in a small knot. "Twenty dollars."

Deeply tanned hands—Jane couldn't help but notice that the hair on the muscular forearms had been bleached golden brown by the sun—were planted on lean, blue-jeaned hips. "Is all of this yours?" he asked, indicating the row of suitcases neatly arranged on the dock.

"It is."

He seemed amused. "Staying long?"

"Possibly." She was going to stay for as long as it took. It could be a week. It could be a month. The Mayfair sisters had promised that she could have the bungalow indefinitely.

The man apparently made up his mind. "Okay. I'll help you out," he said, brushing past her.

"Thank you." Jane knew she sounded relieved. She *was* relieved. "I'll take the train case and the smaller carry-on, if you think you can manage the other bags."

"I think I can manage." He tucked one suitcase under his arm, picked up the other two in his hands and started off down the street in the direction of the Mangy Moose.

Jane quickly grabbed what remained on the dock and hurried after him, skirting around first a mud puddle left behind by the recent rain and then several scrawny chickens pecking in the dirt.

Without slackening his pace, the man tossed back over his shoulder, "What do you have in here?" He obviously meant the largest of her suitcases. "Rocks?"

Jane's reply was deliberately nonchalant. "Just a book or two."

"Feels like an entire set of encyclopedias," he grumbled, almost good-naturedly.

Actually it was her research on the Spanish galleon, *Bella Doña*, including a copy of the ship's manifest that had been translated from the original Spanish. But he didn't need to know that.

Jane felt a trickle of perspiration start between her shoulder blades, run down her back, and settle in the small indentation at the base of her spine. "It's warm," she commented.

"No wind."

A minute later: "I don't see many people."

"The locals are too smart to be out in the heat of the day. They're taking their *siestas*."

That was the extent of the conversation between them until they reached their destination. It was a nondescript wooden building that had once been fire-engine red. That was before the sun and the wind and the salt spray had weathered the paint to a dull salmon color. There were four wooden steps leading up to a covered porch and a small plaque that read: THE MANGY MOOSE.

Her suitcases were deposited by the front door.

Jane held out a twenty-dollar bill. "Thank you."

The man raised his hands, palms up, and backed away. "This one's on the house."

"But I promised to pay you for your trouble," she insisted. "After all, there were three suitcases and you said yourself they were heavy.'' She decided to try a slightly different tack with him. ''I've always believed in paying an honest wage for honest work.'' Besides, he looked like he could use the money.

The man still refused. ''This is Paradise, lady. Not the St. Regis in New York. In the future, five dollars is a more than generous tip by island standards.'' He gave her a meaning-filled smile. ''You wouldn't want to give a man the wrong idea.''

Jane drew a blank. ''The wrong idea?''

It was spelled out for her. ''By overpaying him. He might wonder exactly what you were hiring him to do.''

Jane Bennett's mouth opened and then closed again. She was usually very quick on her feet, but for once she couldn't think of a single clever retort.

Maybe it was the heat.

Or maybe it was the man.

There was something about him. Something she couldn't quite put her finger on. He gave every appearance of being nothing more than a drifter, but Jane had learned a long time ago that appearances could be deceptive.

''Your luggage will be perfectly safe out here.'' He gave her an offhand salute. *''Adios.''*

Jane Bennett took a deep breath and pushed open the swinging doors of the Mangy Moose. As soon as she stepped inside the saloon, the temperature dropped twenty degrees.

Dark glasses weren't needed. She slipped hers off, gave her eyes half a minute to adjust to the interior light, and then took a good look around.

Appearances *were* deceptive.

The inside of the Mangy Moose was all stained wood, polished brass, and shiny copper. The ceiling was hammered tin; it appeared to be the original. An ornate, turn-of-the-century mirror hung behind the bar. There was an antique pinball machine against one wall and a vintage jukebox against another.

Jane could hear the quiet swoosh of the ceiling fans overhead, and somewhere in the background Randy Travis was singing about how it was just a matter of time.

Three men were seated at a table in the far corner. They were speaking in low voices and drinking beer from bottles. The man behind the bar appeared to be washing glassware, and a young woman was intently polishing the brass railing around the countertop.

"Excuse me," Jane said, approaching her. *"Buenas tardes."*

The girl looked up. *"Buenas tardes, senorita."*

"I'm looking for someone."

"Who is it you seek?"

"The boss."

"El patrón?"

"Yes. *El patrón*. Where can I find him, please?"

The girl pointed behind Jane. "He is just coming in the door now, *senorita*."

She turned her head. It was him, of course. The man from the ferry; the beach bum who had lugged her suitcases all the way from the dock to the Mangy Moose.

Jane found her voice. "You're the boss?"

The man nodded and sauntered toward her. "The name is Jake Hollister."

chapter *Three*

"El patrón?"

Jake had seen that expression before: feminine dismay, quickly followed by disbelief, possibly even incredulity. It wasn't the first time. Chances are it wouldn't be the last.

"Calling me *el patrón* is Rosey's idea of a joke." He glanced down at the grinning girl who was busily polishing brass. "However, I do own the place."

Such as it was.

"Why didn't you tell me?" It sounded more like an accusation to Jake than a question.

"You didn't ask." He raised an eyebrow. "What can I do for you, Ms. . . . ?"

"Bennett. Jane Bennett."

"What can I do for you, Ms. Jane Bennett from Buffalo?"

"The man who unloaded my luggage at the dock told me to ask for the boss."

"Tommy Bahama?"

The young woman nodded, took out a tissue, and delicately dabbed at her upper lip. "I need transportation to the Four Sisters Inn. I understand you have a Jeep.''

''I do.'' So this was the inn's newest guest. Rachel Mayfair had mentioned an impending arrival to him several days ago, but frankly Jake had forgotten about it until now.

''I've been traveling nonstop since my plane left Heathrow at six o'clock yesterday morning, Mr. Hollister. I'm tired and I'm hot and my sense of humor deserted me somewhere in the middle of the San Juan airport last night. So if you don't mind, I would like to leave for the Four Sisters Inn as soon as possible,'' Jane Bennett informed him politely but firmly.

This was a woman who was used to getting her own way. Jake didn't doubt that for a second.

He nonchalantly hooked a thumb through the belt loop of his jeans. ''The Jeep's out back.''

''My luggage is on your front porch,'' the lady reminded him unnecessarily.

''I'll bring the Jeep around to the front.''

''Thank you,'' she said a shade haughtily.

''It'll be a few minutes. I have to make sure my supplies are being inventoried. Would you care for a cold drink?''

''No, thank you,'' she said, sitting down on the nearest chair, smoothing out a wrinkle in her skirt and crossing one long, shapely leg over the other. ''I'll wait here.''

''I'll honk.''

Jake seriously doubted if this woman had ever responded to a car's horn before in her life. But after he'd loaded her luggage into the back of the Jeep and had secured it with a length of rope, he reached in the driver's side and leaned on the horn.

Jane Bennett emerged through the swinging doors of the Mangy Moose, took one look at the beat-up, 1980-

model Wrangler with no top, no door handle on the passenger's side and a cracked windshield—it also had more than one hundred thousand miles on the odometer—and said, with a definite flair, Jake thought, for understatement, "It's not quite what I'd expected."

He helped her into the front seat—God, she had great legs!—came around the back of the vehicle, slid behind the wheel and, patting the steering wheel, announced, "The yuppie vehicle of choice stateside, or so I'm told."

"Are you a yuppie, Mr. Hollister?" she asked, fanning herself with a road map of Oregon that had been stashed in the side pocket of the door. The map had come gratis with the Jeep.

"Why don't you call me Jake?"

"Are you a yuppie, Jake?"

"Not the last time I checked." A minute later: "How about you, Ms. Bennett?"

"Just plain Jane."

Anything but plain Jane. "How about you, Jane?"

"I don't believe I qualify either."

"Better hold onto your hat," Jake warned her as he made a U-turn in the middle of Purgatory's main street . . . Purgatory's *only* street.

"Where is the inn?" she asked him as the front left wheel of the Wrangler sprayed through a mud puddle.

He pointed to the large, white, Victorian house overlooking the bay. "There."

They were out of town and starting up the winding hillside road before either spoke again.

It was Jake who decided to break the silence. "What do you know about Paradise?"

" 'A heavenly paradise is that place where roses and white lilies grow,' " she quoted.

"We have both roses and lilies on the island, so this

must be the right place," he said with a facsimile of a smile. "But I meant what do you know about the history of the island?"

"Very little, I'm afraid."

"Then let me enlighten you."

"I was also afraid you were going to say that," she quipped.

Apparently Jane Bennett's sense of humor hadn't deserted her altogether.

"The island was pretty much uninhabited until about a hundred years ago," Jake began. "The first prominent family to settle here was the Lovatos. They started a sugar cane plantation on the far southern tip of Paradise, which is predominantly flat, fertile land."

"Don't tell me. The Lovatos eventually built a house which today is called the—"

"Hacienda. It's where your friends are staying."

"I was introduced to the St. Cyrs as we boarded the ferry in Charlotte Amalie this morning," she informed him.

"In that case, it's where your acquaintances are staying." Jake ducked his head as the Jeep skirted past a low-hanging vine. "Anyway, along with the Lovatos, came a handful of Spanish, Caribe, and Chinese workers. They were originally imported to build roads and cut sugarcane. Some eventually left the island; others stayed and started their own small businesses."

"I believe I met an island woman on the ferry," the elegant creature beside him commented.

"The fortune-teller?"

"Yes."

Jake ran his tongue along his bottom lip; he could almost taste the Hershey's chocolate on his mouth. "Anyway, the second prominent family to arrive on the island—some forty years later—was the Mayfairs: the Reverend Ezekiel Mayfair, his Southern-belle wife, Lareina, and their four young daughters.''

''Hence, the Four Sisters Inn,'' Jane Bennett concluded.

''Exactly.''

''Why hasn't the island ever been developed for tourism?'' It was a logical question.

Jake pulled over to the side of the road and pointed to the stretch of pristine white sand and azure water directly below them. ''That is some of the most beautiful, unspoiled beach in the entire Caribbean. It's also owned and controlled by the Mayfair sisters.''

''Who apparently aren't interested in selling or leasing it,'' his passenger correctly surmised.

Jake nodded. ''So no hotels. No posh resorts. No eighteen-hole golf courses. No tourists.''

Jane Bennett inclined her head slightly. ''If the Mayfairs did agree to sell or lease their land to the developers, Paradise would very quickly become like a hundred other islands in the Caribbean.''

''Yup.''

She drew a deep breath and let it out slowly. ''Maybe it's just as well they haven't, then.''

''Maybe it is just as well.''

''Paradise would be lost.''

His mouth curved humorlessly. ''And never regained.''

It was a minute or two before his companion asked: ''How long have you been on Paradise?''

''About a year.''

She seemed genuinely curious. ''What brought you here, Jake?''

He was circumspect. ''Let's just say a business deal

went sour. I ended up on this particular island more or less by accident.'' Now it was his turn. ''What brought you to Paradise, Jane?''

''I wanted—needed—a vacation.''

He rubbed his hand back and forth along his chin. ''I would have thought St. Lucia or St. Thomas or even Barbados would have been more your style.''

''I wanted someplace different. Someplace secluded. Someplace where I wouldn't run into someone I knew every time I turned around,'' she said, taking off her sunglasses and looking at him.

For the first time Jake saw her eyes clearly. He was tempted to call them brown, but their color was far more complex than simple brown. They were the illusive shades of the agate: cinnamon, saffron, and beryl-green, with a hint of gold and a streak of blue so dark that it bordered on black. He could see the intelligence in Jane Bennett's eyes, and the curiosity, and something akin to . . . sensuality.

There was far more to this woman than met the eye. Although there was nothing wrong with what met the eye either, Jake decided.

''So you, more or less, ended up here by accident as well,'' he prompted.

She fingered the gold watch on her wrist. He could tell it was expensive and Swiss and no doubt carried the name of Piguet or Constantin. ''More or less.''

The lady was lying.

It was a particular talent of his: knowing when someone was lying. Jake Hollister couldn't explain how he knew, he just did. It had been one of his most potent weapons as a businessman. It was certainly one of the reasons he had been so successful.

He put the Jeep into gear, pulled back onto the dirt road, and headed for the inn.

"Tell me about the Mayfair sisters," his passenger urged.

Jake laughed in the back of his throat. "And ruin the surprise?" No way.

The creature that fluttered down the front steps of the stately Victorian house and across the expanse of lush, green lawn toward them reminded Jane of a pink butterfly. Indeed, the woman was a vision in pink from the bow in her bouffant hair to the flower pinned at her waist to the satin slippers on her feet. Her hair was white, her figure plump, her face round and unlined.

A pink organza fan, trimmed in delicate pink lace, was produced from somewhere on the creature's person— Jane didn't see exactly where—and was wafted in front of an ample bosom.

"I do declare," came a voice softened by the remnants of a Southern accent, "this must be Miss Bennett."

Jake Hollister was surprisingly solicitous. "It is, Miss Naomi. May I do the honors?"

"You may indeed, young man."

"Miss Naomi Mayfair, may I present Miss Jane Bennett. Miss Bennett, Miss Mayfair."

"Please call me Miss Naomi. Everyone does."

"Then I will too." For a moment Jane felt as if she should curtsy. "You must call me Jane."

"Oh dear." The fan hovered in midair. "Well, yes, I suppose I must." The fan began to move again, faster, in an almost agitated manner. "Perhaps in a day or two." The woman was visibly flustered. "I should let my sisters know that you're here."

"No need to fuss, Naomi," came a deep, calm, androgynous voice. "I heard the Jeep pull into the driveway."

The second woman was the opposite of the first. She was tall, angular, no-nonsense, dressed in a pair of serviceable trousers and a man's shirt, garden shears in one hand, a bunch of stalwart flowers in the other. She was wearing the equivalent of English "wellies" on her feet; they were covered with mud and bits of wet grass and other plant debris.

The gardening shears were deposited into a deep pocket and the flowers were transferred to the opposite hand before the newcomer grasped Jane's hand and gave it a vigorous pump. "You must be our guest," she said in greeting.

"I am."

"I'm Esther Mayfair."

"Miss Mayfair."

The woman spoke to Jake Hollister. "You're back."

"I'm back."

"How was your trip?"

"Uneventful."

"I see you found Miss Bennett all right."

"I did. Or, I should say, she found me." Jake looked around. "Where's Miss Rachel?"

"I'm right here," came a lilting soprano from behind them.

Jane turned her head. Rachel Mayfair was still an attractive woman, although her age was somewhere between a well-preserved seventy and seventy-five. She wasn't tall and she wasn't short. She wasn't thin and she wasn't fat. She moved like someone of half her years, but her hair was definitely more salt than pepper. The lines on her face attested to a life that had experienced its share of sorrows.

Her handshake was firm but friendly. "I'm Rachel Mayfair. I see you've met my sisters. Welcome to Paradise, Miss Bennett, and to the Four Sisters Inn."

It was on the tip of Jane's tongue to inquire why there were only three sisters but something held her back.

"We mustn't keep Miss Bennett standing out here on the front lawn," scolded Miss Naomi, with a click of her tongue and with more than a hint of disapproval. "It isn't seemly."

"Then we'll go inside directly." Her eldest sister smoothed over the moment.

Naomi Mayfair snapped her pink organza fan shut, looked up at the sunlight as it filtered through the treetops overhead, shaded her eyes for a moment with a plump, pink hand, and remarked, "I do believe it's nearly teatime." Then she added: "I've baked a special lemon cake in honor of Miss Bennett's arrival."

Rachel Mayfair extended an invitation. "Won't you join us for tea and cake, Jake?"

"I'm afraid I can't today. Supplies for the Mangy Moose came in on the afternoon ferry. I've got to get back to business."

Miss Naomi sighed in a most ladylike fashion. "What a pity. I know how much you favor my lemon cake too."

Rachel reached out and patted his arm reassuringly. "Don't worry. We'll see that a piece or two is saved for you."

Esther Mayfair thrust the handful of flowers at her sibling. "Take these inside, will you, sister? The vase is on the kitchen counter. Fill it halfway up to the top with water from the spigot before you add the flowers. I'll arrange them myself after I help Jake with Miss Bennett's luggage."

"We've put you in Delilah," Miss Naomi informed

their guest, fan clasped in one hand, the bouquet of flowers in the other.

Jane was puzzled. "Delilah?"

As they made their way up the front steps, across the old-fashioned wraparound porch and into the vestibule of the grand Victorian house, Rachel Mayfair explained. "Delilah is one of our two rental bungalows. Samson is the other."

"I see." Although Jane wasn't altogether certain that she did see, of course.

"The Book of Judges, Miss Bennett," Naomi Mayfair flung over her shoulder as she disappeared down a long passageway—although the floors of the house were covered with an array of throw rugs, underneath they were wood and polished to a rich patina—and through a door into what Jane assumed was the kitchen.

"Our father was a renowned Virginia orator turned preacher," Miss Rachel said to her. "As a matter of fact, the Reverend Ezekiel Mayfair is still listed in the *Guinness Book of Records* for having preached the longest sermon on the subject of original sin."

Original sin.

Adam and Eve. Temptation. The serpent. The apple. Adam's Fall. Eve's culpability.

Good heavens, Jane Bennett thought to herself as she recalled her own early childhood teachings.

Her hostess laughed good-naturedly. "It was our mother who named the bungalows after the Hebrew strongman, who wreaked havoc among the Philistines, and his mistress and betrayer." Rachel Mayfair entered the parlor, sat down on an authentic horsehair sofa and patted the spot beside her. "I've never been certain," she confessed, "if Mama was serious when she named the bungalows after Samson and Delilah, or if she was only playing a joke on Daddy.''

"Do you enjoy gardening, Miss Bennett?" Esther Mayfair inquired some time later that same afternoon as the four women sat in the formal parlor sipping tea and eating lemon cake.

"I enjoy flowers very much," Jane answered honestly. "Regrettably I've never had the time for gardening."

Miss Naomi balanced her cup and saucer and cake plate on her lap like an expert. "How do you spend your time?"

Jane chose her words with care. "I travel. I do some charity work. And I'm a consultant."

Rachel Mayfair set her teacup down on the rococo table at her elbow and leaned toward Jane. "What kind of consultant, my dear?"

Jane realized the Mayfairs were curious about her. Surely it couldn't hurt to tell them something about herself. She would stick to the truth whenever possible, of course. She'd made that decision long before leaving London for the Caribbean. When the truth wasn't feasible, when she was afraid it would expose her, Jane only hoped the worst sin she would be guilty of was the sin of omission.

"I authenticate antique furniture, silver, objets d'art. My services are offered to private collectors and museums, as well as to the large auction houses like Sotheby's."

"How fascinating," exclaimed Miss Naomi, although it was obvious she had only a limited grasp of what Jane was talking about.

Esther Mayfair was clearly disinterested.

It was Rachel whose eyes lit up with interest. "Do you

mean you can tell if an object is genuine or a counterfeit?''

Jane nodded her head. ''For example, if I were examining a piece of antique English furniture I might ask myself: are all the legs original? Has the hardware been replaced or extensive repairs been made? I thoroughly research the history of its construction and ownership. I may even find the particular piece of furniture portrayed in paintings of the era. In the end, I usually manage to confirm whether or not it's the genuine article.'' Jane took a sip of tepid tea. She decided not to mention that her skill was considered by many to be uncanny. ''I was recently asked by Sotheby's to take a look at a pair of George II 'Peacock' tables. The auction estimate on the pair was almost five hundred thousand dollars.''

''My word!'' Rachel gasped. ''Were they real?''

''Very real and quite magnificent,'' Jane assured her.

''Then you're a kind of detective.''

''I suppose you could say so.''

Without further ado, Esther Mayfair changed the subject. ''I believe your letter said you live in New York City, Miss Bennett.''

''I have a brownstone in New York and a flat in London.''

''I've always wanted to travel and see the world,'' came the admission from Rachel Mayfair. ''I do envy you.''

'' 'From envy, hatred, and malice, and all uncharitableness, Good Lord, deliver us,' '' intoned Miss Naomi.

''Amen.'' Esther helped herself to another piece of cake, popping the entire thing into her mouth at once.

''What made you choose our little island for your holiday, Miss Bennett?''

''I wanted a quiet spot, a place of unspoiled beauty, a

retreat that wasn't teeming with tourists." It was the truth. It simply wasn't *all* of the truth. "Perhaps it was the name of the island that first attracted me: Paradise."

" 'To day shalt thou be with me in Paradise,' Luke 23:43," intoned Miss Naomi again.

Esther swallowed. "Amen."

"No doubt this has been a long, tiring trip for you, Miss Bennett," Rachel suggested.

"It has been."

"Perhaps you'd like to retire to your cottage to unpack and refresh yourself before supper."

"I would like to very much."

"I'll show Miss Bennett the way to Delilah," Esther offered.

"That would be most kind, sister," Rachel said. "If you need anything we haven't thought to provide, please don't hesitate to tell us."

"You've been most gracious. Your tea and cake were delicious, Miss Naomi. The floral arrangements in the house must come from your garden, Miss Mayfair. I don't believe I've ever seen such wonderful flowers. You've all made me feel welcome."

"We have our evening meal at seven in the dining room, but perhaps for tonight you would prefer a tray brought to your bungalow?" Rachel said at the front door of the great Victorian house.

"I am rather tired."

"Then I'll have Benjamin leave a tray on the screened-in front porch. In case you decide to take a lie-down."

"Thank you, Miss Rachel."

"This way, Miss Bennett," said Esther Mayfair as she took off across the green lawn with long-legged strides.

*　　*　　*

Rachel Mayfair chewed on her bottom lip in an uncharacteristic and nervous fashion as she watched the elegant Miss Bennett and her sister, Esther, walk toward the rental cottages.

Naomi voiced aloud the question on both their minds. "I wonder who she is."

"I don't know."

Eyes of vivid blue—far too often they were vague of thought and intent—followed the retreating figures. "Perhaps Miss Jane Bennett is exactly who and what she appears to be."

"Perhaps."

They stood side-by-side for another minute or two. Then Naomi remarked, "Although appearances can sometimes be deceptive, can't they?"

Rachel Mayfair noticed her hands were trembling slightly as she opened the screen door and waited for her younger sister to proceed her into the house where they had lived together nearly all their lives. "Yes, my dear, I'm afraid they can be."

chapter*Four*

*I*t was a perfect night on Paradise.

Her first night on Paradise, Jane thought to herself as she strolled along the deserted beach.

The temperature was a balmy eighty degrees. The breeze off the Caribbean was no more than a soft caress against her skin. The sand was small-grained, silky to the touch and washed clean by the sea; it was still warm from the day's heat.

The scents in the air were those of the wild orchids growing along the embankment behind her, the deep purple bougainvillea and the bright yellow hibiscus that cascaded over a nearby stone wall, and the coconut palms lining the beach between land and sea.

Jane picked a spot at random, lowered her mesh bag to the ground, and went to stand at the water's edge. She looked out across the inlet toward Preacher's Bay. There was an occasional flicker of light in the distance: perhaps from a house in Purgatory, a lantern swinging on a fisherman's boat, or a tropical firefly.

The velvet blue skies overhead were punctuated with the lights of thousands of stars. A sliver of moon was on the rise, casting just enough silvery glow to illuminate her way.

Waves washed up onto shore, lapping gently at her feet. The caftan she had slipped over her head upon awakening billowed around her ankles. The hem was getting wet. She didn't care.

"So this is your precious Paradise, Charlie," she whispered. "Blue sky. Blue water. White sand. The moon and the stars. Tropical flowers, palm trees, and seaweed."

Jane bent over and retrieved a seashell from the beach. Tiny bits of glass, sharp edges worn smooth by the endless ebb and flow of water—or perhaps they were merely small, colored pebbles—glittered like gemstones as they spilled into her outstretched hand.

" 'The truth shall make you free,' " she said out loud, tossing the pebbles back into the sea. "That's what you used to preach to me all the time, Charlie. Well, I'm here on Paradise to find out the truth, and it damn well better set both of us free."

Jane felt the sting of tears in her eyes and a sudden thickness in her throat. "I still miss you, Dad," she confessed.

What did she remember of her father?

Charles Bennett had been a good-looking man, a charming man, a man filled with *joie de vivre*. She'd loved the sound of his voice; walking in the park with him, her hand in his; the way he'd always called her Cordelia when they were alone.

According to Welsh legend, she'd learned from her father at an early age, Cordelia was the daughter of King Lear, ruler of the sea. Indeed, the name meant "jewel of the sea." In Shakespeare's play, Cordelia was the only one of King Lear's three daughters who loved him.

Cordelia Jane Bennett was the only one of Charles

Bennett's three daughters who even remembered him. She had been ten years old when her father vanished. No one had called her Cordelia since.

What did she know of her father?

He had flunked out of three prestigious universities by twenty, married an heiress at twenty-five, much against her family's wishes, produced his first daughter and insisted upon naming her Cordelia—two more daughters, identical twins, would follow some years later—managed to run through his entire fortune but not his wife's, by the time he was thirty-five, and disappeared from the face of the earth before the age of forty.

Vera Gladstone Bennett Worthington (her mother had remarried some years ago), only daughter of *the* Gladstones of Buffalo and Palm Beach, had always referred to her erstwhile first husband as a ne'er-do-well, a dreamer, Peter Pan.

Jane had never blamed her mother. She still didn't. Vera had only done what she'd had to do to protect herself and her three children. She could scarcely allow Charles Bennett to use her money to finance his "little adventures."

So, good-time Charlie, handsome devil that he was, had resorted to schemes and stratagems. He had always been looking for the pot of gold at the end of the rainbow, whether it was a risky investment on Wall Street or a sunken treasure off a Caribbean island.

Jane wiped the back of her hand across her cheek; it came away damp. She hadn't realized she was crying.

"I think it's time for a toast," she proposed, swallowing her tears.

She dipped into the mesh bag and brought out a bottle of vintage champagne and a crystal champagne flute. She uncorked the bottle of Krug Collection 1973 and poured herself a glass.

"What should we drink to first, Charlie?" she said aloud and with no small measure of bravado in her voice.

Silence was her answer.

"To truth? To freedom?" Cordelia Jane Bennett raised her glass toward the open sea. "Yes. Let's drink to truth. For the truth shall make us free."

Jake Hollister slipped out of bed, into a pair of jeans, and started toward the beach.

Whenever he found sleep eluding him or whenever the dreams came—hell, there was no sense in kidding himself, they were nightmares—he headed for the secluded cove and a nighttime swim. There was something about the sound of the waves as they lapped the shoreline that eased his restlessness. In fact, on more than one occasion he had awakened the next morning to find that he'd fallen asleep right there on the sand.

He was about to take his usual shortcut down to the water's edge when he heard voices.

A voice.

A woman's voice.

Jake went down on his haunches, toes digging into the soft sand, rubbed one hand back and forth across his bare chest in a habitual and absentminded gesture, parted the flowering rhododendron in front of him with the other hand and peered through the fuchsia-colored blooms toward the beach.

The voice belonged to Jane Bennett. She was talking to someone named Charlie. Jake looked up and down the shoreline. There was no one named Charlie with her. There was no one with her at all. The lady was alone.

He watched as she tugged at the hairpins that held her

chignon in place. One by one they were pulled from her hair and dropped into a mesh bag on the beach. Then she gave her head a shake and golden-brown waves cascaded down around her shoulders. She kicked off her sandals and left them where they landed.

She was wearing a loose, flowing garment similar to a caftan. There was a crystal champagne flute clasped in her hand. "To freedom, Charlie." The glass was raised in the air. "This time let's drink to freedom."

Without warning Jane Bennett let the caftan slip off her shoulders; it caught at the bend of her elbow and then at her waist. She switched the champagne glass to the opposite hand and wiggled until the material slid down over her hips and pooled around her ankles. She took one step sideways, gave the undoubtedly expensive garment a nudge with her foot and then stood naked, facing the sea.

Jake blew out his breath and rocked back on his heels. Thanks to the shadows cast by the nearby palm trees and the pale moonlight, he couldn't see everything.

But he could see enough.

The woman was exquisite. Her skin was alabaster, porcelainlike, flawless. Her figure was slender, yet she had curves where curves were desirable and muscles where every woman should have muscles. Her abdomen was flat, her hips rounded, and her breasts full and uptilted. Her legs were as long as he had imagined them to be.

Jake knew he should do an immediate about-face and slip away into the night, giving Jane Bennett her privacy. After all, that's why she had come to Paradise. But he had learned the hard way there were two things that didn't mix: alcohol and the sea. God knows he'd tried to drown his sorrows in both on more than one occasion when he had first arrived on Paradise. If it hadn't been for the intervention of Doc Gilmour he wouldn't be here tonight watching this young woman celebrate. Or perhaps she was trying to drown her own sorrows in what he assumed was very expensive champagne.

In vino veritas.

Only there wasn't truth in wine, of course. He'd found that out as well.

There was only one thing for him to do, Jake decided. He would have to stay and stand guard.

Jane Bennett dipped her big toe into the water and drew back. Maybe she had more sense than he'd thought. Maybe she would drink her bubbly, romp nude on the beach, and go home.

He was wrong.

She drained her champagne glass, poured herself another drink from the bottle she had propped up in the sand and began to walk directly into the water.

What was it she had toasted?

Freedom.

What was more freeing, perhaps, for a woman like Jane Bennett than to shed her clothes and her inhibitions? Jake simply had to make sure that she didn't drown in the process.

She was waist deep now. She held her glass out to one side, in an attempt not to spill its contents, and dipped her head back until her hair was wet. The action arched her spine. Jake could clearly see her pale breasts and their darker, puckered centers.

"Sonofabitch," he swore softly under his breath.

He wasn't an oversexed adolescent. It took more than a pair of mammary glands, however perfect in size and shape, to turn him on. In fact, Jake liked to think that he was a man of discriminating tastes when it came to women. He wanted to know what was going on inside a woman's head, not just admire her physical attributes.

The truth was—whether it was the result of his own self-imposed celibacy or the lure of Jane Bennett's breasts rising above a nighttime sea was irrelevant—he was getting hard. His jeans were tight, and he was damned uncomfortable. Suddenly he felt more like a Peeping Tom than a guardian angel.

"Better cool off, Hollister," Jake admonished himself.

He had always believed in mind over matter; the brain in control of the body. He exercised that control now, consciously willing the tension to ease from his muscles until he was relaxed again.

At the same time, Jane Bennett seemed to lose control. A wave slapped up against her backside, tossing her body forward. Cold wine sloshed over the rim of her glass and spilled onto her bare breasts, eliciting a startled gasp. Then she lost her balance and the glass in her hand went flying. She made a grab for it and missed. Jake could hear her dismayed "Oh no!" as the crystal champagne flute disappeared beneath the water's surface.

She stood there for a minute, then shrugged her shoulders, waded into shore and picked up the champagne bottle. She turned and headed back into the Caribbean.

It was time Ms. Bennett realized she wasn't alone.

Jake stood, stretched his legs, and started down to the beach, whistling an aimless tune as he went. He saw the woman's head come up. She'd heard him.

Forewarned was forearmed.

By the time he reached the shoreline, Jane Bennett was out of the water and into the caftan that had obviously been hastily tugged on over her head. She was clutching the champagne bottle in her hand and peering into the darkness. "Who is it?" she demanded to know, her words slightly slurred.

"Jake Hollister." He waited for the information to sink in. Then, discretion being the better part of valor in his opinion, he inquired, as if he didn't already know the answer, "Who are you?"

"Jane Bennett." Her eyes narrowed as he approached. "How long have you been there?"

He fibbed. "Just got here."

Apparently she still wasn't convinced of his motives. "What are you doing?"

"I often come down for a late swim when I can't sleep." That much was the truth.

She went very still. "Couldn't you sleep?"

Jake took in and let out a deep breath before he replied. "Nope. How about you?"

She thought about it, then shook her head and finally asked, "Why couldn't you sleep?"

A simple question, perhaps. But the answer was so damnably complex. How could he explain in a sentence or two what his life had been like the past several years?

Jake lifted his shoulders and dropped them again. "Must have been something I ate." He ran his hand back and forth across his abdomen. "How about you?"

"I forgot to eat," she stated, frowning, her light brown eyebrows drawing together.

"Hunger will do it to you."

"Will do what?"

"Wake you up. Keep you awake. Make sleep difficult, if not impossible," he told her.

"I think Rachel Mayfair mentioned there would be a dinner tray left on my front porch, but I forgot all about it," Jane Bennett admitted after due consideration.

Jake threaded his fingers through his hair—he hadn't bothered combing it before he'd left his bungalow—and indicated the magnum in her hand. "Champagne?"

"Yes."

Taking a step closer, he studied the label. "Krug Collection 1973." He arched one brow in a knowing fashion. "I would venture to guess you didn't buy that around here."

"I brought it with me."

"Celebrating?"

Her chin came up. "Yes."

"Do you mind if I ask what you're celebrating?"

"Not in the least. I'm toasting truth and freedom," she claimed.

A flicker of a sardonic smile came and went from Jake's face. "I'd drink to that."

Jane Bennett chewed on her bottom lip. "I had a glass." She gazed out toward the water. "I lost it." She hesitated for an instant, then handed the magnum of champagne to him. "We'll just have to drink straight from the bottle."

"What should we toast?" he inquired.

The young woman looked baffled. "Freedom?"

"I thought you already had," he pointed out.

She scowled. "Did I?" Her expression cleared. "So I did." She quickly came up with another suggestion. "How about to putting the past behind us?"

"I'll drink to that," Jake responded with genuine enthusiasm. He took a swig and passed the sparkling wine back to her. " 'No man is an island,' " he quoted.

"And no woman," Jane Bennett agreed, taking another sip.

" 'Don't ask for whom the bell tolls . . .' "

" 'It tolls for thee,' " she finished.

"John Donne."

"To John Donne."

The bottle of imported champagne was passed back and forth between them.

"*Dum vivimus vivamus,*" Jake proposed next.

"I speak fluent French, a fair smattering of Italian, and some Spanish. I do not speak a word of Latin," Jane Bennett informed him. "You'll have to translate for me."

Jake was only too happy to. " 'While we live, let us live.' "

"To life."

In his opinion, the lady had had quite enough alcohol for one evening. But it was her celebration, her bottle of expensive vintage champagne, and her first night on the island.

"Why don't we walk along the beach?" Jake said in a deliberately neutral tone.

She started to gather her things together.

"We'll come back for your bag," he assured her.

"But we'll take the champagne," she insisted.

They hadn't gone far before one melodic birdsong after another came from the trees lining the shore.

The woman beside him stopped dead in her tracks, put her head back, and listened intently. "That's beautiful," she said with a sigh. "What kind of birds are they?"

"It's one bird."

"One bird?"

Jake nodded. "He has no song of his own, so he imitates every other bird in the forest."

Jane closed her eyes and shuddered. "How terribly sad."

He gave her an appraising glance. "Do you think so?"

Her face was almost bleak. "Yes."

They walked on. It was perhaps a dozen yards farther down the beach when she paused by a great sprawling tree. She handed over the bottle of Krug in order to take a closer look.

"Most unusual," came the declaration.

"Yes, it is," he concurred.

"I wonder what kind of tree it is."

Jake could help her there. "Strangler fig."

"Really?"

"Really." He went on. "There wouldn't be any strangler figs without the pollinating wasps."

Her expression was one of puzzlement. "Pollinating whats?"

"Wasps. The adult males are wingless and virtually blind. Their entire existence is for two purposes: to mate and to cut a hole in the fig to allow the pregnant females to escape."

She gave him a measuring look. "You seem to know a great deal about everything."

"Not everything," he said with a degree of modesty.

"More than I do," she modified.

"Perhaps."

She took the large bottle of champagne from his hands, raised it to her lips, took a drink and announced: "I went to a very exclusive and very expensive women's college."

"I went to a state university."

"I missed the sexual revolution," she informed him feelingly.

That wasn't what Jake had expected her to say, but he recovered admirably, he thought. "How old are you?"

"Twenty-nine." Jane lowered her voice to a conspiratorial whisper. "But I'll be thirty on my next birthday."

"Too young."

"Who is?"

"You are. You're too young. That's why you missed the sexual revolution."

Jane gave him her full attention. "What about you?"

"Huh?"

She studied him, head cocked to one side, as if trying to divine his age. "Are you too young?"

"I'm thirty-seven."

"Then you didn't miss it."

"Miss what?"

"The sexual revolution."

Jake twisted his mouth into a self-deprecating smile. "Oh, but I did."

Jane Bennett was a curious creature. "Why?"

At least the answer to this question was simple and straightforward. "I was busy building a career for myself," he told her.

"I thought sex was all men were interested in." It was impossible to tell whether or not she spoke ironically.

"Men are interested in the same things women are," Jake said, voice and manner serious.

Jane arched a skeptical eyebrow. "Panty hose that won't run?"

"Well, perhaps not everything. But a great many of the same things interest both sexes."

"Like sex."

The woman had sex on the brain. Jake wondered momentarily whether or not she was wearing the sign that read: LOOK, BUT DON'T TOUCH.

Jake Hollister should have known better, of course.

He should have known *not* to take her arm when she tripped over a fallen palm branch on the beach. He should have known *not* to allow her to lean against him. After all, he was well aware that she was naked under the caftan: he'd been watching her swim—if you could call it swimming—in the nude.

The memory of what Jane Bennett looked like without any clothing on didn't help matters.

Then she said something that surprised him. "Were you watching me while I was in the water?"

Jake swallowed. "Yes."

She seemed more curious then offended. "Why?"

"I was afraid for you."

"And . . . ?"

"And I couldn't take my eyes off you. You're a beautiful woman, Jane Bennett."

She went up on her tiptoes and pressed a light and rather sweet kiss to his lips.

"You don't know what you're doing," he warned.

"Yes, I do," Jane declared.

"Well, I sure as hell don't," Jake grumbled as he brought his mouth down on hers.

chapter *Five*

*D*anger.

Jane should have seen it coming. She didn't.

In the natural world, an encounter with the enemy usually resulted in "fight or flight." Detecting danger—whether it was through sound or scent or instinct—was often a matter of life and death, a matter of survival.

Crazy.

That's what she was for kissing Jake Hollister. For once she'd started, she didn't want to stop.

Jane realized, through the lovely haze created by the champagne she had consumed, how much she liked the way Jake held her: one hand at her waist, one hand in her hair, his grasp strong yet gentle.

He was tall—probably an inch, maybe two, over six feet—and the perfect height if she went up on her tiptoes.

He was muscular. She could feel the strength in his shoulders, his arms, his chest, his legs. She could also feel the control. This was a man in control of himself.

It registered somewhere in the back of her mind that Jake Hollister was wearing a pair of faded denim jeans and very little else. His chest was bare, except for the smattering of brown hair that circled his nipples, arrowed down his flat abdomen and finally disappeared into the waistline of his jeans.

She could hear the sound of his breathing, the rhythmic beat of his heart, the waves that washed up onto shore and licked at their feet.

Her hands were clasped behind Jake's neck. His hair was long, slightly unkempt, and certainly uncombed. It brushed back and forth along his nape with each movement of his head. She ran her fingers through the strands of his hair; they had the feel of silk.

The stubble on his chin and along his jawline was another matter altogether. It was like fine sandpaper. Yet the sensation of his beard scraping her skin was surprisingly erotic.

Jane opened her eyes and studied the dark arch of his brows, the suggestion of an aristocratic nose, the ears tucked close to his head. She knew from this afternoon on the ferry that the color of his eyes was hazel. She was surprised she remembered. At the time she hadn't thought that she'd noticed such an insignificant detail.

Jake opened his eyes and stared down into hers.

What did she see? Intelligence. Interest. Curiosity. Strength. Determination. This was a man who was used to being in charge of himself, of the situation, of those around him. Perhaps calling him *el patrón* wasn't a joke, after all.

The heat radiated from Jake Hollister's body as if he had stored up warmth from the tropical sun all day. He smelled of the night and of the sea. He tasted of champagne.

"You taste like champagne," she murmured, leaning her head back and looking up at him from within the circle of his arms.

He laughed huskily. She could feel the suggestion of movement in his chest, even in the taut muscles of his stomach. "Let me guess," he said. "Krug Collection 1973?"

Jane nodded. Then she wet her lips with her tongue and drew in a deep breath. "What do I taste like?" She'd never asked a man that kind of leading question before.

"Like no one else," he told her.

She laughed. It was a gigolo's line. She didn't believe him, but she wanted to.

"You taste of sweetness and sadness, innocence and seduction," Jake said, lowering his head and kissing her again.

It wasn't the kiss of an inexperienced man. There was no hesitation on his part, no lack of self-confidence. His lips were neither too hard nor too soft, not too gentle or too demanding. They were, however, unabashedly curious about her, blatantly interested, sexually hungry.

It wasn't the kiss of a man on the make. He didn't grind his lips against hers. He didn't try to thrust his tongue into her mouth and halfway down her throat. There was no indication that it was an act. He wasn't pretending passion.

The passion was real.

How little she knew personally of passion, Jane thought with a sigh. Oh, she had encountered collectors with a passion for Old Masters, antique furniture, objets d'art from jeweled Faberge eggs to one-of-a-kind Tiffany lamps. There was often a desire, a need, a *passion* to possess in the world in which she had grown up, lived, and now worked. But it was a passion for things.

Had anyone ever felt passionate about her?

Or was a man's desire for her really a desire for her privileged background, her impeccable pedigree, her money—she had her own fortune thanks to her maternal great-grandmother's will—perhaps her classic looks, her ice princess appearance, or her body, when any body of reasonable attractiveness would do?

Had anyone ever loved what she was in her heart, in her mind, in her soul?

Love and passion, of course, were far from interchangeable, Jane reminded herself.

There was no love, but there was passion in the way Jake Hollister kissed her. Her body was flattened against his from breast to thigh; she could clearly feel the outline of every bone, every muscle. Only the thin material of her caftan and his worn jeans separated her flesh from his.

He didn't try to caress her, to insinuate his hands into those most private places. Yet there was something incredibly intimate about the way their bodies touched. There was no doubt about the state of his sexual arousal: he was erect.

Jake offered no apology, no explanations, no excuses. The situation simply was what it was.

She must be losing her mind.

"This is crazy," Jane finally said aloud. But it came out as a soft, breathless whisper and with no particular inclination or conviction to stop what they were doing.

Jake lifted his head for a moment. "Yup."

Her head was spinning. "Why are we doing this?"

He seemed willing to offer an explanation. "We've discovered that we like kissing each other."

That simple.

That complex.

Jane felt she had to set the record straight. "I don't make a habit of kissing strangers."

Jake put a hand—just the tips of his fingers—against her lips. "Neither do I."

She tried to make some sense of it. "Could it be the champagne?" she wondered out loud.

He answered her question with a question. "Have you drunk champagne before?"

"Yes. Naturally. On numerous occasions." Although she scarcely thought of herself as even much of a social drinker.

Jake didn't appear to be joking when he asked her: "Has drinking champagne ever 'inspired' you to kiss a stranger before?"

He was being ridiculous, and they both knew it. Jane scoffed. "Of course not."

He shrugged his broad shoulders. "I would say that it's not the bubbly."

Jane was still determined to find a rational explanation for her behavior. "Is it the tropical night? The scent of exotic flowers? The balmy breeze off the Caribbean?"

"Weather? Botanical influences?" He pondered the possibilities, then shook his head. "I wouldn't think so."

"Then why?" She had to know.

"I don't know," Jake murmured, nuzzling her neck. The caress sent shivers coursing through her. She couldn't stop shaking. She couldn't *start* breathing. "Do you?"

Her mind was a blank. "Do I what?"

"Do you have any idea why we're behaving like this?"

"We're both crazy." It was the only thing that popped into Jane's mind.

"Maybe we are," he conceded.

"I've never done anything like this in my entire life," she blurted out. It sounded trite, but it was true.

He lifted the wet, loose hair from her neck and combed through the tangled ends with his fingers. "Never?"

"Never." She gave a dramatic sigh.

Dark, masculine eyes sought and held hers. "Frankly, I figured as much."

She gave him her undivided attention. "Did you?"

He grunted. "You're not the type."

She had to ask. "What type am I?"

Jake Hollister didn't mince words. "Cool. Classy. Calm and collected. Hands off." His mouth curved humorlessly. "Definitely hands off."

He was right, of course. At least about the latter. It had been her experience that men, in general, were unreliable. They were best kept at arm's length.

Turnabout was only fair play in her estimation. "What type are you, Mr. Hollister?"

"Jake."

"What type are you, Jake?"

He was serious and sober. He took in and let out a deep breath before he replied. "I can tell you what I'm not. I'm not a man who believes or engages in promiscuous behavior. I'm not a man who tries to bed every willing female who happens along. It isn't healthy in this day and age. Hell, it never has been." There was a dark smirk on his face. "And I have nothing to prove about my manhood. I know who I am, and I know what I want," he stated unequivocally.

"What do you want, Jake Hollister?"

He wanted her.

But Jake had no intention of admitting it at this stage of the game. It was bad enough that a certain portion of his male anatomy was literally shouting the fact. Unfortunately, a man couldn't hide his arousal.

Jane Bennett was trouble with a capital *T*.

He'd known it from the first moment he'd caught sight of her on the island ferry this afternoon. Hadn't he learned his lesson when it came to her kind of woman?

Maybe in the past he'd never had his heart broken, but it had been cracked wide open in several places. This time might be different. This time he might not survive. He was a different man, after all.

He was different, and yet he was the same.

He'd always had an imagination. At the moment, his imagination was running wild. He pictured Jane Bennett as he'd seen her earlier that night in the Caribbean, wet hair dripping down her back.

He imagined making love to her on the beach, her skin covered with granules of pristine white sand. He would have to brush the stuff from her breasts and watch her nipples respond to the unintentional caress. Well, perhaps not so unintentional at that.

His bare knees and his feet would dig into the wet, gritty pebbles, of course. He wouldn't care. Soon, very soon, he figured, he wouldn't even notice.

Or maybe he'd choose to save the lady's precious and—from what he had witnessed—perfect backside. She could straddle his hips, wrap her long, lovely legs around his waist, lower her body inch by inch and impale herself on his eager and waiting flesh. He would fill her with excruciating thoroughness until she had taken every inch of him and he had given as much as he had to give.

Then it would begin.

Slowly at first, with a gentle rocking motion. Then a thrust of her hips, then his, then another thrust and another, stronger, deeper, driving them both to the brink.

Sweet Jesus, Jake silently intoned, he could almost taste her, feel her. His penis was pressed painfully to the front of his jeans, and the situation was downright explosive. If he thought one more erotic thought, if he kissed Jane again, if he moved against her body, he was going to come in his pants like a randy teenager.

"You sorry sonofabitch," he mumbled.

Jane blinked. "I beg your pardon."

Jake covered his tracks as fast as he could. "I said, I'm sorry. It's late and we've both had a little too much to drink." Hell, he hadn't had enough! "I think we'd better call it a night."

They retraced their steps along the stretch of deserted beach and retrieved Jane's mesh bag and her sandals. Then they started to climb the pathway that led to the Four Sisters Inn and the rental bungalows.

"You don't have to escort me to my door," she spoke up.

Jake had his mind on other matters. "I know."

"You're going to anyway."

"Yes."

There was an unmistakable edge of nervousness to her voice. "I don't want you to go out of your way."

"I'm not."

They reached Delilah.

"I'm not going to invite you in," she informed him.

"Good idea," he said with a touch of sardonic humor.

"Good night, Jake."

"Good night, Jane."

She opened the door of the screened-in porch and stepped inside. Her hand was wrapped around the doorknob of the cottage when she paused and turned around. "You never mentioned where you live."

"No, I guess I didn't." He might as well confess to her now. She'd find out sooner or later as it was. "I'm in Samson."

Jane Bennett appeared to choke on her saliva. "You're in the other bungalow?"

Jake nodded his head.

Her voice rose half an octave in disbelief. "You're right next door?"

"Yup. That's me," he drawled with a wicked grin. "The boy next door."

Jake didn't think the lady heard the "Sleep well and pleasant dreams" that he tossed over his shoulder as he strolled along the sandy path to the neighboring cottage.

chapter Six

"This place is in the middle of frigging nowhere."

Tony swept into her *alcoba* the next morning and stood at the end of the massive four-poster Spanish-style bed.

Megs St. Cyr pushed herself up into a sitting position, plumped the pile of antique, lace-trimmed pillows at her back, adjusted the strap of her nightgown—the material was finest silk and had been hand-stitched by a seamstress who operated an exclusive little shop in Marseilles—and then gave her attention to the man who had barged, unannounced and uninvited, into her bedroom.

Tony was obviously in one of his snits.

Megs dismissed the housemaid with a wave of her hand. She waited until the door of her suite had closed; she even counted to ten for good measure before she spoke. "You're going to have to watch yourself." She didn't bother to disguise the criticism in her voice. "The servants have ears, you know."

"They don't understand English," Tony claimed with his usual arrogance about such matters.

Maybe the Hacienda staff did; maybe they didn't. But

Tony had a decided tendency to overestimate his own abilities and underestimate everyone else's.

"They may understand more than you give them credit for," Megs said.

Tony grunted and stuffed his hands into the pockets of his fawn-colored jodhpurs. He frequently wore riding breeches and knee-high leather boots even when he had no intention of going anywhere near a horse. Somehow he was convinced the "look" made him appear dashing.

"I didn't come here this morning to discuss the servants," he said after an interval.

Megs waited patiently while he paced back and forth at the foot of the ornately carved bed, knowing that he would tell her what was on his mind when he was good and ready.

Tony suddenly stopped pacing, turned, and declared, "You've made a mistake."

"*I've* made a mistake?" Megs raised her eyebrows fractionally; that's all it took.

"All right, *we've* made a mistake."

"About what?"

"About coming here."

"*Here* being the Hacienda? The island of Paradise? The Caribbean? Or all of the above?"

"Very amusing." But it was obvious Tony wasn't in the least amused. "It was a bloody awful mistake wangling an invitation out of Don Carlos to visit his family's plantation."

"I thought we agreed it was a good idea."

"I've changed my mind."

"I'm afraid it's too late for that."

"I don't like it here," he whined. "There's nothing to do."

Megs took in and let out a deep breath. "I thought Don Carlos had horses."

"*Had* is the correct terminology. The old fart told me this morning that he sold off his best polo ponies when he became too old to play. All he has left is a small herd of broken-down nags."

"And the plantation?"

"Apparently it was once a thriving sugarcane operation," he informed her. "I don't know what you would call it at present."

"Surely there must be something entertaining to do on Paradise," she ventured.

"Fishing. That's what Don Carlos tells me he does in his spare time, of which he must have plenty," Tony groused.

Sometimes Tony's attention span rivaled that of a five-year-old. "Well, we're here, my dear," Megs said with a sigh. "And we're staying—at least for now."

"I don't see why we have to."

She would try to explain it to him once more, in simple words that he could comprehend. "Free room and board."

His usually sensuous lips compressed into a thin, unattractive line. "Money."

"Money."

"It's always about money," he complained bitterly.

"You like expensive things," she felt compelled to point out.

"So do you," he shot back.

Megs didn't deny it. Indeed, she would be the first to admit that she wanted—no, that she *needed*—the finer things of life. "We're running a bit low on funds this quarter."

"We're always running low on funds," Tony griped. "When is our next check due?"

"Not for two months."

"Christ! Two interminably long, dull months." He slowly walked around the end of the massive bed, leaned over, lifted the jewel dangling from a gold chain around her neck, took its considerable weight in the palm of his hand and inquired with a smirk on his handsome face: "Real or fake?"

Megs was tempted not to tell him the truth. He might suggest they sell the stone, and it was her personal insurance policy; one of the few remaining she had.

"Real," she finally admitted.

Ice-blue eyes were openly assessing. "I'll wager it's worth a pretty penny or two."

"A penny or two," she said lightly.

Tony's expression became one of disdain. "Refresh my memory, dearest Megs. I seem to have forgotten. Exactly who did you sleep with in order to 'earn' this little reward?"

She managed not to wince at the deliberate cruelty in his voice. After all, they had been through this scenario before.

She sat up straighter in the huge bed. "Jealous?"

Tony scoffed. "Hardly." He slowly lowered the stone until it once again nestled between her breasts, knowing full well that his knuckles brushed across one of her nipples in the process.

"Behave yourself," Megs scolded.

His careless stance—legs spread wide apart, hands resting on his hips, muscular thighs and groin aimed at her eye level—was a blatant masculine challenge. "Why?"

"You know why, dear *brother*."

Tony snickered. "That was your idea, not mine."

"You agreed to it," Megs reminded him.

Tony shrugged. "Frankly, it seemed titillating at the time." He lowered his voice to an intimate level. "There's no one here at the moment but the two of us."

With that announcement, he dove down the front of her nightgown, clamped one hand around her breast and squeezed hard. Her body reacted in a predictable fashion. Almost immediately Megs could feel the pleasure bordering on pain in her nipples, the tingling in her lower pelvis and the sticky dampness between her legs.

"We can't," she protested.

Tony's nostrils flared. "We can," he insisted, tweaking her nipple again.

"It's too late to change our story." She slapped at his groping fingers. "We've made our bed . . ."

"And now we must *lay* in it?"

Something like that. "Yes."

"Perhaps I'll see if the pretty young maid who makes up my bed would like to *un*make it as well," Tony threatened.

It wouldn't be the first time he'd strayed. Megs was certain it wouldn't be the last. "You have more important things to tend to," she reminded him.

"Like what?"

"Like keeping your eyes and ears open. Whatever you may think of Don Carlos and his depleted herd of polo ponies, the Lovatos are reputed to be a very old and a very wealthy family."

Tony made a face. "Did you take a good look at the car we were collected in yesterday at the dock?"

"You must learn to see beyond the obvious," Megs stated. Then she added, "The Rolls is a vintage model."

"Vintage model?" Tony's tone was incredulous. "The

bloody thing has to be at least twenty years old.''

"Don Carlos may collect classic automobiles.''

Nordic blue eyes narrowed to slits. ''The Hacienda is filled with old furniture.''

''They're called antiques.''

''There's nothing of value here, Megs.''

''Perhaps not. But we needed a place to stay and Don Carlos' offer was the perfect solution.'' Or so it had seemed at the time. ''Besides, you should know by now that appearances can be deceptive.''

''That's for damned sure.'' Tony sounded almost savage. ''Look at you, my sweet.''

The skin around her mouth grew taut. ''What is that supposed to mean?''

Tony was quite willing, even eager, to expound on the subject. ''You appear to be such a lady, yet underneath it all you're a slut through and through.''

Megs hastened to return the compliment. ''And you, my darling, give the impression of being a perfect gentleman when you're nothing but a first-class bastard.''

''Being a bastard doesn't necessarily prevent a man from being classified as a gentleman, my dear.''

There was a knock on the door.

''*Entre*,'' Megs called out.

It was the housemaid. She was carrying a heavy silver tray with a silver coffee urn, a pair of cups and saucers, and several silver salvers which, when uncovered, revealed a variety of sliced fresh fruits and homemade breads.

''*Desayuno*,'' she announced with a slight bow of her head.

''Breakfast,'' Megs translated. Then she employed one of the few other words she knew in Spanish. ''*Gracias*.''

Once they were alone again, Tony helped himself to a

slice of succulent papaya. "I must say, Megs, the service is excellent, and the food."

"At least we won't starve," she pointed out, their argument seemingly forgotten.

Tony was still chewing, and wiping the juice from his chin with a pristine linen napkin, when he went on to comment, "Frankly, I don't see how we can plan our next move from here."

Megs poured two cups of coffee and held one out to him. Usually she only told Tony as much as he needed to know and only when he needed to know it. But there was always an exception to her own rules. "Opportunity presents itself when you least expect it to," she said with a sly smile.

He accepted the cup of *cafe* and sat down on the edge of the mattress. "What opportunity?"

The idea had first occurred to Megs on the ferry ride from St. Thomas yesterday. Perhaps it was time to try it out on her partner. "Two words," she said cryptically.

"What two words?"

"Jane Bennett."

The handsome head came up. Tony searched her face to see if she was serious. Apparently he decided she was. "What about Jane Bennett?" he inquired.

"She knows Victoria Storm."

A furrow appeared between the man's dark blond eyebrows. "I'm sure a lot of people know Victoria Storm."

Megs was merely trying to put two and two together and somehow come up with four. "Jane Bennett mentioned that they had been college roommates."

"So?"

"So Torey Storm is one of the wealthiest young women in the United States."

"That, I assume, is common knowledge. What does it have to do with us?"

Megs was still thinking out loud. "I was watching our friend Jane on the ferry yesterday."

That brought a smile to Tony's good-looking features. "You weren't the only one."

"I know you had your eye on her."

"So did some beach bum in tattered jeans."

Megs remembered the man: tall, dark, and handsome, intense and unshaven. Although there had been something else about him, something that had caught *and* held her interest. Under other circumstances, she would have been tempted to introduce herself to him.

Temporarily she put the stranger out of her mind and concentrated on the point she wished to make. "There's more to Jane Bennett than meets the eye."

Tony slapped a muscular thigh with his free hand. "I was about to say the same thing."

"I'm talking about money."

His ears perked up. She'd counted on that getting his attention. "Money?"

She dropped her little bomb. "A lot of money."

"How can you tell?"

"The signs are subtle but, nevertheless, they're there." Subtlety, she realized, was an alien concept to Tony. "I think it's just possible that Ms. Jane Bennett is in the same league as her friend."

"You believe she's a bloody heiress, as well."

Megs nodded her head. Then she paused and tapped a perfectly manicured fingernail against her lower lip. "I wonder what she's doing on the island?"

Tony merely shrugged and grunted something unintelligible.

"I think we should find out," she concluded.

"Why?"

"Because it isn't logical."

His laugh was disparaging. "There's a good reason if I've ever heard one."

Tony St. Cyr was a man of limited imagination. She'd known that from the very beginning. On the other hand, she was a woman of unlimited vision.

Megs put her coffee cup down on the table beside the bed and grabbed his arm. "What would a woman like *that* being doing on an island like *this*?"

He gave her the obvious answer. "She's on holiday."

Megs cast him a skeptical glance. "Why would Jane Bennett holiday on Paradise?"

He didn't know; he admitted as much.

"There's something else going on here, Tony."

"What?"

"I don't know." She fell silent for a minute or two. Then she shuddered. "That disgusting creature on the ferry."

"The fortune-teller?"

Megs nodded.

"I thought the jig was up when she called you *senora*," Tony confessed with a nervous laugh. "It was almost as if the old woman knew the truth about us."

"Trust me, she didn't. It was nothing more than a lucky guess on her part," Megs assured him. "Something interesting was said to our traveling companion, however."

Tony remembered. "The old lady claimed that Jane Bennett was seeking someone."

Megs nodded again. "A man. And she predicted that Jane would find him."

He snickered. "It's all nothing more than superstitious mumbo jumbo."

"Danger."

"Danger?"

"The fortune-teller advised Jane there would be danger, and she warned her not to come between the dragon and its wrath."

"The demented old fool spouted a bunch of nonsense about virtuous wives too."

Megs chose to ignore that last remark. "Our newfound friend didn't deny a word of it. She's here on Paradise for a reason and I'll bet my bottom dollar that it isn't for a vacation."

"What are we going to do?"

"Keep an eye on Ms. Bennett."

"How do you propose we do that since we're *here* and she's *there*?" Tony pointed in the general direction of north.

Where there was a strong enough will—and hers was one of the strongest—there was always a way, Megs had found. "Someone must need a little extra cash."

"We're going to hire ourselves a spy?"

"In a manner of speaking. We're going to buy ourselves some information. From the looks of it, I suspect information comes cheap on Paradise." She was anxious to get started now that she had a plan. Megs threw back the covers and began to get out of bed. She found Tony was in her way.

He leaned toward her with a lascivious grin. "Where do you think you're going?"

"I'm getting up."

"I'm already up," he said with a suggestive laugh.

"That, I'm afraid, is your problem."

Tony pinned her to the bed with his heavily aroused body. He buried his head between her breasts. She could feel the heat of his breath on her bare flesh.

"I think it's your problem as well," he mumbled meaningfully.

Megs kept a cool head. God knows, one of them had to. "The housemaid could walk back in here at any moment. Would you care to explain what you're doing to your *sister*?"

Tony swore under his breath, rolled off the bed and crossed the bedroom to the open window. "This whole bloody brother/sister scam is trying my patience."

"We agreed it was a good idea," Megs reminded him.

Tony didn't respond to that. He simply stood and stared out at the tropical gardens and the fountain below.

"Now what?" he finally asked.

"Now you leave, and I get dressed."

Tony glanced at her over his shoulder. "You don't have anything I haven't seen a few hundred times before."

"That is beside the point. Get out. I have to think."

Megs started to make a list in her head as soon as the bedroom door closed behind him. She was very good at getting what she wanted and what she wanted was information about Jane Bennett. That would require a small bribe, an indiscreet servant or two, one here at the Hacienda and another at the Four Sisters Inn.

It could be arranged.

It would be arranged.

But it wasn't Jane Bennett that Megs was thinking about as she began to dress for the day. It was the man on the ferry.

"I wonder what his name is," Megs St. Cyr murmured to herself as she slipped into a pair of skimpy panties and a lacy bra.

chapter *Seven*

"My name is Brilliant Chang," announced the slightly built man standing on the doorstep of the Delilah bungalow. He gave an excruciatingly polite bow of his head and greeted her in perfect English. "Good morning, Miss Bennett."

Jane gave a similarly polite bow of her head in return. "Good morning, Mr. Chang."

"No doubt you are wondering what the two island boys behind me are doing," the man said without preamble.

Jane glanced over his shoulder. There were two young boys—she put their ages at ten and twelve—pounding a pole into the ground in front of her cottage. There was a small wooden structure at their feet. It appeared to be a birdhouse.

"You're right," she told him. "I am wondering what the two boys behind you are doing."

"Do you know what day this is, Miss Bennett?"

Jane raised her eyebrows a fraction of an inch and ventured, "Thursday?"

The man who called himself Brilliant Chang gave her an inscrutable smile. "It is Visakha Day."

"You will have to explain Visakha Day to me."

Her visitor seemed only too happy to oblige. "Visakha Day is the holiest day of the year in Thailand. It is the day when incense wafts skyward as worshipers hold their joss sticks and lotus blossoms in the air to mark the observance of the Lord Buddha's birthday, his enlightenment, and his death."

"I see." A moment passed. "Are you originally from Thailand, Mr. Chang?"

"My revered grandfather was from Bangkok," he stated as if that explained the familial connection.

Jane supposed it did.

The hammering grew louder. She stepped outside, closed the screen door behind her, and approached the hardworking boys who were sinking the pole into a foot-deep hole dug in the sandy earth. She studied the miniature structure waiting on the ground, then glanced up at her unexpected visitor. "Is it a birdhouse?"

Brilliant Chang shook his head from side to side—she did not miss the look of fleeting amusement on his ageless face—and folded his hands in front of him. "It is a spirit house."

Again, Jane was forced to plead ignorance.

"I have come to repay kindness with kindess," he said to her with another polite bow.

She was puzzled. They had never met before. Of that she was quite certain. "What kindness could you possibly feel you need to repay, Mr. Chang?"

"You arrived on Paradise a week ago," he began.

Had it been a week already? Jane felt as though she had been on the island no more than a day or two at most. She had been sleeping a great deal, and napping every afternoon in a hammock located beneath a giant shade tree that separated the two bungalows. She had lost track of time, she realized belatedly.

"Yes, I suppose I did," she finally agreed.

"You traveled here from St. Thomas on the ferry."

"That's correct."

"There was an old woman on that ferry."

Jane furrowed her brow. "Was there?"

His head bobbed up and down.

Then Jane remembered. "She was selling candy and fruit and telling fortunes with the toss of a shark's teeth."

Brilliant Chang showed neither approval nor disapproval of the fortune-teller's activities. He simply observed: "You were most kind to the woman called Niu."

Jane had treated her as she would any human being. That's what she explained to Mr. Chang.

He watched her with thoughtful eyes. "Which is precisely why I am here today. Nui is my mother's favorite cousin's wife." He turned and spread his arms wide, as if to encompass the entire bungalow before him. "If you will permit me, I would like to bless this house and the woman who lives within it."

Jane assumed the gentleman meant her. She didn't see how it could hurt. She gave her permission.

"The spirit house will be raised thus," he explained as the island boys affixed the miniature building atop the pole. "I will say a blessing upon this house where you reside and ask that the spirits come out and dwell in the spirit house. This will leave you in peace."

"In that case, I welcome your blessing."

The small, elegant man went through his ritual, chanting in a language that may have been Thai or Burmese or a hill tribe dialect.

When the ceremony was concluded, Brilliant Chang

turned to her and declared, "This house is now blessed by the Lord Buddha."

"Thank you, Mr. Chang."

Apparently he wasn't finished. "I will now say a Christian blessing as well, in honor of the ladies who reside in the Big House."

Jane assumed he meant the Mayfair sisters.

Eyes were closed, chin lowered to chest, hands raised palms out. Then, from the Book of Numbers, came the recitation, " 'The Lord bless thee and keep thee. The Lord make his face shine upon thee and be gracious unto thee. The Lord lift up his countenance upon thee and give thee peace.' "

"Amen," Jane murmured. She raised her head. "Thank you again, Mr. Chang."

"We are not finished, Miss Bennett."

"We aren't?"

"As my grandmother's sister's husband would say: A house is not a home if one skilled in the art of *feng shui* has not gone within and made certain the surroundings are in harmony."

"*Feng shui?*" she repeated.

"*Feng shui* is the ancient Chinese belief that objects should be in harmonious relationship to one another to maximize good fortune. The literal translation is 'wind and water.' " He looked at her as they paused by her front door. "May I enter?"

"Of course."

Jane followed him inside the bungalow.

Brilliant Chang paused in the middle of the sitting room. "What is the date of your birth?"

She told him.

The gentleman took what appeared to be a large compass from a leather pouch hanging from his right shoulder. "This is a magnetized *luopan*. I will use it to determine the bungalow's orientation. Once I have done that, I must analyze the effects of the structure's unlucky spots based upon your birth date. We are all assigned one of the elements: wood, earth, metal, fire or water. You, Miss Bennett, are water." He paused and studied the morning sunlight as it flowed in the bank of windows on the east side of the cottage. Then he announced, "This is good."

Jane was relieved.

He stopped in front of a small ugly glass vase sitting in the center of what she used for a dining room table since there was no official dining room. He picked up the vase and handed it to her. "This is not good. You may wish to put it away in a closet somewhere."

Jane was in complete agreement.

One chair was rearranged, two small tables and several stacks of books. Finally, with a broad grin and a flash of teeth, he announced, "This house is now in harmony. You will enjoy peace and happiness as long as you live here."

"Thank you, Mr. Chang." Jane only hesitated briefly before adding, "I was about to make myself a cup of tea. Would you care to join me?"

"That is most kind of you."

It was perhaps fifteen minutes later. They were sitting on the screened-in front porch, sipping tea and enjoying the morning breeze gently wafting off the Caribbean.

As if he could read Jane's mind, her guest spoke up. "You may ask me any question you wish, Miss Bennett. I will not be offended."

"Do you believe in any of the blessings you bestowed upon this house today?" she inquired.

"I believe in all of them. I believe in none of them," he told her cryptically.

"That isn't an answer," she pointed out.

He confided in her. "I grew up far from here in another part of the world, Miss Bennett. Our family were outcasts because my parents were of mixed blood: Thai, Burmese, and Chinese. When I was ten years old, my family moved here to the island of Paradise. At the time my father's cousin worked for the Lovato family on their sugarcane plantation."

"The Hacienda."

He nodded. "I was happy here for a time. Then, as a restless young man—as restless young men so often do—I decided that I must see more of the world. So I left this island."

Jane was fascinated. "Where did you go?"

"I attended school in your United States of America."

"Where did you attend school?"

"Several places, but eventually I ended up at Harvard University where I studied philosophy."

Jane heard herself asking, "Did you like Harvard?"

Brilliant Chang shrugged his narrow shoulders in a classic gesture of disinterest. "The great country of America, Harvard University, the island of Paradise: they are all the same."

"How can you say that?"

"The world, like Paradise, has both its light and dark sides," he philosophized. His eyes met hers. "Tell me, Miss Bennett, what have you seen of our island?"

She realized that she had seen very little of Paradise. "Preacher's Bay. The dock and the town of Purgatory. The Mangy Moose. The Four Sisters Inn, of course. The beach below. The blue bay. A rainstorm. A rainbow."

"You have only seen one small part of the island, then."

"Tell me about Paradise," she urged.

He seemed inclined to grant her request. "Some of it is wonderful: the tropical forest, the waterfall that is called the Veil of Mist, and Jacob's Ladder."

She was curious. "What is Jacob's Ladder?"

"A set of natural stone stairs that lead up to the very top of the waterfall. There is also the Raining Room, a cave where incredible stalactites and stalagmites grow from both above and below." He took a sip of his tea before he continued. "But be warned that beyond the waterfall are volcanic mountains and beaches with black sand, strange rock outcroppings with knife-sharp edges fashioned by the wind, the cavern the native Caribes once called 'the place from which nothing returns' and which, according to local legend, is the home of a great and terrifying sea monster."

Jane shivered but confessed, "It sounds intriguing."

Her companion looked at her askance. "You are your father's daughter."

Jane froze for an instant. Then she shrugged and went on nonchalantly, "Who else's daughter would I be?"

Brilliant Chang said, "I meant literally. You are the daughter of Charles Bennett."

Jane had difficulty breathing. "How did you guess?"

"I did not guess. I simply knew." He held up one graceful hand. "There is no need to trouble yourself. I will say nothing. It is for you to decide if and when you reveal your parentage."

Her thoughts were chaotic. "Did you know my father?"

"I did not know him. I knew of him. But I'm not surprised to find you here now."

The words stuck in her throat. "Why aren't you surprised?"

"It will soon be twenty years since he disappeared, will it not?" her guest said.

"Yes, it will be."

"An anniversary."

"Of sorts," she replied.

"A desire to put the past behind you."

"Yes."

"Time is an illusion," he stated, putting his teacup down on the small table before him. "There are those who believe the past, the present, and the future are as one."

"You speak in riddles, Mr. Chang."

"Sometimes it is what I do best. But remember, Miss Bennett, some questions have no answers."

She was beginning to understand that.

The man rose to his feet. "Thank you for the cup of tea and thank you for your hospitality."

"You are most welcome," she said, walking him to the front door. "Thank you for your many blessings on this house."

"Kindness should beget kindness." Brilliant Chang was halfway down the path when he stopped and looked back over his shoulder at her. "You must be careful what you seek on Paradise, Miss Bennett."

Her brow wrinkled. "Why?"

There was another inscrutable smile on the ageless face. "You may well find it."

chapter *Eight*

180,000 silver coins.

1,300 silver bars weighing between 70 and 100 pounds each.

1,200 doubloons (Spanish, late 17th century).

40 variously shaped gold ingots.

215 gold bars.

500 feet of gold chain.

3,000 emeralds.

1,000 pearls of every shape and size.

Personal jewelry and possessions belonging to the noblewoman known as Bella Doña, and said to include one shell-shaped gold box, the engraved scene on the base depicting the Spanish galleon christened in her honor, a gold hair comb embossed with her name, a gold-and-emerald cross on a gold chain, a one-stone emerald ring (said to be a priceless 15-carat stone by today's standards), and a gold brooch with the setting of a heart clasped by a hand and the inscription "No tengo mas que darte" ("I have nothing more to give thee"), presented to the lady by her father before she set sail for Spain where she was to marry a high-ranking nobleman.

The handwritten note at the bottom of the list was dated two months earlier and read:

Dear Ms. Bennett,

I've added a few comments of my own to the translation from the original Spanish, otherwise this is the ship's manifest of valuable objects, as far as historians know, from the *Bella Doña*, which sank in a hurricane somewhere off the coast of Hispaniola in 1692. The wreckage of the *Bella Doña* has never been found, but it was a treasure trove beyond our imagination.

I hope this is what you were looking for.

Yours truly,

Oscar Reinhardt, PhD

Jane refolded the letter and slipped it into a pocket of the leather briefcase lying open on the desk in front of her.

It was exactly what she'd been looking for. The ship's manifest was another important piece of the puzzle. It helped to explain what her father had been doing on this remote Caribbean island. He had been searching for the wreckage of the *Bella Doña*.

The next item Jane removed from the briefcase was a postcard. Faded and slightly out of focus, the corners dog-eared, it was a black-and-white picture of a sprawling Victorian house. Four women, their faces too small and grainy to be distinguishable, posed on a large, wraparound porch. The sign in front of them read THE FOUR SISTERS INN. The words scribbled on the back had been written in a hurry. The message was brief: "My dearest Cordelia, Paradise regained. I have, indeed, seen the Beautiful Lady. Love, Charlie."

The postmark was nearly twenty years ago to the day.

Jane reached for the framed photograph she had propped up on the mahogany desk. It was a color snapshot of a handsome, debonair man in his late thirties and a girl of nine or ten. They were both grinning from ear to ear. The familial resemblance was unmistakable. She was the little girl. Her father was the man. It was the last photograph taken of them together. She never traveled anywhere without it.

"Oh, Dad—" Jane's voice broke off.

Sometimes she still thought of what might have been and was not to be. She had been the last one to give up hope, the last one to accept the fact that her father must be dead.

The official investigation had revealed very little at the time. According to the police report filed on St. Thomas—and the private detective hired by her mother— Charles Avery Bennett was presumed to have drowned or died by "misadventure." His abandoned boat had been discovered several miles offshore with the anchor dropped. Evidence suggested that he had been scuba diving alone. It was just the kind of dangerous and foolhardy stunt good old Charlie would have pulled. And everyone knew it.

Then what was she doing on Paradise?

Jane Bennett asked herself that question for the umpteenth time. The answer was always the same. She wanted to find out what had occurred on that fateful day nearly two decades ago. She *needed* to know for her own sake, for her own peace of mind, exactly what had happened to her father.

For some reason an image of the native fortune-teller who had spoken to her on the ferry ride from the Virgin Islands to Paradise sprang into Jane's head.

What was it the woman had predicted?

Jane closed her eyes and thought for a moment, trying to reconstruct their conversation from memory.

The shark's teeth had been tossed and dutifully examined before the old woman had stated: *"You seek something. No."* She had paused and then corrected her own prophecy. *"You seek someone. A man. You will find him, senorita."*

"But . . . ?" Jane recalled prompting.

"But there is danger. For it is said: 'Come not between the dragon and its wrath.' "

The fortune-teller had been at least partially correct. Jane was seeking a man. Well . . . information about a man anyway. She only wished that she had some idea of what the native woman had meant by the dragon and its wrath.

"Yes, and if wishes were horses, beggars might ride," Jane muttered under her breath as she took a stack of maps from the briefcase and spread them out in front of her on the desk.

It was time to get down to business.

The heart of the Caribbean was the archipelago known as the West Indies or the Antilles. The Greater Antilles consisted of the large islands of Cuba, Jamaica, Hispaniola, and Puerto Rico. The Lesser Antilles were the Leeward and Windward Islands: St. Thomas, St. John, Tortola, St. Kitt's, Antigua, Montserrat, St. Lucia, Martinique, stretching all the way down to Grenada. And, there, to the west of the better-known islands, and no more than a mere speck in the Caribbean Sea, was the tiny and remote island of Paradise.

The second map was an enlargement of Paradise and the surrounding islets; some of which were too inconsequential to even have names. Some were no more than coral reefs rutting dramatically from the sea. Others existed only at low tide.

A third map was color-coded with dates and symbols representing the site of every historically significant shipwreck found during the past quarter century, including the *Nuestra Senora de Atocha*, discovered by salvor Mel Fisher in 1985 after an exhaustive, tragic, and sometimes deadly sixteen-year search.

Where to begin?

That was the question, of course. If Jane were honest with herself—and she did try to face the truth straight-on, sometimes to the point of being unforgiving and ruthless with herself—she knew full well that she wasn't here simply to ferret out information about her father. She wanted to locate the legendary treasure of the *Bella Doña*. She was convinced that its discovery had been the final and crowning act of Charlie Bennett's otherwise seemingly squandered life.

Danger.

As the ferry had approached Paradise on that first day, the island seeress had warned her of the probability.

Danger.

Had her father located the watery grave of the *Bella Doña* and its unfathomable wealth that had lain buried for three hundred years and then paid the ultimate price for his discovery?

Danger.

There was always the possibility of life-threatening danger when a king's ransom in gold and silver and precious gemstones was at stake. Greed had a way of bringing out the worst in people. God knows, Jane had seen enough of greed in her twenty-nine years to last a lifetime. Indeed, several lifetimes.

So what had happened to Charlie?

Had the scuba diving incident been no more or no less than a tragic accident? Had her father fallen overboard, perhaps hitting his head on the side of the boat, and drowned? Had a devil-may-care man, one known to take foolhardy risks, taken one too many risks and paid with his life?

Jane wanted answers.

"Some questions have no answers."

Brilliant Chang had cautioned her of that this morning as the two of them had enjoyed a cup of tea together on the front porch of the Delilah bungalow.

Was she prepared to ask questions, awkward questions, decades-old questions, painful questions, even dangerous questions, for which there were, and might never be, any answers?

Jane sighed, rubbed her eyes wearily, then glanced up from the stack of detailed and intricately drawn maps and gazed out the west-facing window and across the expanse of lush, green, tropical lawn toward the neighboring Samson bungalow.

Why had she kissed Jake Hollister that first night after she had arrived on Paradise?

There was a question without an answer.

Since that encounter on the beach, Jane had managed to avoid being alone with the man. It hadn't been difficult either, now that she thought about it. She occasionally ran into Jake at mealtimes, but the conversation always seemed to be centered on or controlled by one of the Mayfair sisters.

A bittersweet smile lifted the corners of Jane's mouth as she recalled the punch line from a greeting card a friend had once sent her: "Men—can't live with them; can't play mind games without them."

She supposed most women formed their basic attitudes

about the male of the human species from the relationship they'd had with their fathers.

Jane had recognized long ago that her lack of faith in men, her distrust of them, was a direct result of her conflicting feelings about Charlie. On the one hand, she had adored her father. On the other hand, she had always known—or at least sensed, even as a young child—that he was unreliable.

Charlie made promises and didn't keep them.

Charlie bought her expensive gifts and then suddenly, inexplicably took them back, making some excuse about the wrong color, the wrong size, or the shoddy workmanship.

Charlie vowed to be there, but he always disappeared from her life when she needed him most.

Charles Avery Bennett had been a boy to the end: too charming for his own good, too handsome for any woman's good, a little wild, a little flirtatious, frivolous, adventurous, fun-loving, and utterly and completely irresponsible.

She would *not* make the same mistake her mother had, Jane vowed vehemently as she continued to stare out the sunlit window in the direction of the nearby cottage. She would *not* allow herself to become attracted to a good-looking beach bum with more brawn than brains, with more form than substance.

Sniffing disdainfully, she lifted her chin a notch higher in the warm, midafternoon air. The notion was ridiculous. She wasn't in the least bit attracted to Jake Hollister.

"Liar," Jane blurted out, without meaning to.

Perhaps she was attracted to Jake Hollister on a certain primitive . . . physical . . . all right, sexual level. But it didn't mean she had to act on that attraction. In fact, she had absolutely no intention under any circumstances of ever doing so again. One kiss had been enough.

More than enough.

The man was no good. He was uncouth, unshaven, ill-mannered, admittedly handsome as sin, but downright irritating from the top of the lush pelt of dark hair on his head all the way down his long, muscular legs to his usually bare feet.

And he was dangerous.

This was a man with a definite past and definitely without a future. He had no ambitions, no plans, no prospects. He wasn't her type. He never would be. He never could be.

Jane suddenly realized that she was vigorously wafting the air in front of her face with one of the maps she must have absentmindedly folded into a makeshift fan. It was a warm, still, and somewhat sultry afternoon. The perfect afternoon for a dip in the blue Caribbean waters directly below her bungalow.

She quickly stuffed the bundle of maps and the other papers relating to the *Bella Doña* and its precious cargo back in her briefcase, and stashed the whole lot beneath the mahogany desk. It took her less than ten minutes to slip out of her clothing and into a bathing suit, grab her dark sunglasses and a terrycloth cover-up, and head out the door of Delilah, making a beeline for the beach.

Thirty-six.

Thirty-seven.

Thirty-eight.

Thirty-nine.

It was exactly thirty-nine steps from the front door of Samson to the front door of Delilah.

Jake was certain of it.

In the past week, he had walked off the distance between the two bungalows more times than he cared to count.

There was a novella entitled *The Thirty-nine Steps*, Jake recalled from his eclectic reading past. Written by a British barrister-cum-author, John Buchan, later Baron Tweedsmuir, just before the outbreak of World War I, it had eventually been made into a classic black-and-white film by director Alfred Hitchcock.

The Thirty-nine Steps was one of the first true espionage thrillers, and at various points in the story, the hero, Richard Hannay, is mistaken for a cold-blooded murderer, a traitor to his own country, a thoroughly disgusting tramp, and a down-on-his-luck bum. He is pursued throughout England and the Scottish border country by both the police and the true villains of the piece.

At least *he* was only being mistaken for a bum, Jake reflected with a self-deprecating smile as he raised his arm and knocked twice on the porch door of the Delilah bungalow.

"Nobody home, mon," a lilting island voice called out from a nearby thicket of oleander.

Taking two steps sideways, Jake peered around the corner of the cottage. "Who's there?"

A young man emerged from the foliage, wielding pruning shears in one hand and clasping a gunny sack in the other. "Benjamin, Mr. Hollister. That's who 'tis."

Jake recognized the young laborer who frequently did odd jobs for the Mayfair sisters.

Benjamin repeated, his dark eyes round with sincerity, "Miss Bennett not at home."

Jake made to leave, then stopped. "You don't happen to know where she's gone, do you?"

Benjamin nodded his head.

Jake reminded himself to be patient. "Where has Miss Bennett gone?"

The younger man raised his right hand—it happened to be the hand clutching the lethal-looking pruning shears—and pointed in the direction of the water. "Beach."

"When?"

Slender shoulders were lifted high and then lowered once again. "A while ago."

"Ten minutes?"

Benjamin brightened. "More."

"A half hour?"

The handsome but simple youth screwed up his features in thought. "Less."

At least he had managed to pinpoint his quarry's departure for the beach within fifteen or twenty minutes, Jake surmised with some degree of satisfaction. "Thank you, Benjamin."

"You are most welcome, Mr. Hollister," Benjamin responded politely before returning to his assigned task of chopping away at the overgrown oleander bushes.

Jake planted his hands on his blue-jeaned hips and stood there, trying to decide which course of action he should take next. Did he follow Ms. Jane Bennett down to the bay? Or did he cut his losses here and now and forget the entire bloody business?

The truth was, the woman had been avoiding him like the plague ever since that night on the beach. He'd only run into her twice, both times over the dinner table at the main house, where the Mayfair sisters seemed more determined than ever to dominate the conversation.

Oh, he'd caught sight of her several times as she napped in the hammock that had been set up among the palm trees that created a small tropical forest between the two bungalows. Somehow Jake had never had the heart to disturb her.

But he confessed he had watched her.

Jane Bennett was different from any woman he had ever met before. Her eyes were fascinating. They changed color, depending on what she was wearing, the time of day, even her mood.

She was quiet but not at peace. Jake could sense the turmoil churning inside her, the brimming curiosity, the roiling emotions. She was a complex creature.

She was also the kind of woman that a man could spend a lifetime finding out about, exploring with, talking to, learning from, loving. She was a challenge, that's what a woman like Ms. Jane Bennett from Buffalo was to a man. He would always be wondering: What was she feeling? What was she doing? What was she thinking?

"I'll tell you what she thinks about you, Hollister. She thinks that you're a dirty, rotten scoundrel; a no-good beach bum," he snickered darkly, jamming his fists into the pockets of his tattered jeans. "Or, at the very least, the lady assumes you're out for only one thing."

Gee, what could that be?

Sex, maybe.

Why would she think that? Just because he'd taken advantage of her slightly inebriated state that first night on the beach and had kissed her to within an inch of her life.

Hell, she'd been damned lucky he hadn't laid her down on the warm sand, stripped off the ridiculously expensive caftan she'd hastily pulled on over her head, spread her long, lovely legs and made wild, passionate love to her right there and then.

Make love.

Interesting euphemsim.

Didn't he mean have sex with her?

Jake stopped cold in his tracks. No, as a matter of fact, he didn't. It might not be love between the lady and himself, but it sure as hell wasn't unadulterated lust either. There was something about Jane Bennett, something that attracted him in a way, and with a strength, that he couldn't recall ever happening before.

Beads of sweat suddenly broke out on Jake's brow.

Jesus H. Christ, maybe he'd been on this island too long. He was beginning to think and act like an over-eager, adolescent schoolboy. He was a thirty-seven-year-old man who had been almost everywhere and done almost everything. He knew exactly who he was and he knew exactly what he wanted.

"Yeah, right," he said, smirking.

That's why he wasn't having any trouble at all making up his mind on the "complex" choice before him. Did he follow Jane Bennett down to the beach now? Or did he seek her out some other time and some other place? Or did he simply forget the whole damned thing?

The decision was taken out of Jake Hollister's hands.

He heard a woman's terrified scream.

It was coming from the beach.

chapter *Nine*

*P*ain.

Agonizing pain.

Excruciating pain.

Overwhelming pain.

Pain all-encompassing, all-engulfing, all-powerful.

Nothing existed but pain.

It was all that she knew, all that she felt, all that she was.

Jane Bennett collapsed onto the hot, dry sand. One thought managed to penetrate through the searing pain in her brain. How had she made it from the water to the beach?

She had no idea.

She heard a terrifying scream in the distance. Then she realized that her mouth was open and the scream was coming from her.

One minute Jane was floating lazily on her back, basking in the bright Caribbean sunlight, gazing up, transfixed, at the bluest sky she had ever seen, allowing herself to be carried along by the gently lapping waves, the rhythmic

sway of the tropical trees along the shoreline and the
sound of exotic birdsongs trilling from treetop to treetop.

The next minute she felt something brush against her
leg.

It was an instant or two before Jane realized that it—
whatever *it* was—was clinging to her skin. She stood up
in the warm, shallow water of the bay and tried to see
what it could be, but it was just below the surface of the
water and the image was distorted.

Jane waded closer to shore. She stopped. She could
see her upper leg clearly now. A nearly transparent mass
of gelatin had affixed itself to her leg between knee and
thigh.

Immediately she knew something was wrong. Very
wrong. The pain was beginning. Initially it was a flushed
feeling, a panicky feeling. Then it quickly became white-
hot needles piercing, not just her flesh, but directly into
her nerve endings.

It was unlike anything she had ever experienced before. The sensation had started in her leg, yet it was rip-
pling out in ever-increasing circles so rapidly that it soon
engulfed her entire body. The pain was a crescendo, like
the great swell of music and the deafening burst of can-
non fire at the conclusion of Tchaikovsky's "1812 Over-
ture."

A snippet of a memory surfaced from somewhere in
the far recesses of her mind. She recalled reading a newspaper account of a small Australian boy who was stung
by a jellyfish, the kind known as a sea wasp, while he
was swimming in only several feet of water. It had been
no more than two minutes from the time he had left the
water until he had collapsed on shore and died.

Was she dying?

Was she going to take her final breath here and now

while she was all alone and a thousand miles from home?

Jane struggled through the thick water toward the shore.

Dear God in heaven, she wanted to cry out, there was so much she had yet to say, to do, to try to accomplish in this life. It wasn't her time. Surely it couldn't be her time.

Tears welled in her eyes and spilled onto her cheeks. Hot as her tears were, their touch was cool on her heated flesh. She was burning up. The fever was even in her head now too.

Jane's brain began to function in fleeting impressions; her thoughts became mere fragments.

Ice-cold.

White-hot again.

Something on her leg.

Jellyfish.

Death.

Rage swelled up inside her. Perhaps for a moment, and only for a moment, it was strong enough to overcome the devastating pain wreaking every cell of her body.

Jane opened her mouth and screamed. She did not recognize the voice as her own. She did not care that she sounded like a wounded animal shrieking at the top of its lungs. She was wounded and she needed help desperately.

She forced her lips apart one last time. A single word emerged: "Jake!"

Jake hit the beach at a full run.

He had always been good in a crisis, but this time his heart was lodged in his throat and his pulse was pounding in his temples like a huge brass drum. He wasn't winded in the least, yet somehow he couldn't seem to catch his breath.

Where was the ice water reputed to run through his veins?

Where was his utter disdain for and his studied indifference to the plight of other human beings?

Back in the old days—and, let's face it, he admitted, the old days weren't all that long ago—John Spencer Hollister III had been known as one cold-hearted bastard.

But this was different.

He was different.

Jake was sorely afraid that the scream coming from the beach might be Jane Bennett's, and the thought was tearing him apart. His guts were twisting into a sickening knot.

His bare feet hit the hot sand. He never slackened his pace.

The bright sunlight reflecting off the even brighter water blinded him momentarily. He blinked several times in rapid succession and cleared his vision.

It was Jane.

She was half-sitting, half-reclining on the beach. God alone knew how she had managed to drag herself out of the water. When Jake reached her side, one look confirmed his worst fear. For there, clinging to her leg, its colorless body still pulsing with life, its myriad tenacles spread across her thigh, its poisonous barbs undoubtedly penetrating her tender skin, was a huge jellyfish.

She was obviously in excruciating pain. Jake could discern it in her eyes, in the tortured expression on her face, in the feminine fists that pounded the sand beside her, in the way she pleaded with him between screams.

"What is it?" Jane demanded to know.

"A jellyfish."

She was growing more frantic by the second. "Take it off! Please, Jake, pull it off! Do something. Do anything. The pain . . ." She groaned louder. "Jake, the pain."

Jake knew she was in extreme pain. He was tempted to tear the damned thing off with his bare hands. But he couldn't. He didn't dare. It would only make matters worse for both of them.

"I can't," he said, wishing he could explain the reason to her, knowing that under the circumstances she wouldn't understand, praying for some way—dear God, any way—that he could take her pain and make it his own.

He would have done anything to spare Jane Bennett this pain, Jake suddenly realized.

She inhaled sharply and looked directly up at him. "Am I going to die?"

A chill went through him. But he found he couldn't lie to her. "I don't know."

They would both have the answer to her question very soon. That much Jake did know. He held her tenderly, his face pressed to hers. He allowed her to sink her fingernails into the bare flesh of his forearms, drawing blood. He didn't care.

Jake tried to gather his wits about him. Dammit, what did he know about jellyfish?

Some were the size of soccer balls. Some were so tiny and transparent as to be virtually invisible to the human eye. Some were huge, pulsating parachutes with hundred-foot-long tenacles. He seemed to recall that size and color had little to do with a jellyfish's level of toxicity, however. The transparent sea wasps in Australian waters were more of a danger to people than any species of shark.

Their venom was the fastest acting and the most potent in the world.

But this was the Caribbean, not Australia, Jake quickly reminded himself.

"Oh . . ." Another groan of pain came from the sweet, hurting woman in his arms. "Jake . . ."

"I know," he crooned to her. "I know."

"Please, help me."

Jake Hollister had never felt so utterly or so completely helpless in his entire life. It wasn't a feeling, he found, that he cared for.

He gazed down into Jane's pain-filled eyes. "Listen, I wish I could do something. But I can't. If I try to pull the jellyfish off your leg or remove its tenacles, it will only end up releasing more poison into your body."

He had to think and he had to think fast.

Hadn't he heard some months ago, upon first arriving on Paradise, about an old island remedy for a jellyfish sting? Assuming the creature involved wasn't a lethal variety, of course.

Yes!

He remembered now.

It was something a local fisherman had related to Jake as the two of them had been trawling for shrimp on a fine summer morning. The old man had spotted a school of white and purple-freckled cannonball jellyfish not far from their boat. The creatures were so thick in the water that they had turned it into a vast polka-dotted sea.

The knowledgeable islander had turned and announced rather grimly to his companion: "Bad sign, Jake. We can forget shrimping for today. When the jellies move in, everything else moves out. The sharks. The rays. The shrimp. Everything."

Jake had dutifully commiserated with the fisherman about their run of bad luck.

"Jellyfish are a bloody marvel, you know," the shrimper had informed him as he turned the boat around and headed for home. "But they all sting, every last variety of them," he had declared, apparently speaking from experience.

"Then I'll be sure to stay away from your bloody marvels," Jake had only half joked.

"By the way, there's an old island remedy if you're ever stung," the old man had added with a toothless cackle. Then he had gone on to explain exactly what needed to be done.

It came back to Jake in a flash.

He gave Jane a reassuring squeeze. "I think I know what to do to get this bloody thing off you."

"Then do it!" she implored.

Jake wet his lips with the tip of his tongue. "It's an old island remedy."

"I don't care what kind of remedy it is," she claimed.

"Try to stay calm," he cautioned.

"I will," Jane vowed, catching her trembling lower lip between her teeth.

"You're being very brave."

Tears welled once more. "Yes, I am."

The words almost stuck in his throat. "You might prefer to turn your head away."

Jane managed to frown through her pain. "Why?"

"Trust me on this one, okay?"

She nodded.

"Will you do exactly as I say?"

She nodded again.

Jake instructed, "Turn your head away and close your eyes. Don't open them again until I tell you to, no matter what you hear and no matter what you feel. Do you understand?''

"Yes, I understand," came her weak yet clear response.

Jake only hoped when it was all said and done that the damsel in distress would understand. He had no other choice. He had to get the jellyfish off her leg and it was the only way he knew how.

It was, after all, a time-honored island remedy.

"Keep your eyes closed." Jake gave her one final warning before he stood up, took a deep fortifying breath, reached for the zipper of his blue jeans and took aim.

The words of the old fisherman echoed in Jake Hollister's head as the warm, pungent, pale yellow liquid sprayed onto the jellyfish and dripped down Jane Bennett's leg.

"You got to pee on her, man. It is the only way."

chapter *Ten*

"*Y*ou're a lucky young lady, Miss Bennett."

Now that the excruciating pain was beginning to subside to a more bearable level—undoubtedly as a result of the shot the doctor had administered upon her arrival at his office—Jane managed to give him a thin smile. "I'm very lucky, indeed, Dr. Gilmour," she agreed. "A jellyfish sting could have proven fatal."

Jason Gilmour allowed his skepticism to show. "Not a sting from the particular species of jellyfish that attached itself to your leg, I can assure you."

Jane moistened her lips. "I know that now, but neither I nor Jake Hollister realized it at the time."

"The resulting paralysis from the *nematocysts*"—here the good doctor hesitated and then had the wherewithal to translate scientific jargon into comprehensible layman's terms—"that is the stinging capsules on the tentacles of numerous *medusae* or jellyfish, is quite severe and often debilitating."

No one needed to tell Jane Bennett about the pain involved. "It is extremely painful," she stated.

Dr. Gilmour continued with his examination. "Fortunately for you, Jake knew exactly what to do and acted quickly,''

''The man urinated on my leg,'' Jane said, without bothering to disguise her revulsion.

Thank goodness she'd had the sense to keep her eyes closed when Jake Hollister had ordered her to. She shuddered at the thought of what she'd almost had the misfortune to witness on the beach.

''It was the smartest thing Jake could have done since it was highly unlikely he was carrying any antiserum around with him. Applying urine is an old folk remedy for a jellyfish sting. It works surprisingly well too. The *medusae* usually drops right off its victim,'' Jason Gilmour told her with a cheerful bedside manner.

Jane felt compelled to point out one vitally important fact to the island's doctor. ''It only helps, of course, if the sting is that of a non-lethal variety of jellyfish.''

The kindly, white-haired and slightly rumpled gentleman cleared his throat. ''Ahem . . . well . . . yes . . . exactly so. Otherwise, the victim would be dead, and it wouldn't matter any longer. Still, only a marine biologist or an aquatic expert could have made a positive identification of the species you encountered in the bay. There are over nine thousand in the phylum *Cnidaria*, which includes jellyfish. And all true jellyfish sting—it's their primary means of capturing food—but the sting of some is far worse than that of others.''

''Believe me, I'm grateful to be alive,'' she confessed to Paradise's solitary medical personnel.

The truth was, Jane could recall only bits and pieces of the afternoon's traumatic events from the instant the jellyfish had clamped itself onto her thigh until she had been carried, quite literally, into Dr. Gilmour's clinic.

The physical pain was an all-too-vivid memory, as

well as the sound of her own agonizing screams, but she also had a vague recollection of Jake suddenly being there, holding her, soothing her.

More memories came flooding back.

Jake dispensing with the jellyfish.

Jake gathering her up in his arms.

Jake running along the beach; straight up the hillside and past their bungalows.

Jake gently placing her in his Jeep and then driving hellbent for leather down the treacherous and twisting unpaved road, his horn blaring as a warning as he raced along Purgatory's single street and across the open countryside to the doctor's office.

Jason Gilmour finished his inspection of her injuries before making his conclusions known. "No doubt about it, you're a lucky young woman, Miss Bennett. There has been no permanent tissue damage that I can ascertain. You may experience some residual pain, especially after the injection has worn off, but that too will pass in a day or two." He paused, turned, and rummaged in the medicine cabinet behind him. Selecting a small bottle, he handed it to her. "These are mild painkillers. Take one tablet every four to six hours, if necessary. You might need one especially at bedtime to help you sleep."

She accepted the tablets with a heartfelt, "Thank you."

"Do you usually have any trouble sleeping at night, Miss Bennett?" the doctor asked nonchalantly as he reached into a drawer and withdrew what appeared to be a tube of ointment.

"No, I don't," she fibbed. Her sleeping habits were frankly none of this man's business, even if he was a physician.

The tube of ointment was placed beside her on the

examining table. "You can see for yourself there aren't any welts or outward signs of where the jellyfish sank its barbs into your leg, but the skin may still prove to be a bit tender. The salve should help." He gave her hand a reassuring pat. "My prediction is that you'll be as right as rain and as good as new by the first of next week."

"Thank you, Dr. Gilmour."

"You're welcome, Miss Bennett." He leaned back against a desk piled high with medical books and an assortment of professional journals, folded his arms across his broadening midsection, and inquired in an amiable tone, "Are you planning to stay long on Paradise?"

"I'm not certain. I came here for a short vacation." She gave a self-conscious laugh. "But I must confess that I seem to lose all track of time at the inn."

"You're staying with the Mayfair sisters, then?"

Somehow Jane had assumed that her presence on the island, and the reasons she had given for being there in the first place, were common knowledge by now. Heaven knew, anyone or anything in the least bit out of the ordinary was considered news on Paradise.

She pulled Jake's denim shirt more closely around her still damp bathing suit—the shirt had been on loan from its owner since shortly after their arrival at the clinic—and looked squarely at the doctor. "I'm renting one of the bungalows."

He nodded knowingly. "Delilah."

"Yes. Delilah."

Of course, Delilah.

Jake Hollister had been the sole occupant of Samson for more than a year. Surely the doctor was aware of that.

Tit for tat, Jane decided. "Have you been on the island long yourself?" she inquired.

Jason Gilmour gave no indication that he had even heard her question. He simply stood and stared out the window at the tall, whispering sugarcane fields on either side of the road.

The sickly smell of newly cut cane permeated the late afternoon air. A small black pig wallowed in the middle of what had recently been a mud puddle, gnawing on a discarded stick of sugarcane. On the opposite side of the road was a tiny stone chapel.

"The chapel is built of lava rocks spewed up by a volcano and hauled a great distance from the other side, the dark side, of Paradise," he informed her. "The building is held together by molasses, lime, sand from the beach, and cow dung." Jason Gilmour turned back to his patient, blinked his unfocused eyes several times in rapid succession, gave his head a shake and said apologetically, "I beg your pardon, Miss Bennett. Did you ask me something?"

Jane wasn't altogether certain that she wanted to, or even should, repeat her question. The expression on the doctor's face had become one of such utter and complete melancholy for a moment. "I was wondering how long you've been on Paradise."

Gentle, capable hands trembled slightly as they were raised to stroke a wavering chin. "I came to the island a long time ago. Twenty-five years ago to be exact." The masculine voice softened. "It was soon after the death of Angelina."

Jane was beginning to regret her intentional intrusion into Jason Gilmour's private life, but if the doctor had been a resident of Paradise for a quarter of a century, then it was possible, even probable, that he had known her father.

"Angelina was my wife," he went on to confide as he

flopped down into the leather desk chair behind him. "She died in childbirth, along with our baby."

Jane sank her teeth into her bottom lip. This wasn't the appropriate time, she realized, to pursue the subject of Charlie Bennett. There would be other opportunities, surely, to ask this man about her father. "I'm so sorry, Dr. Gilmour. I didn't know."

"Of course you didn't know. How could you, my dear? Think nothing more about it," he consoled her. Nevertheless, Jane noticed that the subject was quickly and summarily dropped. "Once your leg is healed, may I suggest that you get out and explore Paradise. It's a lovely island. There aren't many like it even in the Caribbean."

"I would like that." Jane drew herself up. "I believe I will."

"You won't find a better guide around these parts than Jake Hollister," the doctor recommended with what appeared to be a twinkle of amusement in his eye. "He spends most of his time searching for the wreckage of the *Bella Doña*—in all the wrong places, I might add— but in the process he's managed to garner an encyclopedic amount of knowledge about Paradise and the surrounding islets."

Jane attempted to swallow her astonishment unobtrusively. "The wreckage of the *Bella Doña*?"

That captured the doctor's undivided attention. "You haven't heard the story of the *Bella Doña*?"

God forgive her, came Jane's silent prayer.

She wrinkled up her face and convincingly pleaded ignorance. "I don't believe so."

Apparently Jason Gilmour was off and running on one of his favorite topics of conversation. "Naturally I'm not a professional in the field," came the disclaimer, "but I do consider myself something of an accomplished amateur historian when it comes to the Caribbean Sea and its famous shipwrecks.''

Again, she implored the Almighty for His forgiveness. ''I take it, the *Bella Doña* was a ship, then.''

The man rose fluidly to his feet. ''She was a Spanish galleon that sank in a hurricane on its way back to Europe from South America in 1692. The cargo of the *Bella Doña* was legendary: gold, silver, and jewels beyond compare. Most salvage experts believe the contents of the treasure ship were scattered across miles of ocean floor somewhere off the coast of Hispaniola.''

Jane passed her tongue along the edges of her teeth. ''But not Jake Hollister.''

The doctor shook his head from side to side in good-natured bemusement. ''Let's just say that Jake Hollister is a man with a definite mind of his own.''

She only hesitated briefly before venturing, ''But surely he doesn't have a reputation for being an expert on the subject of historic shipwrecks or sunken treasure.''

''No, he doesn't have a reputation for being an expert on either subject—at least not as far as I know. But you can ask him for yourself. He's still in my waiting room.'' Jason Gilmour headed toward the connecting door. ''I was about to ask Jake to join us anyway. When he brought you in for treatment, I noticed that his arm was bleeding. He may require a stitch or two and a tetanus shot.''

''I'm afraid it's all my fault,'' Jane hastened to confess, feeling sheepish, even a little contrite, about the matter.

Kindly eyebrows were raised in a questioning arch. ''All your fault, Miss Bennett?''

''When I was half out of my mind with pain, I believe

I may have dug my fingernails into Jake Hollister's arm.''

"Miss Bennett seems to have done a pretty thorough job on your arm, Jake," observed Jason Gilmour as he finished disinfecting the set of nasty three-inch-long abrasions. "I'm going to give you a tetanus shot on the basis of it's better to be safe than sorry. But I don't think you're going to need any stitches."

"Whatever you say, Doc." Jake felt the faint pinprick of the needle as it went into his muscle. A sterile, white bandage was then applied to the wounds on his forearm.

"Try to keep your arm clean and dry for a couple of days," the older man instructed.

"No problemo," he said.

Jake was trying to act especially nonchalant about the whole business for Jane's benefit. The young woman appeared uncomfortable enough as it was. She was perched on the very edge of her seat. Her hands were clasped tightly together on her lap. Her lower lip was worried, then gnawed, then tugged on with the sharp, serrated edges of her front teeth as she intently watched every procedure and every move that Dr. Gilmour made.

She was also as white as a sheet.

"Have you ever been stung by a jellyfish, Doc?" Jake asked, once his medical treatment had been concluded.

Jason Gilmour peeled off his sterilized gloves, deposited them in the waste container beside the sink, and began to wash his hands. "Can't say that I have, Jake."

"Well, I haven't either. But from what I observed this afternoon we've both been damned lucky. Miss Bennett was in the most physical pain of any human being I've ever seen. A few minor scratches aren't much in comparison."

Jake hadn't really intended to come to the lady's rescue again, yet she looked like she could have kissed him . . . out of sheer gratitude, if for no other reason.

He wouldn't have minded.

Then again maybe that wouldn't be such a good idea. Jane Bennett had kissed him that first night on the beach, and he had kissed her back: thoroughly, completely, eagerly, passionately, and in just about every other way known to Man. It had been wreaking havoc with his peace of mind and his sleep ever since.

A simple but polite thank-you was in order, however, and that's what he received from the usually prim and proper Ms. Bennett.

"Thank you, Jake," she said with a tremulous smile.

He looked down at her from his position on the examining table, hoping like hell that a dazzling smile would make up for his uncombed hair, his bare chest—she was still wearing his shirt—and his unshaven face. "Anytime, Jane."

The "anything" and the "anywhere" part remained unspoken, but it was definitely there between them nonetheless.

"Well, now that I've got you both patched up and on the road to recovery, would you care to join me for a glass of cold lemonade?" Jason Gilmour inquired.

All of a sudden Jake realized he was incredibly thirsty. "It depends on how well Jane is feeling."

"I'd love a cold drink," she said.

"Then it's settled. Cold lemonade for three coming right up." The doctor removed his official white coat and called out to the woman sitting at the reception desk by the front door of the clinic. "We're going into the house for a few minutes, Mrs. Ortega."

"All right, doctor," came the reply.

Jason Gilmour worked and lived in the same white-washed stone building. It was a convenient arrangement that seemed to suit him well. His medical practice was at the front of the house, and he lived in several large rooms at the rear. There was a living room, a small study, a kitchen, one bedroom, and a bath.

"Please make yourselves comfortable." Their host indicated a trio of overstuffed armchairs arranged haphazardly around a coffee table. The table was piled high with books, stacks of unread newspapers, and unopened mail. There was a bowl of fresh fruit in the center. Several pieces of the fruit had been nibbled on and then returned, half-eaten and complete with visible teeth marks, to the bowl.

Once they were alone, Jane raised a questioning eyebrow in Jake's direction.

"China," was his reply.

Jane was obviously puzzled. "China?" She frowned prettily. "China as in fine china? China as in the country of China?"

Jake was almost enjoying himself. "China as in the monkey," he said.

"Monkey?" She bent forward slightly from the waist, reached out, and placed her hand on his uninjured arm, deliberately keeping her voice pitched to a confidential level. "Do you mean a monkey literally?"

Jake never had the opportunity to answer her. A small, brown, furry creature skipped into the room, across the tabletop, swung up onto the back of Jane Bennett's armchair and proceeded to gave her shoulder-length hair a playful tug.

"What in the world?" She laughed out loud.

Jake found himself simply sitting there and openly staring at her.

"What is it?" Jane asked, still laughing aloud with delight as the tiny, nimble, macaque monkey scampered down the side of the armchair and settled on her lap.

"I've never heard you laugh before."

Her face was suddenly awash with color. She was blushing, Jake realized belatedly.

"Of course you have," Jane said with a dismissive sniff.

Jake was adamant. "I have not."

Evidently she wasn't about to take his claim seriously. "How can you be so certain?"

"Because when you laugh, Miss Jane Bennett, you are the most beautiful thing I have ever set eyes on," he proclaimed.

Her cheeks went from pale pink to bright red in the space of a single breath. "What in the name of male sanity—or is that an oxymoron?—did Dr. Gilmour put in your shot?" she finally said, attempting to make light of his compliment.

Jake refused to back down. "It was a tetanus shot, as you damn well know."

The subject was abruptly changed. "Is this China?" Jane asked, indicating the tiny animal on her lap.

"Ah, Miss Bennett, I see you've met China," Jason Gilmour called out to his guest as he entered the room with a tray of ice-filled glasses and a plate of cookies. "China doesn't take to everyone. And, frankly, not everyone takes to China. Please feel free to scoot her off your lap if she makes you uncomfortable."

"She's wearing a diaper and she seems content. I see no reason why China can't stay exactly where she is," came the reply.

Their conversation centered, at least in the beginning, on the tiny creature.

"Where did China come from originally?" Jane inquired of their host as she carefully sipped her drink, making certain, Jake noticed, not to spill any cold lemonade on the trusting animal.

"She was smuggled into the States from India as a baby," the doctor explained. "When the smugglers were arrested by the authorities, I ended up taking her in."

"How long ago was that?"

Jason Gilmour thought for a moment. "It must be nearly twenty-six years ago now." He nodded his head affirmatively. "It is. China has a birthday coming up soon."

"And she'll be . . . ?"

"Twenty-six years old."

"You've been together a long time," Jane observed.

"Longer than some marriages." There was a pause. "Longer than Angelina and I had together."

Jake found the expression on Jane Bennett's face unreadable, but he wondered if she was thinking the same thing about Doc Gilmour and China that he had on more than one occasion: the tiny creature had become wife, baby, companion, and pet all rolled into one.

"That's enough about little China." Jason Gilmour shoved a stack of newspapers aside, set his glass down on the table in front of him, leaned back in his easy chair, gave Jake a shrewd look, and suggested, "Why don't you tell Miss Bennett the legend of the *Bella Doña*?"

"Hey, I'm just a crazy treasure hunter, Doc, you know that. You're the true historian. Why don't you tell her the story?"

And so he did.

"Once upon a time," Jason Gilmour began. Then he stopped and took a minute to explain that since everything he was about to relate couldn't be proven to be historically accurate, and because he liked to add a flourish or two of his own, he always began with "once upon a time."

"Go on, you old fraud," Jake urged with an affectionate smile.

"Once upon a time, several centuries and more ago, there lived a beautiful young Spanish lady. Now, unfortunately, the young lady's mother had died giving her birth, but she grew up, nevertheless, the apple of her father's eye."

Jake reached out, plucked a fresh apple from the bowl on the coffee table, and juggled it several times in the air.

The doctor ignored him and continued. "The young lady's father was a rich and powerful man. Indeed, he was the governor of a large Caribbean island claimed by the Spanish government."

Jake bit into the crisp apple, chewed noisily several times and swallowed.

"Her *padre* was not a selfish man, however," declared the storyteller.

"Of course not," interjected Jake. "The *padres* in your stories never are."

Jason Gilmour raised his voice momentarily. "In fact, he was a very generous man, especially when it came to his only child and beloved daughter." Here he paused, took a sip of lemonade, and resumed telling the tale in a normal tone of voice. "The governor bestowed upon the lovely *senorita* rich fabrics from the east, which were then fashioned into the latest styles for her to wear."

"Wear where?" Jane asked.

"I'm coming to that," he assured her. "The governor imported scholars to instruct his daughter in languages, history, mathematics, and the sciences. The finest artisans sailed across the ocean from cities all over Europe to teach her painting, singing, dancing, and the pianoforte. When she grew to maturity, the lady's father also presented her with the jewels that had once belonged to her mother. And, upon the occasion of her eighteenth birthday''—here Jason Gilmour raised his right hand in the air, index finger pointing toward the ceiling for emphasis—''the governor christened the newest and greatest ship of the Spanish fleet in her honor, calling it the *Bella Doña*.''

Jane Bennett's lips parted in a smile. ''The beautiful lady.''

Both men nodded.

''The day came, of course, when even these accolades weren't enough for the lovely creature known throughout the islands as Bella Doña. She wanted a title, a grand palace, a place at court, and even greater riches. Her wishes became known to the king, Charles II, and it was suggested that the lady should set sail for Spain. There she would assume a coveted position at the royal court and marry a suitably high-ranking nobleman. The necessary dowry was arranged, the betrothal officially announced, and Bella Doña prepared for the journey that would take her from the New World—the only world, in truth, that she had ever known—to the Old World where she was to become a *duquesa*, a wife and one day, undoubtedly, a *madre* herself.''

Jake noticed that Jane was completely enthralled by the story. She was leaning forward in her chair—making sure not to disturb the tiny creature asleep on her lap—her gaze never once wavering from Jason Gilmour's face.

''Do you suppose the *duque* was in love with Bella Doña?'' she asked, making a hopeful sound.

''I doubt if the gentleman had ever seen his future

wife,'' Jake piped up. ''In those days marriages were nearly always arranged, especially among the upper classes.''

''It is possible, nevertheless,'' Jason Gilmour hastened to add, ''that the prospective bride and groom had exchanged portraits of each other. It wasn't an uncommon practice at the time.''

''Do you think Bella Doña's father loved her?'' Jane asked, unaware, Jake was certain, how wistful her tone had become.

Jason Gilmour chose to say the right words. ''I'm certain that he did, my dear.''

''It must have broken his heart to give his child to another man, to watch her sail away, knowing that he might never see her again.''

''I'm afraid he lost Bella Doña in the end anyway.'' The doctor seemed reluctant to finish the story he had begun.

''Go on,'' urged Jane. ''Tell us the rest.''

He shrugged and went on. ''As far as we know, from available historical records, the ship known as the *Bella Doña* set sail on a fine summer day in 1692. It was carrying a vast treasure in gold and silver coins and ingots, gold chains, and enormous quantities of emeralds and pearls, riches beyond any man's imagination.''

''Of greater importance,'' Jane reminded them, ''it must have been carrying Bella Doña herself.''

Dr. Gilmour shifted in his armchair. ''Among her personal possessions was a brooch presented to the lady by her father just before she set sail. It was inscribed with the words: '*No tengo mas que darte.*' ''

'' 'I have nothing more to give thee,' '' Jane whispered.

The doctor threw her a glance. "I see you know your Spanish, Miss Bennett."

She appeared slightly flustered. "Only a little."

"Your strength in languages, if I'm not mistaken," Jake spoke up, "is French and Italian, with a smattering of Spanish and next to nothing of Latin."

"You have an excellent memory for details, Mr. Hollister."

So it was back to *Mr.* Hollister, was it?

"You might be surprised what I have an excellent memory for, Ms. Bennett," Jake muttered under his breath, knowing full well that Jane had heard every word.

"Please finish your story, Dr. Gilmour," she requested.

"The ending, I'm afraid, is an unhappy one. The *Bella Doña* set sail on a clear day, but the ship encountered weather-related problems only a day or two out of port. Historians believe that the ship could have reached Hispaniola."

"Or one of a hundred other islands in the Caribbean," Jake butted in, advancing his own theory.

"Or perhaps one of a hundred other islands," Jason Gilmour repeated with a tolerant smile. "It makes little difference to us and it made absolutely no difference to the passengers and crew aboard the *Bella Doña*. The ship sank during a hurricane and all lives were lost."

"The treasure, as well," Jake added.

Tears welled unwillingly, unknowingly, in Jane Bennett's eyes. "Her poor father."

The doctor raised his glass to his mouth, drained the last of the lemonade, and concluded with the statement: "It's said that he died of a broken heart within a year."

Jake refused to give in to such mawkish sentimentality. "And men have been searching for the wreckage of the

Bella Doña ever since. So far unsuccessfully."

Jane was obviously curious, in spite of herself. "Why do men seek treasure, Jake? What is the allure?"

He took in and let out a deep breath before he replied. "For some, I suspect, it's the thrill, the rush of pure adrenaline, that comes with discovery."

"Go on," she urged.

"There has always been a lost thing, a lost time, a lost place, cut off from the rest of the world, Jane. Legendary cities of gold. Ancient cities buried beneath the sea, buried beneath the rubble of a mountain or a volcano, buried underneath other cities. The quest for the lost has always held a fascination for some people."

People like him.

Jake continued. "For others it might be the satisfaction of finding a clue to the past, a missing piece of history." Here, he paused. "For others it's simple greed."

Brown eyebrows were arched above intelligent brown eyes. "Is greed ever simple?"

Jake grinned and held up both his hands in mock surrender. "Hey, I give up. I know when I'm getting in way over my head. If it's philosophy you want to discuss, you should see Brilliant Chang."

"As a matter of fact, I met Mr. Chang only this morning," Jane informed him. "The gentleman paid me a visit and erected a spirit house outside my bungalow."

"Fascinating man, Brilliant Chang," offered Jason Gilmour.

Jane put her hand to her mouth and stifled a yawn.

"It's time you took Miss Bennett back to her bungalow, Jake," the doctor advised as he lifted China from her lap. "The shot I administered may make the lady a bit drowsy. She should get a little extra rest, anyway." He said to Jane, "I'll stop by tomorrow and see how you're faring. In the meantime, if you need medical help, don't hesitate to send someone to fetch me.''

"Thank you, Dr. Gilmour." Jane stifled another yawn. "And thank you again for the lemonade."

At her insistence, a suitable donation was left with the clinic receptionist. It was nearly dark when Jake tucked her into the passenger seat of his Jeep and headed for home.

Jason Gilmour watched from his window as the Jeep sped down the dirt road, leaving a cloud of dust in its wake.

"You liked her, didn't you, China?" He found the tiny monkey's favorite spot behind her left ear and gently scratched it. Then he exhaled on a sigh and admitted, "I liked her too."

The doctor stood there for another minute or two. "It can't be merely coincidence that she's here on Paradise. I wonder how much she knows. Poor Charlie Bennett. Poor Mary Magdalene. The past is never really dead and buried. It always comes back to haunt the living."

For on a night much like tonight, twenty years before, unspoken passion had flared and unspeakable deeds had been done; all in the name of love. But the past—especially the sins of the past—refused to remain buried.

Jason Gilmour recalled a quotation that he had read forty years before in a college class on the ancient Greek philosopher, Heraclitus. He had wondered if it were true then; he knew it to be true now: *A man's character was his fate.*

chapter*Eleven*

Jane knew someone had been there the minute she walked into the bungalow.

She hesitated for a moment or two just inside the front door of Delilah. It wasn't as if the cottage had been ransacked, or the tables and chairs overturned, or even at a glance that anything appeared to be missing or out of the ordinary. It was simply that as she had crossed the threshold, a chill had run down Jane's spine. Somehow, in some way, something hadn't felt right to her.

There was an absence of *rightness*.

Obviously Jake hadn't anticipated her stopping so abruptly or without a word of warning. He ran into her from the back with a soft thud. "What is it?"

"I don't know," she said without inflection.

He was standing so close to her that Jane could feel the muscles in his arms and legs tense in anticipation. She sensed the sudden and heightened awareness in his body.

Survival instincts must have cautioned him to lower his voice to a whisper. "What do you *think* it is, then?"

Jane turned her head to the side; she was barely breathing. "Someone has been here."

He was perfectly serious when he asked: "Are they here now?"

She relaxed. "No."

That didn't entirely satisfy Jake. "How do you know?"

She shrugged. "I don't know how I know. I just do." She felt foolish saying it out loud. But the truth was someone *had* been in the bungalow, and they weren't there now.

Jake lifted and then lowered his bare shoulders—she was still wearing his shirt—before offering an opinion. "Maybe it was the woman who comes in to tidy up."

"She cleaned the place from top to bottom yesterday and told me that she would return next Tuesday."

Jake tried again. "Perhaps it was one of the Mayfair sisters." He didn't sound convinced of that option himself. "Although I've never known our landladies to trespass once they've rented out a bungalow. They're very respectful of personal privacy."

"Yes. They are."

"So, all we've got to go on so far is this 'feeling' of yours," Jake clarified.

That was about the size of it.

There was a minute of silence. "Do you get these feelings often?" he inquired.

"Only sometimes," she confessed, rubbing her arms. "And usually it's about furniture."

Jane could just imagine the expression on the man's face; she could certainly hear the skepticism in his voice.

"I really don't want to be having this conversation," Jake muttered. But, of course, he had to finish what he'd started. They both knew that. He gave a long-suffering sigh. "Why, pray tell, do you get feelings about furniture?"

"I authenticate antiques."

"So?"

"I'm very good at it."

"Congratulations," he said dryly.

The time for modesty had passed. "Actually I'm one of the leading experts in the field. I have a near photographic memory when it comes to antique sofas and chairs, tables, highboys, armoires, commodes, writing desks—"

Jake cut her off. "I think I get the idea."

Jane went straight to the point. "There have been occasions when all the expertise and all the knowledge in the world hasn't been enough."

"Not even for you?"

"Not even for me."

"And . . . ?" he prompted.

"And somehow I still always know."

"Are you clairvoyant?"

"I suppose you could say I am in a way. But my clairvoyance only seems to apply to furniture or perhaps a piece of rare old silver or sometimes the occasional—"

"Rug," he finished for her.

Jane was forced to bite her tongue to keep from laughing. "Very funny."

"I've just never heard of a psychic antique dealer before," Jake confessed with a deep-chested chuckle.

She shouldn't have told him. "I shouldn't have told you," she said out loud.

"Don't worry. Your secret is safe with me." He whistled soundlessly, then said, "I think it might be a good idea for me to look around anyway. I'll sleep better if I know everything is all right here before I head back to Samson.''

She'd sleep better, as well, Jane admitted to herself.

''Don't turn the lights on yet, and stay here,'' he ordered as he glided through the darkened room. He was back in less than five minutes. ''The coast is clear.''

She'd known it was. ''Now what?''

''Now let's turn the lights on.'' Jake reached for the lamp on the table beside him. The room was soon aglow with light. ''I'd like you to take a good look around if you feel up to it.''

''I feel fine,'' she assured him. Her drowsiness had vanished the instant she'd entered the bungalow.

''Our goal is to see if anything is missing.'' He paused and then placed a protective arm around her shoulder for a moment. ''How's the leg feel?''

She smiled up at him. ''No pain.''

It was the truth. There wasn't any pain. She was aware of the inch-wide streaks on her thigh where the jellyfish had attached its tenacles, but the pain itself had faded to a kind of tenderness, as Dr. Gilmour had predicted.

Jake went from room to room, turning on every light in the place. Then he stood in the center of what served as the living room, with his hands on his hips, and scrutinized the interior of the cottage.

Jane's heart took a leap.

The man was magnificent.

Even with heavy five o'clock shadow on his jaw (he probably hadn't shaved in two or three days), even with thick, dark, tousled hair that he never seemed to comb (its texture was that of fine black silk), even with a faint streak of what appeared to be blood smeared across his midsection (his abdomen was all hard, taut muscles and tanned skin), even with brown stains on the knees of his jeans (no doubt from kneeling in the damp sand to care for her), Jake Hollister was still the most attractive man she had ever set eyes on.

Jane nearly choked on her own saliva.

She must be losing her mind.

Jake Hollister wasn't her type. He never would be. He never could be.

Her type was impeccably groomed from the top of his fashionably styled hair to the tips of his highly polished, handmade Italian shoes. Her type was well-dressed, well-educated, well-mannered, and certainly well-off. Her type knew what wine was the perfect complement to poached salmon and which port should always be served with a wedge of Stilton and a slice of pear.

The men in her life seemed to be equally comfortable in tweeds or tails. They played golf, tennis, polo, or squash—with athletic skill and, above all else, of course, with sportsmanship.

The men who populated her world were interesting and knowledgable. They could converse on a wide range of topics from the talents of the leading soprano at La Scala that season, to the best place to rent a villa along the Mediterranean.

They knew how to treat a lady like a lady. They were polite. They were cultured. They were considerate. They were respectful.

They were boring.

Jane's mouth dropped open.

"What is it?" Jake demanded to know. "Have you noticed something missing?"

Only in her life; not in her bungalow, she nearly blurted out the damning truth.

Jane snapped her teeth together. Then she opened her

mouth again long enough to explain, "I haven't looked yet."

"What have you been doing?"

She wondered what Jake Hollister would say if he knew that she'd been standing there daydreaming or—since it was already after dark—nightdreaming about him.

She ignored the question the man had asked—a talent every smart woman learned sooner or later—and answered the one she wanted to instead. "I was wondering if Brilliant Chang would be kind enough to return and bless the house a second time since its peace and tranquility have been disturbed."

"I suggest we worry about peace and tranquility in the morning," Jake grumbled impatiently. "For now, let's simply find out if any of your belongings have been pinched."

Jane immediately came to attention and snapped her heels together. "Yessir."

"We'll approach this in a logical manner."

Jane batted her eyelashes at him. "What an excellent idea. Why didn't I think of that?"

Jake gave her a speculative glance. "What in the hell did Doc Gilmour put in your shot?"

"It was a painkiller, as you well know," she answered offhandedly.

He shook his head. "I guess that explains it."

"Explains what?"

"Your behavior." He refused to expound further. Instead, he started firing questions at her. "Is any of your money missing?"

Jane checked her handbag. "No. It's all here."

"Credit cards?"

"They're here too."

"Travelers checks?"

"Ditto."

"What about jewelry?"

"Well, I rarely wear any jewelry," she explained, "but when I do I prefer yellow gold or occasionally a touch of platinum or white gold."

Jake blew out his breath expressively. "I meant, has any of your jewelry been stolen?"

Jane's mouth formed a perfectly round *O*. "I'll have to check," she informed him.

Dark, masculine eyes were raised heavenward, as if praying for patience. "You do that."

Jane trooped along to her bedroom, opened the top bureau drawer, delved under a pile of silk undergarments and located the small velvet pouch where she stashed her jewelry. It took only half a minute to verify that the few pieces of gold jewelry she had brought with her on this trip were safely where she had left them.

"Everything's here," she called out to her interrogator as she replaced the velvet pouch, straightened her panties and bras, and sauntered back into the living room.

A lightbulb seemed to go on over Jake's head. He snapped his fingers together. "What about your passport?"

"It's in my handbag," she stated.

"Better double check."

She double checked. Her passport was exactly where she had expected it to be.

Jake's eyebrows snapped together. "Are you certain someone was in here?"

"Yes."

He waggled his head. "And you don't have any idea what they might be looking for?"

That's when it hit Jane.

Good Lord! There was something of immeasurable value that she hadn't even considered since returning to the bungalow. It was the contents of her leather briefcase. Inside the briefcase were a copy of the ship's manifest, all of her detailed maps, her father's postcard, that last photograph taken of the two of them together, the professor's letter, and her copious notes on the wreckage of the *Bella Doña.*

Jake made an impatient sound. "Well, do you or don't you?"

She tried to stall. She needed time to think. It was difficult enough to keep a semblance of her wits about her, but between the painkiller administered by the good doctor and Jake Hollister standing there, beautifully bare-chested and staring down intently into her eyes, she was sunk.

"Does she or doesn't she?" Jane repeated.

A muscle in Jake's face began to twitch. "Jane, do you have any idea what the thief was looking for?"

She told a bald-faced lie. "No."

He came a step closer. "Jane . . ."

It was the way he said her name. He knew she was lying.

"Dammit."

It wasn't until he laughed aloud that she realized she'd given herself away.

"Gotcha!" he declared and took another step toward her.

She caught her bottom lip between her front teeth. "Do I have to tell you?" she groaned.

"It'd make it a whole lot easier on both of us if you did. Sooner or later, you're going to have to trust somebody."

He was right.

And, after all, he had saved her life this afternoon.

Well . . . in a manner of speaking.

He had been kind and considerate and concerned. He had rushed to her rescue. He had been her salvation, the only thing, the only one, who had stood between her and potential disaster.

She might be a little afraid of him. Any woman with an ounce of intelligence or common sense would be. Jake Hollister was entirely too sexy, too attractive, too uncivilized, and far too irresistible for his own good.

Not to mentions hers.

But underneath that gruff and unshaven exterior was a decent and honorable man, she just knew it. He might even be described as a gentleman in some circles. She believed that he was a man she could trust with her life . . . if not her heart.

She had to face it. She had to trust someone and her choices on the island were rather limited. If not Jake Hollister, then who else could she put her faith in?

No guts, no glory.

Nothing ventured, nothing gained.

Jane moistened her lips and drew a fortifying breath. "I'm not sure where to start."

He ran a weary hand across his eyes. "Since it's getting late and we've already had a hell of a day with not much to drink or eat besides a glass of lemonade and a stale cookie—"

"You had an apple," she reminded him.

"I had several bites of an apple," Jake corrected. "Why don't we cut to the chase?"

So she did. "I'd heard of the *Bella Doña*."

He smacked his forehead with an open palm. "Now there's a frigging revelation."

There was no need for him to be sarcastic. Nevertheless, she continued. "I knew about the shipwreck."

"And the treasure?"

"Yes, and the treasure. But I'd never heard the entire story."

"You mean the fairytale that Jason Gilmour entertained us with this afternoon?"

She eyed him warily. "I was aware of most of the historical facts."

"Why didn't you let on?"

She raised her hands waist-high and then let them drop again. "Dr. Gilmour seemed to be having so much fun telling us about the *Bella Doña*." She added, "It was a fascinating story."

"Most of it was pure fiction."

"Well, I enjoyed his version," she said, coming to the doctor's defense.

Jake rubbed a hand back and forth across his bare stomach. "Do you have anything to drink around here?"

"Tea."

"Anything stronger?"

"Coffee."

He winced.

She was immediately solicitous. "Are you in pain?"

For some reason Jake didn't answer that question.

She tried again. "Does your arm hurt?"

"Naw."

"Now who's not telling the truth?"

Jake ran his hand through his hair and assumed an air of almost casual indifference. "I know it's late and we're both tired and hungry, but I'd like to ask you a question."

"Ask away."

"I want an honest answer."

Jane swallowed hard. "All right."

"Who's Charlie?"

chapter *Twelve*

"Charlie's full name was Charles Avery Bennett," Jane said to him. There was a slight catch in her voice.

Jake immediately picked up on her use of the past tense. "Was?"

"Charlie's dead," came the cryptic response.

"I'm sorry." It was a socially acceptable expression of sympathy on his part, yet Jake felt like a hypocrite for using it. He wasn't really sorry that Charlie Bennett was dead. Not if it meant that Charlie Bennett *alive* would have stood between him and what he wanted.

And what he wanted, Jake realized, was this woman.

He was beginning to feel like something of a heel, as well. "I shouldn't have asked."

She stood a little straighter. "It's all right. Truly it is."

"You have my deepest condolences."

"Thank you," she responded with excruciating politeness.

"Who was he? Your husband?"

Jane turned and looked at him with an incredulous expression on her face. "Charlie was my father."

Jake was momentarily speechless. "Your father?" he finally said, mostly to himself.

"Yes, my father." She shot him a frown. "By the way, where did you learn his name?"

"I heard you mention it that first night down on the beach," Jake admitted, trying to quickly adjust his thinking and correct the misconception that he had been carrying around in his head for the past week and more.

Charlie was Jane's father!

He wasn't her lover, or her boyfriend, or her husband, or even her ex-husband. He had been her father.

It changed everything.

She cast him a sidelong glance. "You look like you could use a drink."

Jake wasn't going to pretend otherwise. "I could."

"Champagne is all I had and it's gone," she said apologetically. "I'm afraid we drank it that night on the beach. I don't have anything else to offer you."

"It doesn't matter."

And it didn't.

Jake had discovered shortly after his arrival on Paradise that alcohol never solved problems; it only created them.

"I can offer you something to eat," Jane said, still seemingly concerned for his welfare. "Why don't we go into the kitchen and raid the fridge?"

It was the best offer he'd had all day. Hell, coming from this woman, it was the best offer Jake Hollister had ever had, period.

"Sit," she ordered, pointing to one of the two chairs at the kitchen table.

Jake sat.

"I'm not sure what supplies the housekeeper has stocked the refrigerator and cupboards with, but I am considered something of a gourmet cook,'' Jane informed him with more than a hint of pride in her voice. "I've been known to perform near culinary miracles with next to nothing available in my kitchen.''

Apparently the woman did everything well.

Jake wondered just how far afield and in what specific directions Jane Bennett's talents took her. He couldn't prevent the smile that appeared on his face as a thoroughly risque image flitted across his mind.

She opened the door of the refrigerator and bent over to examine its contents. Meanwhile, he seized the opportunity to study her lovely derriere and her lovely long legs. She was still dressed in her swimsuit and his denim shirt. The shirt reached midthigh on her, but there was plenty left to admire.

"I'm so hungry,'' he confessed upon hearing a loud growl coming from his stomach and knowing that she must have heard it too, "that I could eat anything right now.''

She tossed over her shoulder, "How does an omelet sound?''

"Great.''

"Do you like grated cheese in yours?''

"Perfect.''

"How about mushrooms?''

Jake nodded his head and gave a grunt.

"Green pepper?''

He grunted again.

"Onions?''

"Yup.''

"Tomatoes?''

"Sure.''

"Artichoke hearts?''

Hell, why not?

Each time he voiced his agreement, Jane plucked the item from the refrigerator shelf and placed it on the kitchen counter next to the container of fresh eggs. She finally straightened and remarked to him, "I must say, Jake Hollister, you're an easy man to please."

She had no idea how easy.

"All we have available to drink with our supper is milk or coffee," she informed him as she went right to work at the stove. "There doesn't seem to be a supply of liquor in the house, not even a little sherry or wine to cook with."

Jake could hear the sizzle of butter melting in a hot frying pan and his belly clenched in anticipation. "I don't think the Mayfair sisters approve of 'spirits.' "

"Yet you own the only bar on the island," she pointed out.

He would attempt to explain. "For the Mayfairs, the world in general—and Paradise in specific—is divided into two parts. There is the town down there where the common folk live, and the hill up here where they reside."

"And never the twain shall meet?"

"Something like that. I don't think they object to alcohol as long as they don't actually have to come into contact with it themselves."

"Oops." Jane stifled a laugh. "I didn't realize alcoholic beverages weren't allowed on the premises the night I decided to celebrate on the beach."

"I'll never tell," he vowed.

"How do I know that?" she teased him.

"My silence can be bought."

She didn't bother stifling her laughter this time. "Ah— 'hush' money."

"I didn't say anything about money, did I?" Jake

threw right back. From the embarrassed expression on her face, he decided a change of subject was in order. "You were toasting your father that first night, weren't you?"

Jane's eyes glazed over. Jake was almost sorry he'd mentioned it, but his curiosity was killing him. He needed to know everything there was to know about this woman. And the place to begin was with her father and just what the hell she was doing on Paradise. That's what his gut instincts told him.

And his gut instincts were rarely, if ever, wrong.

Her eyes cleared. "Yes, I was."

He shifted in his chair and stretched his legs out under the table. "If you don't want to talk about it, I'll understand. After all, it's none of my business."

She glanced at him over her shoulder. "I promised I was going to tell you the truth, Jake, and I am."

Thank God, he silently intoned.

Using her right hand, and a graceful flick of her wrist, she broke one egg after another into a mixing bowl. "I'm not on this island by accident, and I'm not here for a vacation," she announced.

He knew that.

She deliberately took in and released a lungful of air. "I'm here to find out what happened to my father."

Dead or alive, apparently.

"Charlie was last seen alive on Paradise," she added as something more than an afterthought.

That didn't make a lot of sense to Jake. He'd been on the island for over a year and he had never heard the man's name mentioned until a slightly inebriated Jane Bennett had raised her champagne glass in a toast to him. "Are you sure your father was here on Paradise?"

She was resolute in her convictions. "He was."

"When?"

Jane's jaw firmed. "Twenty years ago."

"You're kidding." But he could see that she wasn't. "The trail is going to be a little cold, isn't it?"

"Yes, it is."

"The odds of finding anything or anyone twenty years after the fact must be . . ." Jake paused and raised his shoulders in a shrug.

"Astronomical," she finished.

Jane Bennett was no fool. She had to know what she was up against. Obviously discovering what happened to her father was important enough to her that she was willing to try, whatever the odds of success or the likelihood of failure.

Jake blinked in astonishment. "The old woman was right," he mouthed.

"The old woman?"

"The one who was aboard the ferry the day we sailed from St. Thomas into Purgatory. Surely you remember. Besides selling candy, fruit, and cigarettes to the passengers, she was tossing shark's teeth and telling fortunes."

Jane turned and jabbed the air for emphasis, using the paring knife in her hand. "Her name is Nui, by the way, and she's some kind of distant relation to Brilliant Chang."

"You don't say."

"I just did."

"Well, Nui predicted that you were looking for a man, and it turns out that that's exactly what you're doing."

With a censorious glance in his direction, Jane returned to her culinary efforts. "You were eavesdropping."

"I didn't have much choice. I was only standing a few feet from you and your friends—"

"If you're referring to the St. Cyrs," she interrupted. "They are not my friends."

"Okay. I was only standing a few feet from you and your acquaintances."

"Unwilling acquaintances, at that," she said blisteringly.

Whew! The lady could be downright bullheaded once she'd made up her mind.

"Anyway, the ferry is public transportation and the fortune-teller made no attempt to lower her voice," he said.

Jane seemed to recover her sense of humor. "She didn't exactly whisper, did she?"

"No, she didn't."

"I suppose everyone on board heard her."

"Only the passengers on the top deck."

"Well, it doesn't matter. Her predictions were nothing more than a lucky guess or two on her part," Jane declared, determined to dismiss the entire incident. "I don't believe in fortune-tellers, or soothsayers, or any of that mumbo jumbo, do you?"

Jake rubbed his hand back and forth along his nape. He suddenly realized that he needed a haircut. "What about your own clairvoyance when it comes to furniture?"

Jane made a funny face. "That's different," she claimed as she expertly went about the business of chopping crisp green peppers and ripe, red tomatoes into bite-size chunks.

Was it?

Jake could be stubborn too. He wasn't about to let her off the hook that easily. "Is it? How?"

His hostess offered up a rational explanation—at least it was rational in her opinion—while she continued cooking. "I don't believe there's any psychic or supernatural ability involved in what I do. It's simply in the blood. I have lived and breathed antiques since the day I was born. I grew up surrounded by them. I've spent a lifetime studying them, learning about them. I love them. And, yes, perhaps I have a special feel for them. But that's all."

Just as he had a special feel for when people were lying, Jake ruminated.

Like now.

Everything that occurred in a man's life couldn't be explained in purely rational terms. That much Jake had learned the hard way. Perhaps his friend, Brilliant Chang, had said it best: There were some questions that had no answers.

Jake raised his chin in the air and breathed in deeply. "Something sure smells good."

"It's almost ready. What would you like to drink? Water? Coffee? Milk?"

He might as well go for the wholesome image. "I'll help myself to a glass of milk. What would you like?"

"I'll have the same," Jane replied as she took two plates from the cupboard above her head and set them on the countertop.

It wasn't long before Jake was wolfing down perfectly toasted bread and the best omelet he had ever tasted. "Your reputation as a cook is well-deserved. This is delicious."

"Thank you," she responded.

"In fact, it's great."

"I'm glad you're enjoying it," Jane said between far daintier bites than his.

He tried not to talk with his mouth full. "It's more than great; it's fabulous."

"Would you like seconds?" she inquired.

Jake immediately held out his empty plate. "If it wouldn't be too much trouble. Yes, please."

"It's no trouble," Jane assured him.

Sometime later, while lingering over a cup of coffee, the subject of the cottage's recent trespasser was raised again.

Jake chose what he hoped was the right moment to remind Jane. "You were going to tell me what you think the thief was after."

"Why don't you bring your coffee and come into the other room with me?" she suggested.

He did, making himself comfortable in one of the overstuffed chairs beside a large mahogany desk, coffee cup in his hand. Jane sat down in the companion chair, but only after she had rummaged under the desk and emerged with a brown leather briefcase.

Her sigh of relief was audible. "It's still here."

Jake regarded the lady and the object in her hands. "You believe someone was after your briefcase?"

She begged to differ with him. "Not the briefcase itself but its contents."

Patience wasn't Jake Hollister's long suit. It never had been. It never would be. It wasn't something that he had been born with or blessed with as he matured. Nor had he ever managed to obtain a sufficient amount of it in his business dealings, no matter how hard he'd tried. But he could be patient, if absolutely necessary, at certain times.

This was one of those times.

Jane Bennett would divulge the contents of her briefcase when she was good and ready.

Apparently she was good and ready now.

She unlocked the brass closure on the front of the

briefcase, opened the top and then proceeded to extract a pile of papers, several manila file folders, a stack of maps, what appeared to be an assortment of business letters, and even a snapshot or two. She sorted through each item, one by one, and then announced, without bothering to conceal her excitement, "It's all here."

"Good news?"

"Wonderful news!" she exclaimed.

Jake was chomping at the bit. He wanted to ask Jane if he could examine the contents of her files. He'd caught a glimpse of what appeared to be a translation of the *Bella Doña's* manifest and wonderfully detailed maps of Paradise and the surrounding islands. She might have information that could be of immense help to him in his search for the sunken treasure ship.

But he couldn't do it.

He couldn't bring himself to sweet-talk this woman into helping him. There was too much at stake. Not gold or silver or emeralds or buried treasure but something of far greater value to him: the chance of a future with Jane Bennett.

Jake sat back in his chair. "So, whatever your thief was after, it appears that he didn't get his hands on it."

"No, he didn't get his hands on it." Jane leaned toward him. "You're looking for the wreckage of the *Bella Doña*, aren't you?"

"In my spare time," he answered, trying to sound nonchalant about it. Hell, all he had these days was spare time.

Jane sat up ramrod straight in her chair. "I have a proposition for you, Jake Hollister."

He didn't move. "Do you, Jane Bennett?"

She scooted closer. "Let's make a deal."

He raised his eyebrows and repeated, "Let's make a deal?"

"I want us to become partners."

chapter *Thirteen*

"*L*oose lips sink ships," Jane cautioned.

"I beg your pardon," Jake said, looking at her as if she'd lost her mind.

"If we're going to become partners in this venture, then it must be understood that whatever we say and whatever we do will be held in the strictest confidence."

"In other words," he recapped, "it will be our secret."

She nodded her head. "Neither of us will breathe a word to anyone of what passes between the two of us."

"We could write it down and sign it in our own blood, if you like," he suggested in a tone that narrowly missed being sarcastic.

He was making fun of her, of course. Jane recognized that almost immediately. "I don't think it's necessary to go to those extremes." She did, nonetheless, have several relevant points she wanted to discuss with him. "I believe we both understand the reasons why I wish to find the *Bella Doña*."

She watched as Jake eased back into the comfortable, overstuffed armchair and took a drink of his coffee before he responded. "I assume it's a kind of tribute to your father."

So he did understand.

"It is."

"Maybe it's also a way of finally putting the past to rest for you and for Charlie."

He understood more than she'd given him credit for.

"That too," she agreed.

"You might even be trying to find the *Bella Doña* so you can prove to the world, in general, and skeptics, in particular, that your father was right for once in his life."

The man was a mind reader.

"It's all of the above," Jane acknowledged, folding her lips into a soft, obstinate line that friends and foes alike would have had no difficulty in recognizing.

"There could still be another reason," her partner theorized.

Jane was at a loss. "Another reason?"

Something flickered behind the brooding hazel eyes. "Maybe you wouldn't mind acquiring a few fabulous jewels and a ton or two of gold and silver for yourself."

"I'm not interested in acquiring jewels of any kind or so much as an ounce of gold or silver," she informed him in no uncertain terms.

There was a huge safe deposit box filled with priceless jewelry back home in the bank in Buffalo. It had been bequeathed to Jane by her maternal great-grandmother. She hadn't even bothered to look at the stuff in years.

Not that it was any of Jake's business.

"I thought every woman was interested in fancy baubles and a huge, and preferably Swiss, bank account; even one born with a silver spoon in her mouth," he ventured.

Was the man intentionally trying to be offensive, Jane wondered with some heat.

If so, he was succeeding.

"How does the saying go?" Jake deliberated for five, maybe ten, seconds, his dark brows drawing together. " 'A woman can never be too rich or too thin.' "

Jane refused to conceal her feelings on the matter. "That is pure hooey."

"Hooey?" he repeated, sounding faintly puzzled. "I don't believe I'm familiar with that term."

She bit the inside of her cheek. "Perhaps you know it best under one of its more common synonyms: bunk, baloney, balderdash, poppycock, drivel, hogwash, or bullshit?"

Jake made a disapproving clicking sound by flicking the tip of his tongue against the back of his front teeth. "Tsk-tsk. Such language, and from a lady."

Fiddlesticks. She had allowed the man to cause her to lose her composure, and that was something she rarely did. Jane wasn't proud of herself or of her crude use of profanity.

"If you will pardon my French," she finally added with a humorless smile.

"I had no idea bullshit was a French word," Jake managed with a perfectly straight face.

Jane decided it was time to move the conversation along. "You're well aware of my reasons for wanting to find the *Bella Doña*. I think it's only fair, under the circumstances, that I know why you're searching for the wreckage."

"You want to understand my motives."

"Exactly," she said.

Jake took her request seriously. "I'd never heard of the *Bella Doña* before I arrived in this part of the hemisphere. Even as a boy, I don't recall having any interest in pirates or buried treasure or long-lost shipwrecks or tropical islands.'' He brushed his hand across his eyes almost involuntarily. "Before I came here, I was another kind of man and I lived in another kind of world altogether.''

Jane found she couldn't move or speak.

Nor did she wish to.

"I left the States over a year ago." Jake paused, then apparently reconsidered his time frame. "I guess it's been closer to two years ago now. Anyway, I wandered from island to island. One was pretty much the same as the next to me. I ended up on Paradise entirely by accident. One day I was feeling slightly under the weather—"

He stopped his narrative cold.

She waited.

He gave a snort. "All right, I'd been drinking. Somehow I ended up on the local ferry. When it docked at Purgatory and the other passengers got off, so did I.'' Jane listened to the resignation in his voice. "I've been here ever since.''

"What made you stay?'' she asked eventually.

"Well, as it turned out, I joined in a poker game over at the Mangy Moose one night shortly after my arrival on the island and I won the damned place.'' His tone was only half humorous.

Jane blinked in astonishment. "You won the Mangy Moose in a card game?''

The corners of his mouth turned up into a smile of self-mockery. "That's about the size of it.''

Why, the whole idea was preposterous.

Jane stared at him in disbelief. "You became a business owner completely by chance.''

Jake gave a little private laugh. "There are any number of witnesses who would argue with that statement."

"Meaning?"

"Meaning the game was probably rigged."

"Rigged so you would win?" Jane was left nonplussed. "But that doesn't make any sense," she pointed out.

"Doesn't it?"

Jake obviously knew something she didn't.

An idea occurred to her. "What happened to the man who lost the Mangy Moose to you?"

There was a flash of straight, white teeth. "The lucky sonofabitch celebrated his good fortune by buying drinks all around and then hightailing it off Paradise and back to civilization."

Jane wanted to make certain that she had the story correct. "You're telling me the previous owner of the Mangy Moose fixed a poker game so you would deliberately win the only bar on Paradise."

"Lock, stock, and barrel. Or should I say lock, stock, and beer bottle?" Jake raised one hand and stroked the growth of beard on his chin. "It's an amazing story, isn't it?"

"Yes, it is," she agreed. "But we have digressed from my original question, Mr. Hollister."

"Ms. Bennett, I can't even remember what your original question was," he confessed.

"I want to know why you're searching for the wreckage of the *Bella Doña*."

Jake became absolutely still. "You want the God's truth?" he said through stiff lips.

Jane steeled herself for his answer, well aware that she might not like what she was about to hear.

"Yes, I want the God's truth."

He put it in the simplest terms. "To have something to do."

Jane didn't understand. "I—ah—I don't understand." She stumbled over the words.

Jake shifted in his seat, accidentally bumped his bandaged arm on the corner of the table beside his chair, and winced. It was a quarter of a minute before he said, "When I arrived on Paradise, I didn't have much interest in anything. Searching for the *Bella Doña* gave me a reason to get up in the morning. It gave my life a purpose."

The man was baring his soul to her.

Suddenly Jane felt like crying.

"I'll be honest with you," her partner went on. "I don't give a flying fig what we do with the *Bella Doña* after we locate it. I simply want the satisfaction of finding the shipwreck, of seeing the project through to its conclusion, of solving a puzzle that so many others haven't been able to solve in over three hundred years."

It was good enough for her.

More than good enough.

"The way I see it," Jane said in a businesslike tone, "I supply whatever information I have—most of which is right here in my briefcase—and any financial backing that we may need."

He sat and he waited. Jake Hollister could do that better than any man she had ever met before.

Jane expounded on their arrangement. "You contribute your vast knowledge of the island and the surrounding waters, your survival skills, and your expertise as a diver."

His expression didn't alter. "And you figure that makes it a fifty-fifty proposition between the two of us?"

She raised her eyes to his. "I think it makes us perfect partners," she maintained.

"I agree," he said. "One more question."

"Shoot."

"Once we find the *Bella Doña*, and I believe that we will, then what?" he asked.

Jane's head shot up. She opened her mouth and immediately snapped it shut again. She heard herself give an unexpected hoot of laughter. "Do you know what?"

"Nope."

"I don't know the answer to your question. I've never thought in terms of what to do with the shipwreck. I was always so preoccupied with planning how to go about finding it."

"That makes two of us," Jake confessed. "I suggest we concentrate on the search and worry about pesky little details like what to do with a few thousand tons of salvage later."

"It's a deal, then."

"We have ourselves a deal," he said with a certain finality.

"I believe we should shake on it," Jane said, reaching out toward him with her hand.

There was a twinkle of something akin to mischief in Jake's eyes when he proposed instead, "Don't you think, under the circumstances, that a partnership like ours should be sealed, not with a traditional handshake, but with a kiss?"

Jane was genuinely caught off guard by his suggestion. Then the perfect solution presented itself to her. She put the leather briefcase down on the floor beside the desk, rose to her feet, crossed the short distance to where Jake was sitting, went down on her haunches by his chair— she was careful not to bump the tender skin on her thigh—bent her head and pressed a kiss on his arm just above the spot where Dr. Gilmour had applied the white bandage.

"Sealed with a kiss," she contended as she straightened.

Jake's eyes were suddenly the color of a midnight-blue sky illuminated by the glow of a silvery moon.

"Jane . . ." Her name was no more than a husky whisper.

She never knew how she had the nerve to say, "Now it's your turn to reciprocate."

Her heart was pounding wildly. Surely Jake could hear its wild pounding. Surely he could feel her pulse racing. He must know that her knees were trembling, that her insides were shaking with one tremor after another like the aftershocks of an earthquake. He must realize that she wanted something from him and that she didn't know what it was.

Maybe it was simply that she wanted him.

"Oh, honey, I would love to reciprocate in kind," Jake said with a thoroughly masculine and thoroughly disappointed sigh as his gaze went to her injured thigh.

A moment passed.

Jake placed his coffee cup on the table beside his armchair and rose to his feet in one long, fluid, powerful motion. He stood directly in front of her. He reached for her hand and raised it slowly toward his mouth. "I think this is as far as I dare go in returning the favor."

There was genuine regret in his eyes as he pressed his lips to the back of her hand, lightly passing them over her skin. He turned her hand over and repeated the caress on the more sensitive underside, brushing his lips across her palm.

Jane was left dazed.

The breath caught in her throat. It was her turn to utter

his name as if it were a struggle simply to speak. "Jake—"

A warning was issued. "We've got to be careful."

Her eyes, Jane knew, were filled with unanswered questions as she gazed up into his. "Why?"

Jake regarded her closely. "We're sailing into uncharted waters."

Was that all? But she knew it was enough and she knew it meant danger.

Jane tilted her head to one side. "Do you mind so very much?"

"It's not that I mind, but there's no predicting what lies ahead. Treacherous currents can suddenly and inexplicably sweep a man under before he knows it. Reefs can scuttle a boat in seconds without warning. We could be getting in way over our heads. Sometimes it's sink or swim, Jane, and we might well sink."

"Or we might well swim," she said with optimism.

"We might." Jake took in a deep breath and let it out again. "Can we afford to take a chance?"

"Can we afford not to?"

"I've never considered it a good idea to mix business with pleasure," he said, stating his opinion.

"Neither have I." She agreed in theory. "This is the first time I've been tempted."

"Me too." Jake seemed anxious to clarify one point. "It's not the painkiller making you act this way, is it?"

Jane hid a smile. "The effect wore off some time ago." She had a question for him to answer. "It's not because you've been stranded on a nearly deserted island for a couple of years, is it?"

Jake burst out laughing. In fact, he couldn't seem to stop laughing.

"What's so funny?" she wanted to know.

"Honey, I've had more offers since I became a worthless beach bum than I ever had in my previous life."

Jane experienced a pang of genuine jealousy. "And . . . ?"

"And what?"

"And did you take any of them up on their offers?"

Jake was suddenly deadly serious. "Not a one."

Jane knew he was telling her the truth, but she found she was a curious creature. "Why not?"

The reason seemed simple enough to him. "I wasn't interested."

"Go on," she urged.

"The women didn't interest me. They didn't tempt me. They didn't appeal to me. I wasn't attracted to them. I'm thirty-seven years old, Jane. I'm not interested in the opposite sex merely for the sake of having sex. I've been waiting a long time now for a woman to come along that I wanted, needed, to make love to desperately."

Jane felt a faint color rise in her cheeks as she recalled Jake's immediate and spontaneous reaction to her that first night on the beach. He had obviously found her attractive. He'd had an erection from their first kiss to their last.

Indeed, she could feel his erection there between them at this very moment.

She finally got up her nerve and asked, "Have you found one?"

His answer was a succinct, "Yes."

She swallowed hard. "Who is she?"

His eyes were on her mouth. "You."

Jane didn't know what to say in response to that, so she decided not to say anything.

"I know you aren't in the habit of taking up with strange men, men you've only known for a week—"

"Eight days."

Jake scowled. "Eight days?"

"We've known each other for eight days."

A smile slowly spread across his features and transformed his face. "In that case, Ms. Bennett, how do you feel about me?"

What was the sense in pretending to be coy at this stage of the game? "I want you, Mr. Hollister."

"Is it because I'm different from the type of men you usually go out with?" he asked her.

Questions.

There were so many of them.

"It's true that you're different from other men I've known. It is one of the things that initially attracted me to you. But this isn't some kind of experiment, Jake. I'm not saying to myself: 'Gee, I usually date civilized men, I think I'll try an uncivilized one just for a change of pace.' "

"What is it?"

Jane wasn't about to say the word love. She wasn't sure if the word entered into it or ever would for that matter. She didn't know how to put what she felt for Jake Hollister into words. It was a feeling. It was a wanting. It was a need. It was a strong sexual attraction. It was all of these things and it was none of them.

"I'm not certain," she finally admitted. "Are you?"

"No."

"Kiss me, Jake. I want to kiss you."

He backed off a discreet inch or two. "I want to kiss you more than you know. But I haven't shaved or showered in a couple of days."

"I don't care."

"Well, I do." He swore under his breath. "Christ, honey, look at me. I'm a mess."

"I'm a mess too," she pointed out to him.

"No, you aren't. You're beautiful."

"Then you're blind."

"They say love is blind," came the quiet response.

There, it had been said out loud. It was there between them now: the word love.

"Jake, one kiss, please," she implored, reaching up and wrapping her arms around his neck.

She could feel him weakening.

"I'm going to kiss you, Jane Bennett, the way I've been wanting to kiss you since the first moment I saw you. I'm going to touch you in places where I've dreamed of touching you. Then I'm going to tuck you into bed, say good night and walk out the door of this bungalow and not look back."

"Why can't you stay?"

"This isn't the right time and we both know it."

Damn the man. He was right, of course.

"Just look at us," he said with a mirthless chuckle at the sight of their bandages and scrapes and cuts and bruises. "Talk about the walking wounded."

"And once we're no longer the walking wounded—"

"I know where I'm going to take you."

Naturally Jane was curious. "Where?"

"It's a private place. No one ever goes there but me. There is a pool of clear water and green grass all around. The sun is always overhead and there is the most beautiful waterfall you have ever seen. Sometimes, if the sun catches the spray of mist just right it creates a rainbow. I'll take you there. That's where we'll know."

"That's where we'll know what?"

"If it's the right time and the right place."

Jake bent his head, then, and nuzzled her neck, his

mouth a soft caress against the exceptionally sensitive skin just beneath her ear.

Jane shivered.

He raised his head. "Are you cold?"

"No. I'm warm."

He gazed intently into her eyes and, almost as if in slow motion, he brought his lips to within a fraction of an inch of hers. "I'm thirsty."

"Then drink," she urged as he took her mouth.

It was everything a kiss should be and rarely was.

It was both hot and cold.

It drove her away, yet it beckoned her closer.

It captured and held her within its unyielding grip, yet it set her free.

It satisfied her, and it made her yearn hungrily, desperately, crazily for more.

It was only a kiss. It was nothing, and it was everything. It was heaven, and it was hell.

Jake's mouth tasted of Jake and just Jake. That's the only way Jane knew how to describe his taste, his scent, the texture of his mouth. It was clean and masculine, slightly spicy, alluring, intoxicating, immediately addictive, inexplicably so.

Jake's kiss was Jake's kiss.

And she loved it.

His fingers went to the buttons down the front of his shirt—the shirt she was wearing.

Some part of her brain must still have been functioning on a halfway rational level. Jane heard herself say, "You'll want your shirt back, of course."

"Not tonight," he murmured as he undid the last button and slipped his hands under the material and around her waist.

He was very gentle with her. He made certain he didn't

brush against the leg that had been injured. He was careful not to scrape his bandaged arm against her body.

His lips found hers.

His mouth blazed a white-hot trail along her bare shoulder and across her collarbone to her other shoulder. He pressed his lips to the swell of her breasts where they rose above the bodice of her swimsuit.

He moved lower and found her nipples jutting against the skintight fabric. He flicked his tongue back and forth across their sensitive tips until they were as tight and as hard as unripe berries and the thin material was soaked through.

Jane heard an aroused groan.

It was her own.

He could do so much to her with so little. It left her frightened and trembling and on fire for him.

She untwined her hands from around his neck. She ran one hand slowly down each bare arm, careful not to press the wounds beneath the bandage. She too could and would give him a taste of his own bittersweet medicine.

Her fingers roamed his upper body, discovered the small, rigid male nipples, the hard muscles, the smooth skin, the smattering of silky soft hair in the center of his chest that formed a directional arrow down his torso, a direction that her hands naturally followed.

When she reached his waist, she felt his indrawn breath, his startled arousal so nearby, his suddenly rigid stance, and she knew that the time had come to put an end to it.

"This is where it stops, isn't it?" she said with a whisper.

"This is where it stops for now." He sighed heavily and rested his forehead against hers. "There will be another time; a better time. There will be another place; a better place. I promise."

"Are you a man who always keeps his promises?"

Jake gazed down intently into her face. "Always. You can count on it."

She hoped so.

He reluctantly released her from his embrace, took her by the hand, and lead her to the bedroom at the back of the bungalow. "I said I was going to tuck you into bed, and that is exactly what I intend to do."

"But, Jake—"

"Don't worry, honey. I'll turn off the lights and lock up before I leave. If you need me, you know where to find me: right next door."

Just as he had on her first night on Paradise after they had returned from the beach, Jake Hollister left her with, "Sleep well," and a wish for pleasant dreams.

chapter *Fourteen*

She was a fish out of water, this woman with the false yellow hair, the cunning eyes, and the blood-red fingernails.

There was a feeling of *wrongness* about her. She should not be here. She did not belong here. He did not understand why she had come to this place.

Not like the other lady, the one who lived in the bungalow at the top of the hill. She belonged on the island. She was welcome here. She gave him a feeling of *rightness*. She spoke to him kindly and gently, and she did not treat him as though he were different from others. There was goodness inside her and loneliness and sometimes sadness. These were things he understood.

They thought he was simple.

He wasn't.

He merely preferred silence and solitude, the companionship of the birds, the tiny lizards that basked on rocks worn smooth by the water and warmed by the sun, the trees, the sky, and especially the sea.

It was his way.

He was awkward and uncomfortable with people, and

so he avoided them as much as possible. He did not speak unless he was spoken to, and sometimes, oftentimes, not even then. He tried to make himself unseen and unheard, and, therefore, he was rarely seen or heard by anyone.

But he saw and he listened. It was all stored in his head—totally useless and unimportant details in his view. It was mostly incidental things: who went where and when they went and what they did and what they said and who they saw and who saw them.

It was there in his memory.

He had been gathering these worthless bits of information for many years.

People tended to think of him as a boy and to treat him like one, as well. Sometimes they even called him "boy." Then he would close his ears and his mouth and his heart. He had not been a boy for a very long time. He was not certain how old he was. He did not believe it mattered. But he knew he was a man.

What did matter to him were the pristine white beaches where he often walked alone, watching a tiny sand crab scurrying on its way as he unintentionally disturbed it.

What interested him were the scores of birds singing in the trees overhead, the blooming hibiscus and bougainvillea, the stirring of the sea breeze against his skin, the sudden tropical storms that brought wind and rain and thunder to his world.

What fascinated him most were the creatures of the sea: the ones he watched over and swam along with and frequently talked to. They were good listeners, he had discovered. They made no judgments and they accepted him exactly as he was.

Not so the woman with the false yellow hair and the voice that betrayed her every time she opened her mouth.

He could hear her speaking now. Her voice hurt his

ears. He wanted to run away or to cover his head with his hands. But any movement might give his presence away. It might reveal to the woman and the man with her that he was there, concealed behind the oleander— he had found himself particularly interested in oleander of late—and discovery could only bring him trouble.

He wanted no part of trouble.

He always tried to avoid trouble.

He would have to stay where he was . . . as he was. He must remain as immovable as the stone wall beside him.

And so he watched, and he listened.

The man was dressed in the traditional clothes for riding horses, but there were no longer any horses to ride at the Hacienda. This he knew from listening to the stablehands and even from Don Carlos himself.

The woman was wearing a lace jacket that could provide no protection from either the sun or the rain and two small pieces of material underneath. There was next to nothing that remained concealed from any eyes that cared to gaze upon her.

"Your so-called spies have come up with precious little useful information," the man complained to her, anger and resentment clearly marking his otherwise handsome features. "You're wasting our precious money, if you ask me."

"Well, I'm not asking you." The woman snapped her blood-red, clawlike fingers together and said quarrelsomely, "As a matter of fact, I don't give *that* for what you think, Tony. So unless I ask, in future, you can keep your opinions to yourself."

"My, my, did Megs get up on the wrong side of the bed this morning?" he inquired, his voice laced with sarcasm.

"Which side of what bed I got up on this morning is none of your business," she stated with an ugly expression on what some people might mistake for a beautiful face.

The man reached out, grabbed her roughly by the arm, and slammed her up against his body. The woman's breasts were flattened against his chest as he deliberately moved his other hand from her reddened cheek to encircle her neck.

The threat was more than implied.

"Maybe I'll make it my business."

"Maybe you'll blow this entire scheme of ours and a lot of money along with it if you do."

It was the mention of money that appeared to make the blond man hesitate. Money, obviously, was a thing of great importance and interest to him.

"Perhaps we get what we pay for in this world, after all," he said, lowering the female to the ground again. "Your cheap spies are providing us with just that—cheap information."

"I paid a great deal more than that for you, the *Honorable* Tony St. Cyr, and the jury is still out on whether you were worth the price," she said, baiting him.

The man's complexion became mottled with color. "It was my money, if you recall correctly."

"You seem to have a conveniently short memory on the subject of money. What other kind did I expect you to have?" she added in an aside. "The money was mine to begin with. It was the inheritance left to me by my grandfather."

He brought his face closer. "I've always wondered what you had to do to convince the old man to leave you more in his will than the other grandchildren."

She took a step toward him, her fists raised to strike. "Why, you bastard—"

"For once, Megs, you're absolutely right."

She stopped and stared up at him. "What do you mean for once I'm right?"

"You believe that no one else is half so clever as you, half so cunning. Well, the truth is, my dear, you aren't always right. You aren't infallible. You do make mistakes."

"I'm well aware of that." She snorted unattractively. "I married you, didn't I?"

His hand flew to her lips. It was too late, of course. "Keep your voice down," he cautioned. "Do you want someone to hear you?"

Someone already had.

She removed his hand from her mouth and said, "What is it that you want to tell me?"

"I'm not the fourth son of an earl, my sweet."

The woman paled beneath her perfect tan. "You'd better explain what you mean by that remark," she insisted.

"Well, I am the earl's fourth progeny. But there are only three legitimate sons, I'm afraid. Just as you suspected, I'm a bastard first, last, and foremost." Here the man called Tony laughed. "You didn't buy the titled gentleman you were so eager to get your hands on, after all."

"You are a son of a bitch."

"Precisely. And, believe me, my mother was a first rate, not a first-class bitch. She was a real down-and-dirty variety of bitch, as a matter of fact. Dumped me on the streets of London and told me to fend for myself when I was only twelve years old."

"What a sad story. Poor, poor Tonykins." The blonde woman could be cruel as well. "I've decided whatever price I paid for you, it was too bloody much.''

Tony gathered her in his arms and began to kiss and caress her. ''Do you think so?''

''Well,'' she said with a throaty laugh, ''in some ways, I'll admit, you earn your keep. Nevertheless, it was my grandfather's money that set us up in business.''

''It was the investment information that I acquired by blackmailing our commodities broker that made it into the fortune we have today. Or it would be a fortune if your grandfather's will hadn't stipulated that we receive it as a quarterly allowance. We're being treated like children whose pocket money has to be doled out to them farthing by farthing,'' he said resentfully. ''Money. It always comes down to the fact that we never seem to have enough of the bleeding stuff. And now we're wasting even more of it on the fools we've hired to find out what Jane Bennett is doing on this godforsaken island.''

''We'll find out one way or another,'' Megs assured him. ''I guarantee you of that. Ms. Bennett has more than met her match in me.''

The man and woman wandered on along the garden pathway and out of sight.

He was free at last to move without being detected.

He quickly left this place, feeling a sudden need to cleanse himself in the sea.

But he did not forget what he had seen and what he had heard. He would never allow any harm to come to the kind lady. He would bide his time, and when the time was right, he knew where to go, and he knew who to tell.

chapter *Fifteen*

Jake lay awake in his bed and fantasized about Jane Bennett.

There was nothing new in that. He spent most of his waking hours thinking about her, and from the condition of his body, he suspected he was dreaming about her during the night too. Every time he awakened, which was often, he had an erection.

It had been four days since the incident involving Jane and the jellyfish. She was on the mend. He was on the mend.

That wasn't the problem.

Or maybe it was.

"Jeez, get a grip, Hollister," he muttered, propping one hand behind his head and punching his pillow with the other. He reached down and pulled the bedsheet over the lower half of his body.

He had to think of something besides Jane for his sanity's sake . . . what little there was left of it.

Color schemes.

Now *there* was a brilliant solution to his problem. Well, maybe not a brilliant solution, but it was a solution readily at hand. The bungalows, Samson and Delilah, were identical in terms of floor plans, square footage, and the layout of their rooms; identical in every detail except their color schemes.

Jake detested the colors used in Samson: cow-dung brown and pumpkin orange. Not that Delilah was much better with its vivid shades of pink and scarlet.

He had volunteered his services last summer, offering to paint the inside of the rental cottages gratis, suggesting something in a nice neutral beige or off-white for Samson, and maybe a pastel green or blue for Delilah. The Mayfair sisters wouldn't hear of it, and he was in no position to argue with them. They were his landladies, after all, and he was simply their tenant.

Their one and only tenant, he'd been tempted to point out on numerous occasions. He had managed to resist the temptation, and he was glad, in the end, that he had.

It was Miss Rachel who had mentioned to him one day, in private, that the bungalows had been faithfully repainted in their original colors every three to five years for as long as she could remember. And she was the eldest of the sisters, having been a girl of ten or twelve when the family moved to Paradise.

"Daddy detested brown and orange, as much, I suspect, as you do," she had said to him. "And scarlet always seemed like such an odd choice to us girls. After all, Daddy had been a well-known and respected preacher back in Virginia where the Mayfairs hail from." Here, Miss Rachel had paused to interject an historical note. "There have been Mayfairs in Virginia since it became a royal colony in 1624, as you no doubt are aware."

He hadn't been aware of it, of course.

"Anyway, Mama was always such a lady, from her lovely hair, which she wore swept up onto the top of her head, right down to the tips of her dainty toes. I do believe that sister Naomi most resembles our mother.'' Rachel Mayfair had permitted herself a small sigh, then. ''We never understood why Mama would choose those particular colors, but she did. In fact, she insisted on them.''

Frankly Jake hadn't had a clue.

She had continued. ''Mama made us promise—and we were each required to take an oath on the Good Book, itself—that the colors would never be changed.'' Miss Rachel had shaken her head from side to side, not understanding her mother's motives anymore as the woman of seventy she was now than she had as a girl six decades before. ''Naturally, we honored Mama's wishes, and we've kept our promise to her all these years.''

So Samson remained an ugly brown and orange; Delilah a garish shade of scarlet.

There had been rumors, of course, about the Reverend Ezekiel Mayfair and his Southern-belle wife, Lareina, and the reason behind their relocation to a remote Caribbean island.

Insinuations.

Whispers.

Intimations.

Sex.

Scandal.

It seemed likely—indeed, it had been broadly hinted—that the Reverend had not only preached to his congregation on the subject of original sin, especially to the ladies among his flock, but had indulged in an ungodly amount of it himself.

Which brought Jake back to the subject of sex. The very subject he was trying *not* to think about as he lay there staring at the putrid brown walls of his bedroom.

The bedroom of Delilah was cotton-candy pink.

Apparently the only ones who didn't seem to mind the atrocious color were the good spirits that Brilliant Chang had guaranteed Jane were still hanging around the cottage and the spirit house that he'd had erected out front.

The gentleman had also informed her that she had been correct in her feelings of *rightness* and *wrongness*, that she was a woman of genuine intuition, and that she should not fear the gifts the gods had bestowed upon her.

Jake, on the other hand, had taken the whole business with a grain of salt.

What was the word Jane had used?

Hooey, that was it.

Jake would be the first to admit that he wasn't a spiritual man. He liked ideas. He liked concepts. He liked proofs. He preferred tangibles. Things that he couldn't see or hear or touch or smell or taste or prove through computer computations made him a little uneasy.

Once it passed into the realm of hocus-pocus, he got nervous, real nervous.

Of course, there was always that sixth sense of his. The one that alerted him to the fact that someone was either telling the truth or they were lying.

He'd always had it, even as a kid.

Hell, what child couldn't tell when somebody was trying to put one over on him?

At the age of seven or eight, Jake hadn't thought about it much. He hadn't tried to figure it out. He hadn't questioned it, and he had certainly never told anyone about it. It had simply been part of him, like his aptitude for math or his ability to see the relationship between ideas that appeared to be unrelated.

He had been good at a lot of things: math, physics, spatial concepts, problem-solving, and eventually anything to do with computers. But only one thing had counted in the small Indiana town where he had grown up: basketball.

And Jake had hated basketball.

Unfortunately his father had loved everything about the game of basketball—loved playing it, loved watching it, loved talking about it, even loved coaching it. He had expected—no, he had *demanded*—that his oldest son feel the same way.

Jake had refused.

It had created a rift between father and son that was approximately the size of the Grand Canyon.

Five years later, his younger half-brother, Joby, had become the star athlete their father had always dreamed of having in the Hollister family. Joby had even gone on to be named the most valuable player of the state championship high-school basketball team.

Next, Joby had been handed a full athletic scholarship and—under the table, from grateful college alumni—a fancy red convertible, plenty of spending money, pretty girls virtually at his beck and call, and all the beer he could drink.

Meanwhile, Jake had worked his way through the state university without a penny of support from his family while often juggling two or three part-time jobs simultaneously. He had graduated with highest honors and a degree in economics.

Job offers had poured in.

He had accepted one halfway across the country with a young, innovative yet prestigious think tank. He had packed up his few belongings, said his even fewer good-byes, and left.

He'd never looked back.

Not once.

In the next several years Jake began to succeed beyond his wildest dreams. He had a natural talent for making money, and he made a lot of it. Before the age of thirty, he had become the president of his own multimillion-dollar corporation.

Joby, on the other hand, had been injured during his second year of college—not on the basketball court but during a raucous fraternity party. He'd lost his athletic scholarship as a result, dropped out of school—he had always been an indifferent student at best—and, at nineteen, found himself a has-been.

Former high-school basketball stars and hometown heroes were a dime a dozen, even in Indiana . . . especially in Indiana. That had been the one, sad, unforeseen truth that Joby Hollister and his proud father had not prepared themselves to face.

Jake never knew why he'd done it.

Hell, he didn't know why to this day.

But he had agreed to take Joby into his company, despite the glaringly obvious fact that his younger half-brother didn't possess the skills, the intelligence, the education, or the ambition necessary to survive in Jake's world.

It was a jungle out there, after all.

Jake had learned that the hard way. He was ruthless. He had to be. He played hard, and he played to win. It was how he'd gotten where he was, and it was the only way he knew how to stay there.

Joby hadn't been cut from the same cloth. That was immediately apparent. He had always had everything handed to him. He didn't have a clue how to get it for himself. He didn't even know how to make money; he only knew how to spend it.

Squander it, in Jake's opinion.

It had simply never occurred to Jake that his younger half-brother would somehow feel he had to live up to the incredible success that Jake had made of himself.

Joby had always been heralded as the star.

Joby had always been regarded as the favored son.

Joby had been the one with the boyish charm, the incredibly broad shoulders, and the blond good looks. Joby had been the one who knew how to throw a great party and show everyone a good time. Joby had been the one who attracted females like bees to honey.

Then Joby had found himself a Hollywood starlet with more bosom than beauty, and more beauty than brains or talent, and had decided to marry her.

Jake had been against it from the start.

He'd seen Charlene's type a hundred times before in sunny California where pretty starlets were less than a dime a dozen. She was a young woman going nowhere fast and she knew it. But Charlene had still wanted the best, and Joby had been the best in her book.

Charlene hadn't been as dumb as she'd looked. It had taken her less than three months to figure out that Joby was second best. That's when she had decided to go after Jake.

Jake had turned her down flat.

The woman was, after all, for better or worse, his brother's wife.

Charlene hadn't believed in taking no for an answer. Jake had come home one night to discover that Charlene had bribed her way into his bed. She was waiting, willing, and naked.

He'd told her to get out.

That was when Joby had shown up looking for his errant wife. He'd been drinking. There had been an ugly scene. Joby had ended up landing a hard right on his older brother's jaw—Jake wasn't about to make matters worse by striking back—before jumping into his expensive sports car and taking off with a squeal of rubber-burning tires.

Charlene had made her exit with tears streaming down her lovely face. Real or otherwise, Jake had never known for certain. The servant who had allowed her into the house—the bribe was a tempting one-hundred-dollar bill—had been summarily fired and sent packing that same night. And Jake had dropped into bed after taking a handful of aspirin and applying an ice pack to his jaw.

Little did Jake realize the nightmare had just begun.

The police had come pounding on his door in the middle of the night. Joby had missed a treacherous hairpin turn on the highway. Witnesses at the scene had estimated that he was going at least ninety when he'd slammed through the guardrail and careened into the canyon below. The sports car had burst into flames on impact.

In a matter of a moment or two, Jake Hollister's younger brother—and his own peace of mind—had ceased to exist.

Charlene had made a beautiful widow. Six months later Jake had read in the newspaper that she'd married the star quarterback for one of the professional football teams.

His father had never forgiven Jake, of course.

Jake had never forgiven himself.

He'd tried to. But it hadn't worked. A few months later he had sold his company to an eager competitor for millions, dumped the money into a bank account, and had taken off for parts unknown.

He had been on the go ever since, wandering from place to place. Looking for what? Repentance? Peace of mind? Forgetfulness? Forgiveness? A way to make some kind of sense of it all? A reason to go on? A reason for anything?

God, he was tired, Jake thought as he lay there staring up at the ceiling of the bungalow.

Tired but not in the least bit sleepy.

Something Brilliant Chang had said to him that very afternoon came to mind. They had been sitting in a small grove of trees and enjoying a cup of green tea together.

It was another of Chang's stories. The gentleman was always telling stories.

"There once was an ancient Chinese philosopher named Zhuangzi," he had begun.

Brilliant Chang's stories frequently began with the mention of an ancient Chinese philosopher, Jake had noted with some amusement.

Chang had seemed in no hurry to go on. He had taken several sips of tea from his handleless cup, brushed a small bug from his arm without causing it harm, and then had finally continued. "One night Zhuangzi dreamed that he was a butterfly."

"A butterfly?" Jake had repeated, mystified.

Brilliant Chang had bestowed an inscrutable smile upon his companion and concluded his unusually brief story with, "For the rest of his life Zhuangzi wondered: Was he a man who dreamed of being a butterfly, or a butterfly who dreamed of being a man?"

That was what Jake Hollister was pondering on this warm tropical night as he lie awake in his bed.

Not the lovely Jane Bennett in the next bungalow.

Not even the tragedy of his step-brother's death.

But the dream of an ancient Chinese philosopher whose name he couldn't even pronounce.

"Dammit, Chang," Jake swore as he turned over and tried to go to sleep.

The nightmare began as it always did.

Jake was a boy again, running through a field of golden grain waving in the wind—as the wind blew only in Indiana—chasing his younger brother, calling out to him to wait, there might be danger ahead. Jake should go first, he always warned Joby. After all, he was the oldest and he knew best.

Joby never listened to him.

He only ran faster, turning back to laugh at Jake, his beautiful, boyish face filled with mischief and the promise of youth and the belief that nothing bad could ever happen to him.

That's how the nightmare always began.

It usually ended on a winding, treacherous, hillside road in California, police sirens wailing shrilly in the distance, flashing lights—red, white, blue, and yellow—in the background, television cameras and reporters everywhere, and there, down below in the desert canyon, the burning and charred remains of what had once been Joby Hollister and his fancy sports car.

Except tonight the ending was different. Tonight the nightmare ended, not with a man standing there staring at the tragic scene before him, but a butterfly.

Jake shot straight up in bed.

The sheets were soaked through and the top layer was twisted around his legs in a stranglehold. He was covered with sweat. He always was when he had been dreaming that particular dream.

"Dream, hell," he swore aloud. "It's a nightmare."

He was suddenly thirsty. He reached for the glass of

water that he kept on the bedside table and clumsily knocked it over. He heard the glass hit the bungalow floor and shatter.

"Shit."

He rolled over and swung his legs off the opposite side of the mattress. He'd clean up the broken glass later. What he needed right now was a swim in the bay. It was the only thing, he'd found, that helped at a time like this.

He was naked. He grabbed a pair of jeans from the chair beside the bed and pulled them on his sweat-slick body. He was out the door of Samson and halfway down the path between the two bungalows when he heard his name.

"Jake?"

He stopped dead in his tracks. He didn't move a muscle. He didn't even breathe.

"Jake, is that you?" The voice was coming from the region of the canvas hammock that was tied to two of the larger trees that grew between the cottages.

"Yeah, it's me," he said, exhaling.

He'd known it was Jane just by the way she had said his name. Nobody said his name like she did. Nobody ever had before, and he doubted if anybody ever would again. Somehow she made it sound like the word Jake was the answer to a prayer.

She floated toward him, through the night, like a ghostly apparition. "Where are you going?"

He'd keep his answers brief. "Down to the beach."

"Can't you sleep?"

"I was asleep."

She was close enough that Jake saw the speculative look she gave him. "Did you wake up?"

He didn't answer her question. Instead, he asked her: "What time is it?"

"Late." Jane laughed disconcertedly. "Early." She finally conceded, "I suppose it depends on how you look at it."

Jake suddenly realized that she was dressed in a short, gossamerlike nightgown and precious little else. Her feet were bare and her hair was down around her shoulders in a wild tumble of silk. "What are you doing out here?"

There was a short, brittle pause. "I couldn't sleep," she admitted at last.

Jake found he was curious. Besides, it was his turn to ask the questions. "Why not?"

Jane quickly turned the tables on him. "Why couldn't you sleep?"

"I already told you"—he stuffed his hands into the pockets of his jeans—"I was asleep."

She was persistent. He wondered fleetingly if she'd ever considered becoming a lawyer. "What woke you up, then?"

"A dream—" He stopped and corrected himself. "—a nightmare about a butterfly."

"Ah, the big, bad butterfly," she declared. "I once had a nightmare about a hummingbird."

"Don't tell me," he said with a sardonic laugh. "It had something to do with one of Brilliant Chang's stories."

She scowled. "Brilliant Chang?"

"Never mind," he said.

Jane swung back and forth from her shoulders like a girl would. "Want to go skinny-dipping in the bay?"

"Aren't you afraid?"

"Of what?"

"Of getting stung again by a jellyfish." It had only been four days since her accident.

She shook her head. "It's like lightning."

"Lightning?"

"How often is it going to strike the same person twice?" It was a logical query, of course.

"Actually the odds of being struck by lightning even once are—"

"Astronomical," she finished for him.

"Yeah, astronomical." Jake smiled meaningfully. "I still don't think it's a smart idea for us to go skinny-dipping together."

"In that case, let's relax in the hammock for a while instead."

Jane didn't say another word. She simply came to him through the night, reached for his hand and urged him toward the spot beneath the trees.

Skinny-dipping would have been the safer alternative, Jake realized belatedly as he stretched out on the canvas hammock and Jane lay down beside him.

chapter *Sixteen*

"*I* was rushing through Heathrow one time and stopped at a bookstall to buy some reading material for the airplane trip from London to New York," Jane remarked to Jake as she stretched out alongside him on the hammock.

He gave a grunt of acknowledgment that meant, she assumed, that he'd heard her.

Jane tended to chatter whenever she was nervous, which, frankly, was infrequent for her at the age of nearly thirty. Yet she was surprisingly jittery at the moment, and so she found herself chattering.

"I picked up a magazine—a copy of *Condé Nast Traveler*, I think—and I still vividly recall the headline for the article advertised on the front cover. It was entitled 'The Dream: How Easy is it to Buy a Piece of Paradise?' " She turned her head to the side and studied his profile in the moonlight. "I've been wondering ever since."

She could feel the vibration of his larynx as Jake spoke. "What have you been wondering ever since?"

"Do you suppose you can actually *buy* a piece of paradise?"

"As opposed to what?"

Jane made a subtle gesture with one shoulder that most closely resembled a shrug. Her other shoulder was firmly wedged in the crook of Jake's arm. "I don't know." Niggling thoughts persisted. "Inherit a piece? Earn a piece? Create a piece for yourself?"

Jake seemed to take her question under consideration. "Or none of the above."

She nodded, but it was such an imperceptible movement that he might easily have missed it altogether. "Maybe if you're lucky—" Jane hesitated.

"Yes . . . ?"

"Well, perhaps, you can get a piece of paradise simply by asking for it," she finished.

"You mean for free?"

"I suppose I do." She didn't know exactly what she meant.

"Wasn't there a saying or a song lyric or something written by somebody sometime about the best things in life being free?" Jake turned his head toward her, and the hammock responded by swaying back and forth with their weight.

"I believe there was."

A firmly chiseled masculine chin was lifted slightly and dark-lashed eyes stared up through the trees overhead at a star-filled sky. There was the merest hint of a tropical breeze and the scent of the sea and the sand and the palm trees.

"It's a beautiful night," he said.

"Yes, it is," Jane agreed.

"It didn't cost a penny."

"No, it didn't."

"I guess that makes it free."

"I guess it does," she said.

"We didn't even have to ask for it either."

"No, we didn't."

Jake exhaled quietly. It was as close to a wistful sigh as she had ever heard from him.

"I wish everything in life could be so simple." He gestured with his hand. "It would just be there, and each of us could decide if we wanted it or not."

"Isn't that how it already works?"

"Isn't that how *what* already works?" he asked.

"Life."

He didn't respond for a good thirty seconds or longer. "I believe most things in life come with a price tag. It's a question of whether we wish to pay the price—or whether we think we can afford to." As an afterthought, he added, "Then there are those times, of course, when we pay the price whether we want to or not."

Jane sensed a hint of melancholy creeping into their conversation and changed the subject. "What would you like to do?"

Her question caught Jake off guard. "Do?"

"Yes. What would you like to do? Right here. Right now," she said briskly.

He laughed huskily. There was something sexually suggestive and rather intimate in his laugh that shot an arrow of awareness right through her. Despite the warmth of the night, Jane found, all of a sudden, that there were goose bumps covering her arms and legs.

"I don't think I should answer that question on the grounds it might incriminate me," Jake replied, his voice a throaty rumble.

"Is that anything like taking the Fifth?" she said, teasing him just a little in the process.

"Something like that."

"Chicken!" she exclaimed.

"Chicken as in poultry?"

"Or fowl."

"Or as in calling foul."

Jane wrinkled up her nose. "That was pretty awful."

"Yes, it was," he acknowledged.

She tugged at the hem of her nightgown. Somehow it had inched up her legs and was presently an immodest six to eight inches above her knees.

Once she had her clothing adjusted, she inquired, "What would you like to talk about?"

"Nothing," Jake said bluntly.

"Nothing?"

"We don't have to talk about anything, do we?"

"No. You're absolutely right," Jane conceded. "We can simply lie here next to each other and do nothing in particular and say nothing at all."

There was a moment of silence.

"Is that what you had in mind?" she inquired. Then she decided to try a different approach with him. "If you were alone, is that what you would be doing?"

Jake appeared at a momentary loss. "I guess so."

Jane didn't see it that way. "I don't think so."

"You don't?"

She was quite capable of being as blunt as he. "You'd be down in the bay trying to swim it off."

"*It?*"

"The effect, the trauma, the distress, the emotional upset, the physical restlessness, the aftermath, whatever you want to call it, of your nightmare."

"Oh."

Jane wasn't finished with him yet. "Or you would be stretched out on the sand trying to analyze what it meant."

Jake actually laughed, although there was no indication

of any humor in the sound of it. "You're probably right."

"I usually am."

"No modesty there."

"I have an intuition for these things, remember?" At least she did according to Brilliant Chang.

Jane decided to try silence.

The silence lasted for perhaps two minutes, possibly three.

"Why in the hell would a grown man dream about a butterfly?" Jake burst out, fidgeting around on the hammock until they were facing each other again.

"Lepidopteraphobia?"

"Fear of butterflies? I don't think so." He gave her a long measuring look. "Are you sure that's an actual word?"

"No," she confessed. Then she went on before she lost her train of thought. "Perhaps the butterfly represents something in your life."

"I can't imagine what."

Jane threw out the first idea that popped into her head. "A desire for freedom."

Jake appeared to be biting his tongue. "Would you care to explain that one?"

"Well, a butterfly has wings. It can fly. Perhaps to a human being that could represent freedom. Or because man doesn't have wings, it might represent the lack of freedom."

"Were you a psychology major in college, by any chance?"

Jane shook her head. "Art history." Her interrogation wasn't complete. Far from it, in fact. "Have you had this particular nightmare before?"

"A version of it."

"Do you want to talk about it?"

"Not particularly."

She studied him for a moment or two. "Any particular reason why not?"

Sometimes Jake Hollister could be a man of irritatingly few words. "It wouldn't change anything."

It was the perfect opening for Jane to quote one of her favorite aphorisms. " 'Nothing endures but change.' " She even added for good measure, "Change is always possible. You might not have the nightmare again."

"Who said that?" Jake wanted to know.

"I just did."

"I mean the quote. Who said it originally?"

"Heraclitus."

Jake frowned. "He sounds Greek—and ancient."

"He is. He was. Heraclitus was a Greek philosopher who lived about 500 B.C. His ideas were said to be a major influence on Socrates, Plato, and Aristotle."

"Ah, the Big Three." Jake appeared mildly interested. "What else did Heraclitus say?"

Jane tried to recall quickly. "Well, I'm no expert—and I can't say that I always agree with him—but Heraclitus also wrote: 'The way up and the way down are the same.' "

"If Heraclitus believed that, then the man was a fool," Jake stated, and they both chuckled, realizing that he was referring to a very conspicuous and obvious state of the male anatomy—his male anatomy—and not some ancient Greek philosophy.

"I don't have nightmares," Jane finally said, returning to their original discussion, "but I do sometimes suffer from what the French call 'nuit blanche.' "

"Translation: white nights," Jake offered.

Her brows came together in a small line of amazement. "You speak French."

"I speak about as much French as you do Latin," he advised her.

"Well, the literal translation is white nights, but what it really means is sleepless nights," she interpreted for him.

"Are you an insomniac?"

Jane didn't commit herself to an answer. "Aren't we all insomniacs occasionally?"

Apparently his curiosity wasn't satisfied. "Does your insomnia seem to be related to having nightmares?"

He was watching her with an intent expression; it made her nervous. "I don't believe so. I just wake up in the middle of the night, and I can't seem to get back to sleep." She curled one arm up under her head. "What about you? Is it caused by your nightmares?"

"Pretty much."

"Does it happen frequently?"

He was silent a moment, evidently mulling it over. "It used to be more often. Maybe once or twice a week. Now it's perhaps only once a month."

"You mentioned that the butterfly was a recent addition to your nightmare."

Jake looked at her appraisingly. "I might as well tell you, huh?"

"You might as well."

"Okay, but I'll make it short and sweet. Except, believe me, the story isn't in the least bit sweet."

She hadn't thought it would be.

Jake took in a deep breath and released it before he started. "I had a younger half-brother named Joby. We were as different as night and day. I was the square peg in the round hole back home in Indiana, and Joby was everything our father wanted a son of his to be.''

Jane could feel her pulse beginning to pick up speed already. ''Which was?''

Jake spelled it out for her in plain and simple words. ''A real man's man. A star athlete. A big-time basketball player.''

''Something went wrong?''

''Something went real wrong.''

''What was it?'' Because it was apparent to Jane that something very tragic and very permanent had happened.

''I went away and became a success in the world I had chosen, and Joby blew it big-time in his. When there were no other choices left for him, he tried to become a part of my world, but he wasn't cut out for it.''

''He failed?''

''He died.''

''Ohmigod, Jake, I'm sorry.''

His head moved. It wasn't a shake and it wasn't a nod. ''It was a car accident. Joby had been drinking. He was driving too fast. He literally crashed and burned.''

''Did you see the accident?''

''I arrived on the scene within a half hour.''

''And since then you have nightmares about it.''

''I blame myself.''

''Why?''

''Because I could have prevented it.'' Jake was very quiet. ''I could have prevented it, and I didn't.''

''Guilt is a heavy burden to carry around with you all the time,'' she observed.

''Yeah, it is.''

''Have you tried to talk to your father and mother about it?''

''Stepmother.''

"Father and stepmother."

He was silent.

"How much time have you spent back in your hometown with your parents since the accident?"

He was still silent.

"You haven't been back?"

"I went back for the funeral. My father made it pretty clear at the time that he didn't want to see me again. Joby was the apple of his eye. He blamed me for Joby's death. He always has. He always will."

"That can't still be true, Jake. Not now that your father has had some time to think it over. He's lost one son. But he doesn't have to lose both of you."

Jake made a noncommittal sound.

Jane wondered if she was talking to a brick wall. "You should go back to Indiana once you leave the island. You should try to make peace with your father and with yourself."

For all she knew, maybe it was the first time Jake had thought of a life—and a world—outside of Paradise since the ferry had docked at Purgatory over a year ago. Maybe it was the first time he had considered going back.

"You're awfully quiet," she commented.

"I was thinking."

She waited.

"Maybe you're right," he conceded. "Maybe I should try again. I did what I could at the time."

"Which was?"

"A few things in Joby's memory."

"Things?"

"Like athletic scholarships. Giving money to the high school to build the Joby Hollister Memorial Auditorium. Things like that." Jake stared over her shoulder and off into the distance. "Everything has a price, even peace of mind."

"Peace of mind can't be bought with money, however."

His eyes came back to hers. "You're a wise woman for one so young."

"I'm not that young," she said stubbornly, "and you don't know how old I am, anyway."

"Yes, I do."

"You're guessing, then."

"I know exactly how old you are, Ms. Bennett. You told me that first night on the beach."

She couldn't seem to recall their entire conversation from that evening. "I did?"

He nodded and gave her a smug smile. "You're twenty-nine going on thirty."

"I don't usually give out that information," she informed him with a haughty sniff.

"Especially not for free," he said with a laugh.

It was good to hear him laugh again.

"*Never* for free," she claimed.

"Well, you did that time. So now I'm curious."

"About what?"

His mood was playful. "I was wondering what else you might be willing to give out for free."

"Did you have anything specific in mind?"

"I might."

"What, pray tell, would that be?"

"You said the best things in life are free."

"I believe you were the one who mentioned that, Jake Hollister, not me."

"Picky. Picky." Jake brought his face closer to hers. "I happen to believe that kissing certainly counts among the best things in life. Don't you agree?"

How could she disagree? "I suppose it depends on whom one is kissing."

"Excellent point. I can see that you're going to keep me on my toes. Let me rephrase that. I believe that kissing *you* is definitely one of the best things in life."

Jane couldn't argue with his logic.

"Kissing you would be paradise," he went on. "In fact, you said, if you're lucky maybe you can get a piece of paradise by simply asking for it."

Jane's pulse was beating double. "Did I say that?"

"Yes, you did." Dark eyes engaged hers. "So, I'm asking, Jane Bennett. I'm asking for a kiss from you."

chapter Seventeen

*H*e was a clever man, Jake Hollister.

Jane leaned toward him. She didn't have far to go. No more than an inch or two separated their heads on the canvas pillow attached to the hammock.

She could smell a distinctive combination of masculine scents: the aroma of clean soap and musky male sweat, something not unlike natural leather—although she had never actually seen Jake wear leather, and it seemed highly unlikely to her that he ever would in this warm climate—something salty, undoubtedly from the sea air all around them, and something indescribably and inexplicably Jake.

Jane dropped a swift kiss on his jaw.

"No wonder it's free," he mumbled.

"There's more," she guaranteed.

The next kiss was a feathery light touch of her lips to a spot just behind and below his left ear. That brought a small, sharp inhalation from its recipient.

The third kiss lingered for a count of three or four at the corner of his mouth, where a frown line might appear one day. At the age of thirty-seven, however, there was no sign of it yet. Jake's bottom lip twitched in response.

The kisses that followed varied from a quick peck on his forehead to a buss to his unshaven cheek to a whispery nuzzle somewhere in the region of his Adam's apple. The last one resulted in a shiver that Jane clearly felt herself.

"You are a tease," Jake proclaimed.

"I'm not teasing you," Jane shot back without the slightest feeling of remorse. It was her belief that he deserved no mercy, under the circumstances. "I'm merely giving you a *free* sample of what's to come," she said blithely.

"It's called torture."

"It's called anticipation."

"What it's called"—Jake paused, as if for emphasis, and grinned at her—"is foreplay."

That's when she decided it was time to shut him up with a bona fide kiss on the mouth. It began as a soft, exploratory caress: her lips brushing back and forth across his. She was taking his measure, whether he realized it or not.

How large was his mouth?

How hard or soft were his lips?

What did he taste like tonight? Did she like the taste of him?

Were his kisses too wet or too dry—or somewhere in between and just right?

Was he going to pressure her for greater intimacy than she desired at the moment? Was he going to attempt to pry her lips apart and stick his tongue into her mouth?

Who was in control of this kissing experiment anyway? That's what it came down to. Jake had done the asking, but she was the one giving the answer.

Jake Hollister was a wise man, Jane decided. At least

when it came to women. At least when it came to her. Somehow he recognized that she wanted, that she needed, to feel in control of the situation. And so he allowed her to set the pace.

The man went up another notch in her estimation.

He waited until she wanted more. Until she was prepared to give more. Until she was prepared to receive more.

The time had come.

Jane was suddenly conscious of the fact that Jake was wearing only a pair of jeans. No denim shirt. No T-shirt. No shoes. No socks. No undershorts.

Were threadbare jeans all the man owned?

She was also aware of her own state of dishabille: she was wearing a sheer nightgown of finest cotton—the kind of cotton that caressed the skin all on its own.

Jake's chest was still slightly sweaty. From the waist up, he was nothing but bare skin and a smattering of dark hair on top of hard muscle and harder bone.

Her breasts had been pressed against him as they lay together in the hammock. Now her nightgown was damp and the material had become nearly transparent. Her nipples were clearly visible, even in the faint light cast by the moon and the stars. He had to be blind not to see her nakedness.

Jake was anything but blind.

Where was she going to kiss him next? How was she going to kiss him? What was going to happen when she did? These were the questions that Jane knew she should ask herself, that she knew she should be thinking about.

But she didn't want to think.

She simply wanted to *feel*.

She made her choice.

Going up on one elbow, Jane leaned over and kissed

the exact spot above Jake Hollister's heart. She could hear its strong rhythmic cadence. She could feel its powerful and steady beat. His heart was pounding sure and fast.

It was a short distance from where his heart lay beneath the surface of his skin to the small, nutlike, and already rigid male nipple on the outside of his body. She touched him first with her mouth, then tugged gently with her lips and finally flicked at the surface of his nipple with the tip of her tongue.

Her reward was the quiver of physical awareness that ran down the entire length of Jake's frame. Jane found she was quite pleased with herself.

Her hair fell in a wild tumble around her shoulders. She impatiently pushed at its unmanageable mass, trying to secure it behind her ears, but several errant strands escaped, nevertheless, and brushed along his bare skin even as Jane dragged her mouth from one side of his chest to the other and back again.

She savored his flesh as if he were her favorite flavor, and she found his taste very much to her liking. She nipped at him with the serrated edges of her teeth, and she could imagine the pleasure that was almost pain, and the near pain that was, indeed, pleasure.

She nibbled and feasted and devoured him as though she were half-starved, and he could somehow satisfy the terrible hunger inside of her.

She heard a moan of sexual arousal. It came from Jake, but it echoed again and again inside her.

With her tongue she traced the pattern of soft, dark hair that encircled each male nipple, and then followed the narrow path it took down the center of his chest to the point where it disappeared beneath the waistband of his jeans. She drew a damp ring around the indentation of his navel and felt his muscles clench.

"Paradise for the asking," Jane murmured as she returned to his mouth at last.

"Paradise for the taking," Jake muttered as he finally drew her beneath him, the canvas hammock swaying wildly with the shifting of their weight.

Then he covered her mouth with a kiss that seemed to have no beginning and no end.

Jake had taken about all he could take.

Jane was so damnably sweet and surprisingly innocent, he'd discovered. He didn't believe for a minute that she had any real concept of the effect she was having on him: on his peace of mind, on his physical condition, his advanced state of arousal, his desperate and urgent need for her.

All in good time, Jake, he reproached himself. Some things only got better with time.

"Ask me," he demanded, raising his head only long enough and far enough to say the words.

"Ask you?" Jane seemed to have difficulty in forming the words. She appeared dazed. "Ask you for what?"

"For the same thing I asked for," Jake insisted, pulling her toward him.

He saw her struggle for a response. "Paradise?"

He smiled in spite of himself. "We may end up with paradise, honey, but what I asked you for was a kiss."

He'd gotten more than he had bargained for, of course. No doubt Jane was about to find herself in a similar position.

She looked at him and made a disbelieving sound. "You want me to ask you for a kiss?"

It was that simple.

And that complex.

"Yes," he stated.

"Why?" Her eyes were huge now and round as saucers. "I obviously want you to kiss me."

"Say the words."

It suddenly seemed to dawn on her. "Of course. I needed to hear the words. You need to hear them too."

Bingo!

"That way we both know where we stand," he stated.

Jane laughed in the back of her throat. "Where we stand? I was under the impression that we were lying down."

Jake laughed along with her. The woman had a sense of humor—or a sense of the absurd—at the most unexpected times.

She stopped laughing, reached up, and ruffled the uncombed thatch of hair on top of his head. She gently grasped a fistful of the stuff and brought his face down to within a single breath of hers, arching her back as she did so, and wrapping her other arm tightly around his neck. "I want you to kiss me, Jake Hollister." Her eyes burned into his. "I'm asking you for a kiss. Will you kiss me?"

"Yes," Jake answered, brushing his mouth against hers, breathing in her scent, touching her lips and teeth and tongue with his own to get a hint of her flavor.

"I like the taste of you," she whispered.

"I like the taste of you," he echoed.

Jake didn't think he had the words to describe exactly what she tasted of: something slightly sweet but not too sweet, definitely not saccharine; something intriguing, something intoxicating, although there was no hint of alcohol on her breath tonight, not even that of a rare and expensive vintage champagne; something altogether, and rather addictive too, damn her.

He had never tasted a woman quite like her.

Not her mouth. Not her skin. Not the strand of silky hair that inadvertently caught on his beard and was consequently drawn in slow motion across his lips.

Jake found himself burying his face in her hair and muttering in a voice he scarcely recognized as his own, "God Almighty, I like the smell of you."

"And I like the smell of you," she admitted.

He breathed in deeply and held her scent in his nostrils, in his throat, in his lungs, savoring it, not wanting to let it go until he was finally forced to exhale out of sheer necessity.

He had never smelled a woman like her.

Not her hair. Not her flesh. Not her scent. It was partly composed of the subtle hint of sandalwood from her own private fragrance that he had detected the first day on the ferry. It was partly composed of her natural essence: an element far more elusive and far more difficult—hell, it was virtually impossible—to pin down.

The bottom line was Jane Bennett smelled like Jane Bennett, and no one else.

Jake went on to tell her, "I like the sound of your voice, the sound of your laughter."

"I like the sound of your voice and your laughter, as well," she reciprocated.

Jake was almost ashamed to admit it to her. But in the end he did. "I especially like the way you say my name."

Jane laughed softly; it was a small, cozy sound. "Jake."

"Yeah, just like that."

Then he kissed her again soundly, seductively, provocatively, a right-down-to-the-toes kind of kiss, hoping and praying that she would say his name again.

She did. "Jake . . ."

It was his favorite way to hear his name spoken.

"I think I could look at you all night," he admitted, staring down into her face.

"I like the way you look too," she confessed, her eyes shining up at him.

"I've seen more of you, however," he told her.

Jake could detect the faint hint of color that rose in Jane's cheeks. He could even feel the slight heat of embarrassment that accompanied it.

"It was my first night on Paradise, wasn't it? I was drinking champagne, making a private toast or two, and taking a dip in the nude. And you were watching me," she scolded him, but there wasn't any real reproach in her tone.

He hadn't apologized then. He wasn't about to apologize now. "I liked what I saw."

"Well, I've seen enough of you to be able to say the same," she informed him in no uncertain terms. "In case you didn't realize it, Jake Hollister, your blue jeans, sans any underwear, leave scant little to the imagination."

"What you see is what you get," he told her with a devilishly masculine glint in his eye.

"I certainly hope so." She took a deep breath and added, "In fact, I'm counting on it."

Fingertips only, Jake traced the outline of Jane's face, feature by feature. He started with the delicate shape of an ear, drew a classically and enviously high cheekbone, moved along to a slightly uptilted nose, up and across the arch of one elegant eyebrow to the other, down the oval shape of her face to the opposite ear.

There was more.

Her not-too-high nor too-low forehead. The tiny crease between her topaz eyes when she frowned. Her mouth with its perfect lips, at least in his opinion. Her exquisite chin. The definitive line of her jaw.

There was even more.

Her long, slender, white, swanlike neck. Her collarbone—not bony and protruding like so many slender women's. The way the silky wisps of her light brown hair defined her nape and tended to curl, with a mind of their own it almost seemed, around her ears.

There was far more.

The lovely full breasts with their rosy pink centers. Nipples perfect in every way: not too large, not too small, flawless in shape, the precise color—a shade somewhere in between the ripe red strawberry and the luscious raspberry, his preferred fruits—that was most enticing to him. Her nipples were already hard, already protruding, already distinct and very apparent against the thin material of her nightgown.

Jake covered her breast, and the passion-hardened tip poked the center of his palm, making his fingers itch to touch her, to tease her, to caress her, to catch her nipple between thumb and finger and squeeze until he heard the breath audibly catch in her throat.

He flattened his hand on her ribcage between breast and stomach, and felt the involuntary reflex of her muscles. He moved lower to her belly and then lower still to that soft, rounded and so sensitive mound between her thighs. Her hips lifted instinctively off the hammock.

The first thing he remembered admiring about this woman was her long, lovely legs. He caressed her now from thigh to knee to ankle and back again, each leg given its due attention in course.

Then he backtracked to the juncture between those

long, lovely legs and settled his hand where her body radiated its own special feminine heat and moisture.

Jane moaned aloud.

"I like the way you feel beneath my hands, my fingertips, my mouth, my lips," Jake murmured. Jane touched her hands to his shoulders, the unmistakable strength in his upper arms, his chest, the taut muscles of his abdomen, the muscles, harder still, of his thighs and, finally with a soft and thoroughly female cry of exclamation—Jake found himself cherishing the sound of it—placed her hand on his jeans where his erection surged toward her.

"I like the way you feel," she divulged.

Jake reached down and, not without some degree of difficulty and no small amount of agility on his part, released the button at the waistline of his jeans one-handedly. Then he eased the zipper down until his penis sprang free.

Jane touched him, soft and tender skin on soft and tender skin. She traced the shape of him from the sensitive tip, with its drop or two of precious male essence, to where it all began in a thatch of thick, dark, curly hair.

She murmured in a low, husky contralto somewhat unlike her usual voice, "I love the way you feel."

He slipped his hand beneath her nightgown, up one long, lovely leg and located the silky nest at the apex of her thighs. He entangled his fingers in the damp hair there. He wetted his hand with her body's natural moisture. He gently flicked her clitoris several times; she jerked with each arousing touch.

He dipped into her, then, just a fraction of an inch. She groaned her need out loud, her desire for more, and so he obeyed and slipped his finger in further.

Her back spontaneously arched, her breasts thrust forward, and her hips rose even higher off the hammock. That was the moment he plunged in ever deeper and deeper, and even followed, after a moment, with a second finger.

Jake realized there were tiny beads of sweat on his forehead and on his upper lip from the effort of maintaining some semblance of self-control. It was one of the hardest things he'd ever had to do in his life.

Hell, it was the hardest he'd ever been in his life, he reflected in a moment of self-deprecating humor.

It was later—he couldn't have said how much later—before Jake found he could speak, or cared to speak.

"I love the way you feel on the inside and on the outside," he managed.

"I love to feel you, your hands, on me, inside me," Jane confessed to him in a whisper. "Make love to me again, Jake."

"I will," he promised. God knew, he fully intended to. "But I can't come inside you the way I might like to, honey. I didn't exactly come prepared for this."

Jake knew she was tempted to say that it didn't matter. He knew because the thought had briefly crossed his own mind.

But it did matter.

They both knew that. And they were too mature to take chances, any chances, all kinds of chances.

"What can we do, then?" she asked, gazing up into his eyes.

"We can kiss and touch and we can bring each other great pleasure and satisfaction."

Jake kissed and caressed her. He brought her to one climax after another with his hands, with his fingers, with his mouth, until Jane cried his name out on a sob, begging for mercy, begging for more, then begging only for him.

She brought him release with her touch and her kisses; even once only by her reaction to him.

They were happy, tired, satiated. They had never known a night like the night they spent together in the hammock beneath the tropical heavens and the tropical trees.

The pale pink light of dawn was stealing across the Caribbean sky when Jake enveloped Jane in his arms for the last time, tucking her head under his chin and falling into a sleep of such peace as he had never known before.

Out of long habit, and due to an occasional bout with insomnia, Rachel was always the first awake, the first up, and the first out of bed in the morning in the Mayfair household. She was usually washed, dressed, brushed and combed for the day, and in the kitchen putting on the kettle even as the first brilliant streaks of dawn began to creep across the Caribbean sky.

This morning was no different.

She filled her favorite copper teakettle with water from the spigot, carried it to the stove, struck a match, and held it to the burner. From years of experience, she knew exactly when and how much to adjust the flame without even looking.

Then, as was also her custom every morning, Rachel crossed to the long row of kitchen windows and gazed out over the expanse of lush, green lawn, the white sandy beach far below, the blue, oh-so-blue Caribbean in the distance.

It was only out of her peripheral vision that she could glimpse the rental bungalows, Samson and Delilah, the grove of trees between the twin cottages and the old canvas hammock.

This morning she realized there was someone in the hammock. Jake Hollister, no doubt. It wouldn't be the first time she had known him to fall asleep there or even down on the beach itself.

She had never asked him, of course.

She would never dream of prying.

But she suspected that Jake sometimes suffered from nightmares and the sleeplessness that often resulted.

That's what usually caused her insomnia: nightmares.

Not so much anymore, of course. It had been twenty years, after all, and surely the God of Abraham was a merciful God.

Pain faded with time. Some images did, as well. Although every now and then, Rachel would still awaken in the dead of night, her heart pounding in her chest, unable to catch her breath and with that terrifying feeling that she was suffocating, her body drenched in perspiration, and the face of her dear sister, pretty Mary Magdalene, sweet Mary Magdalene, innocent Mary Magdalene, lying there in death, eyes wide open and staring unseeing up into hers.

Hands clutched to her breast, Rachel squeezed her eyes shut against the memory and the pain. When she opened them again—dear Lord, how long had they been closed?—the sun was on the rise and so was Jake Hollister from his makeshift bed.

He wasn't alone.

There was a second person in the hammock.

Rachel watched as Jake bent over and swept a half-sleeping form into his arms. It was a young woman.

It was Jane Bennett.

He cradled her with great care and tenderness as he

carried her toward the Delilah bungalow, only to emerge a few minutes later and make his way toward Samson.

" 'Judge not, that ye be not judged,' " Rachel murmured under her breath.

Perhaps the world would be a better place if more of its people, even its pious people, especially its pious people, remembered those words. Not just remembered them but lived them.

Certainly the Mayfairs would have been better off if they had practiced those words every day of their lives, not just read them from the Good Book, recited them from memory like some platitude and then immediately forgotten them.

Jake Hollister and Jane Bennett: Were they lovers? Did they seek strength and solace and a few minutes of forgetfulness in each other's arms?

So be it.

She would not stand in judgment. She would not name it sin. There had already been too much naming of sin, too much pain, and not enough, not nearly enough loving in this house.

Mama.

Daddy.

Charlie Bennett.

Poor sweet but deluded Mary Magdalene.

The childhood nursery rhyme echoed through Rachel Mayfair's head as she picked up a watering can and began to moisten the soil around the plants that her sister, Esther, was nurturing on the window sill.

> *Mary, Mary, quite contrary,*
> *How does your garden grow?*
> *With silver bells and cockleshells*
> *And pretty maids all in a row.*

chapter *Eighteen*

"Do you have hiking boots with you?"

"No."

"Sturdy walking shoes?"

"Sort of."

"Sort of?" The expression on Jake's face was one of skepticism. "What are they? Sneakers?"

Jane shook her head from side to side. "Better than sneakers. Reeboks."

Jake made an impatient sound and checked his list again. "They'll have to do."

"Well, I didn't realize I was going to be tramping through the forest primeval when I packed my bags back in London three weeks ago," she grumbled under her breath.

At the very least she had assumed there would be a general store on the island. Well, there was a general store of sorts on Paradise: Maxwell's. But currently he was all out of hiking boots in her size—or in any size, for that matter.

Jane planted her hands on the hips of her newly purchased blue jeans. They were two sizes too large for her.

But both Jake and Maxwell himself had assured her that they would shrink to the correct size with repeated laundering. By her calculations that would be somewhere in the vicinity of one to two hundred washings, or tropical drenchings, depending on which came first.

"Tell me something," she said, pulling her newly purchased cap down over her eyes.

At least it made sense to Jane to protect herself from the sun. She was wearing plenty of protection too: a long-sleeved shirt, jeans down past her ankles, sunblock with an SPF of forty-five, dark sunglasses, and the attractive khaki cap with a bill that extended a good four or five inches past the end of her nose.

If her friends could see her now . . .

"Tell you what?" Jake said briskly as he walked around the heavily loaded Jeep, checking every item on his list, not once, not twice, but a minimum of three times.

"What were you in your previous life?" she inquired as she followed in his footsteps.

"My previous life?" he said, frowning at her. "You mean like what was I in my last reincarnation?" Jake tightened the ropes that secured their scuba gear and air tanks. "To tell you the truth, I'm not sure I believe in that kind of thing."

Jane stood a little straighter, not that she had ever been one to slouch. "I meant what did you do for a job, a profession, before you decided to hang it up and take off for parts unknown and landed here on Paradise?"

Sometimes one had to be very specific when speaking to the male of the species, she noticed.

Jake's mouth formed a round *O*. "I was in business. I was a businessman."

That narrowed it down to two or three thousand possibilities. "Were you any good as a businessman?"

Jane knew he had been good on some level. She recalled the night they had been lying in the hammock, baring their souls—along with a number of other things—and Jake had mentioned that he'd donated the money for scholarships and a building at the local high school back home in Indiana in memory of his halfbrother.

"I was good enough."

"You were successful?"

"That depends on your definition of success," he said noncommittally as he checked and double-checked the supply of food and water they were taking along on this excursion into the interior.

Was Jake merely impatient to be on their way? Or was he getting philosophical on her again? She wondered if he'd been hanging out with Brilliant Chang in between meetings with her.

There was no other way to describe the time they had spent together for the past week. They weren't dates. They weren't assignations. They weren't even appointments, and they certainly weren't romantic trysts.

They were meetings.

Planning meetings and strategy sessions during which the two of them pored over maps, studied charts, scanned historical references, debated theories, and did just about every other darned thing two people could do who were making plans to search for a treasure ship that had been lost for more than three hundred years.

Jake kicked the front left tire of the Wrangler several times with the toe of his boot—the tire had been giving him a little trouble, he claimed, for the past twenty thousand miles or so—and threw her a sharp glance. "If it makes any difference"—inferring, of course, that it made absolutely *no* difference—"I made a great deal of money in my business."

He obviously didn't spend any of it on clothes, Jane mused as she noted the latest pair of shabby jeans he was wearing. No doubt there was an identical pair in his knapsack.

"Were you happy at what you were doing?" she asked.

"Happy?" Jake repeated the word as if it were an alien concept to him. "I guess so."

"Did you love it?" Jane honestly wanted to know his feelings on the subject. "Could you hardly wait to get up in the morning so you could start doing it all over again?"

Jake stopped what he was doing.

He removed his dark aviator glasses and slipped them into his shirt pocket.

He came around the side of the Jeep, leaned one elbow on the edge of the passenger's door, pushed his hat back from his face and brought his mouth down right next to hers.

Jane could feel his breath stir the tiny hairs that had escaped from her ponytail. She could see every eyelash framing his eyes, every color that made up his irises—and there had to be at least a half dozen different shades of brown and green and blue—even a tiny scratch on his chin where he had apparently cut himself shaving that morning.

Jake was that close to her.

Then he announced in a voice laced with innuendo: "Honey, there is only one thing I can hardly wait to get up in the morning so I can start doing *it* all over again."

Jane understood immediately.

Heat flooded her face and rushed down her body.

She was speechless. Not because she couldn't think of a single thing to say, but because there were suddenly so many feelings, so many sensations, so many words all ajumble in her head that not a single one sorted itself out in time for her to utter it before Jake dropped a hard, swift kiss on her mouth and went back to his packing.

A delayed "oh" was the extent of what she finally managed to vocalize before they climbed aboard the Jeep Wrangler, drove along the dusty street of Purgatory—sending squawking chickens flying in several different directions—and out into the countryside.

The lady was a class act.

She was a damned good sport too.

Of course, at the moment, she looked ridiculous in the getup she was wearing: jeans that hung down her backside, and just about every other side of her, and had to be held up with a belt cinched tightly around her middle, fancy running shoes that would have been more at home in a fitness spa than out here in the middle of the jungle, and a cap that hid about everything but the occasional thrust of a defiant chin and the swing of a girlish ponytail.

"Tell me again where we're going?" Jane shouted over the roar of the engine and the noise of the tires digging into the dirt road.

"Up to a spot that I know of in the hills," Jake answered, keeping both hands on the steering wheel.

"What's it called?"

"Redemption."

That brought a raised eyebrow from his passenger. Not that he actually saw Jane's eyebrow arch, but Jake could certainly imagine such an occurrence beneath the cap and the sunglasses.

"As in 'Thou wilt be condemned into everlasting redemption for this'?" she quoted.

"Don't forget," he reminded her, keeping his eyes straight ahead on the road. "The Mayfairs were churchgoing people and some of the very first settlers on Paradise. They named most of the island, as a matter of fact."

"What I quoted from was Shakespeare; specifically, *Much Ado About Nothing*," Jane informed him. "Not the Bible."

"Thank God," he muttered under his breath.

"What exactly is Redemption?"

"A pool of clear water beneath a magnificent waterfall called the Veil of Mist."

She wrapped one arm around her knee. "That doesn't sound very biblical to me."

"It isn't," he said. "The waterfall was named centuries ago by the native Caribe Indians passing through on their way to a more hospitable island."

Jane glanced around and observed, "This island seems hospitable enough to me, assuming you don't mind a little jungle and the lack of certain amenities."

"Apparently the Caribes felt otherwise. But the name stuck anyway. There is also a set of natural stone steps leading up to the top of the waterfall, which the Mayfairs named—"

"Jacob's Ladder," she finished for him.

"How did you guess?"

"I didn't guess. Brilliant Chang mentioned it to me one day while we were drinking tea."

"Speaking of Brilliant Chang," Jake said as he turned onto an even steeper grade of road. "Have there been any more signs of trespassers or evil spirits?"

"Not a one." Jane must have picked up on something in his voice, however. "Why?"

There wasn't much he could hide from the lady these days, Jake had discovered. He had to admit it was a little disconcerting at times, but she seemed to have developed a sixth sense when it came to him.

He didn't want to worry her unduly, but he might as well tell her. She always seemed to have a way of getting it out of him eventually, anyway.

"I've had the feeling we're being watched," he confessed as he ducked his head to miss a low-hanging vine.

"Since when?"

"Since"—here he decided to display some tact, or at least some care in his answer—"not long after you arrived on the island."

"Are *we* being watched? Or am *I* being watched?" she asked, cutting straight through to the heart of the matter.

Jake hated like hell having to tell her. "I think you're the one being watched."

"Why would anyone be spying on me?"

"Why would anyone be in your bungalow?"

"The *Bella Doña*. They do know about the *Bella Doña*," she exclaimed, her hand flying to her mouth as if she shouldn't have said the name of the ship out loud.

"I don't think that's it."

"You don't?"

"I don't believe it's anything that specific."

"Oh, you mean someone is spying on me simply for the pleasure of spying on me?"

"Maybe they're being paid to find out whatever they can about you," he advanced.

"Which takes us back to why?" She was quiet for a

minute or two. "Why don't you think it's because of the *Bella Doña*?"

"Because everyone on this island knows I have these crazy theories about the shipwreck, and I've been searching for the bloody thing for over a year, and nobody has bothered to spy on me in all that time," Jake informed her.

"In other words, the islanders think you're a crackpot."

"Something like that."

"Actually it must come in handy."

"It does. They don't pay any attention to me, and I'm allowed to go about my business without being disturbed."

"Being crazy often helps in cases like this," she stated. "Or so I'm told."

They drove through the forested countryside, gradually climbing higher and higher. At one point Jake stopped the four-wheel-drive vehicle, and they simply sat and gazed out over the landscape before them. It was all lush, green vegetation below, hills in the distance, mountains behind the hills, and blue skies overhead.

"It's breathtaking," Jane murmured.

"Yes, it is." Jake sat back for a moment. "There is a fabled flower which grows here called *tiare apetahi*, which, despite attempts at transplanting it, will grow no place else. The flower's blooms, which pop like firecrackers two hours before dawn, are said to ward off evil spirits." He went on with a wry expression on his face. "Some claim that smoking the dried leaves of the *tiare apetahi* will enable a true believer to see 'inside of inside.' "

"Dr. Gilmour was right," Jane said quietly.

"About what?"

"About you." She pressed her lips together briefly. "He said you had gained an encyclopedic knowledge about this island in your search for the *Bella Doña*."

"But he's still convinced I'm looking in all the wrong places," Jake said with a chuckle as he put the Jeep into gear and drove on.

Once they were underway, Jane asked him again, "Who do you think is watching me?"

"I don't know," he answered truthfully.

"It could be almost anyone," she speculated.

"It could be."

"I wish I knew who—or at least why."

"So do I, sweetheart."

Their journey lasted another ten or fifteen minutes. Soon after they reached their destination. Jake pulled the Jeep off the road and into a high grassy meadow.

He turned to Jane and took her hand in his. "I won't let anything happen to you."

"I know you won't."

"I promise," he vowed. "And I always keep my promises."

chapter Nineteen

"You have to promise that you'll keep me in your sights every second during this dive," Jake instructed as they stood on the edge of the large, clear pool.

"I promise," Jane vowed, knowing how important it was to her own safety, to Jake's and to the success of this venture that she do exactly as she was told.

They had already changed into their wetsuits and scuba gear. The rest of their belongings and equipment were stored in the Jeep, which was concealed behind a thicket of nearby bushes. Not that there was another human being within thirty miles.

"The cardinal rule of scuba diving is that you always have a companion diver or 'buddy,' and you keep the other diver in view at all times," Jake informed her. "I'm your buddy. Don't let me out of your sight."

She had no intention of doing so.

Life was uncertain. Life underwater was even more uncertain. There was little, if any, margin for error. And the price of making a mistake was high, indeed.

Jake went on to explain. "We're practicing in wetsuits instead of dive suits for one reason and one reason only.

When we find the *Bella Doña* and take our first dive down to the site of it we won't know ahead of time what the water temperature is going to be. Lycra and similar materials would protect us from abrasions from rock, coral, even the shipwreck itself, but it would provide no serious thermal protection.''

"In other words, the dive suits might not keep us warm enough," Jane said in plain English.

"Exactly." Jake nodded his head in approval. "This dive is your final exam, in a manner of speaking, and I believe you're prepared for it.''

Jane certainly hoped so.

He ticked each point off, one by one, on his fingers. "You've proven to me that you're scuba-certified.''

She was. She hadn't done a lot of diving in the past year, but Jane didn't consider herself a novice either.

He ticked off point number two. "You showed that you could handle yourself well when we dived in the bay just below the Four Sisters Inn and even the Caribbean itself at the tip of the island.''

At the time Jane hadn't realized it was some kind of test. She'd assumed that they were practicing for the Big Dive, as they referred to the one they would be making in search of the *Bella Doña*.

Jake marked off one final point on his fingers. "I've been watching you closely.''

Jane flashed him a bright smile.

"I don't mean watching you like that, honey," he said, relaxing his militarylike stance for a moment.

He did watch her like *that*, of course, and they both knew it.

"I meant that I've observed the way you handle yourself in the water, the way you take charge of maintaining your own diving gear. That's important for a good diver.

I don't trust anybody else to check over my equipment and neither do you." He gave her a congratulatory pat on the back. "I like that."

"It's my life at stake every time I go diving," Jane pointed out. "Since my life means more to me than it does to anyone else, it only makes sense that I should check and double check my own apparatus."

Jake obviously agreed with her.

The next topic of conversation was their current locale. "I picked Redemption for this dress rehearsal for a very important reason," he told her.

Jane honestly tried to keep her attention on what Jake was saying, but this was one of the most breathtaking and beautiful settings she had ever beheld.

Redemption was a crystal-clear pool where you could see right down to the bottom. The bottom wasn't sand or mud, as might be expected, but was comprised of stones of various shapes and hues. The stones had been worn smooth by centuries, perhaps millennia, of water rushing over, around, and under them.

On three sides of the tranquil pond there were meadows of abundant green grass. Beyond the rich grasslands were trees of every color and size and type indigenous to the island, and beyond the trees were the hills of Paradise.

On the horizon, and no small distance away—enveloped in a blue haze that reminded Jane of the Great Smoky Mountains of Tennessee—she could make out the silhouette of majestic mountains, but they were miles and miles away, on the other side, the dark side, of Paradise.

A shiver coursed through her.

The other side, the dark side, of Paradise is where she and Jake would soon be headed.

The fourth perimeter of Redemption was the waterfall,

the Veil of Mist, and it was literally a curtain of mist. Water cascaded thirty, perhaps forty feet down the hillside and a fine spray was created where it met the tranquil pool.

To one side of the waterfall were the stone steps carved by Nature herself and named Jacob's Ladder by the Mayfairs. The other side was a sheer face of rock. Only rock climbers or perhaps mountaineers would even attempt that side of the cliff, and there had been virtually none since the island was first founded.

As Jake had said to her, he was one of the few people who ever visited Redemption. It was such a beautiful place that Jane found it difficult to believe until she remembered there weren't any tourists on Paradise. Apparently the native inhabitants had little time or interest in exploring the more remote regions of their own island. Or perhaps they simply took the natural beauty of Paradise for granted.

"As I was saying . . ." Jake cleared his throat and made certain he had her complete attention.

"Yes . . . ?"

"I picked Redemption for one very important reason."

"The waterfall?"

Jake shook his head, but it wasn't a definite no. "Not so much for the waterfall as for what is beneath it."

"And what, pray tell, is beneath the waterfall?"

"A cave."

"Of course!" Jane exclaimed, slapping her forehead with the flat of her hand. The whole idea of an underground cave jelled with Jake's favorite theory about the location of the *Bella Doña*.

"I see you get my drift."

"I certainly do."

"What you need—and what we both could use more

of—is the experience of diving into a cave.''

''Into the unknown,'' she hypothesized.

''It will be more than into the unknown, Jane,'' he warned. ''It will be into darkness.''

''Darkness.'' She repeated the word and shivered.

''This is the only place on the island that I know of where you can get the experience of diving into a cave that is without a direct source of light.'' Jake had been all business. Suddenly he was human again. ''Are you afraid?''

Jane would be a fool not to answer him truthfully. ''I'm not so much afraid as apprehensive.''

''Good,'' Jake said, putting a reassuring arm around her shoulder for a moment. ''It'll help you stay on your toes.''

Not literally, of course, since Jane was wearing swimming fins on her feet.

''Now let's run through the basic rules one last time before we dive,'' Jake said, and he meant business. ''We will use no more than a third of our air going in and during the time we spend in the cave. We will use another third for the journey back out of the cave. And one third of our air is always held in reserve for emergencies. You got that?''

''I've got it,'' Jane stated emphatically.

''We will do everything by the book, and nothing will go wrong,'' he predicted. ''Any questions?''

''No questions.''

Jane knew for a fact that Jake Hollister hadn't always done it by the book. A mutual friend of theirs—the good doctor—had alerted her to the fact that Jake used to be a risk taker. He had even been known to dive alone. Diving without a buddy was supposed to be the cardinal sin, after all, in scuba diving.

Jake had apparently learned his lesson the hard way, according to Jason Gilmour.

The story was not an unfamiliar one in diving circles. Jake had been down in eighty or ninety feet of water and had whacked his air tank on an overhanging rock. Unbeknownst to him the air had started leaking out. He was usually very conscious of his gauges—as any good diver was—and he still thought he had fifteen hundred pounds of air.

Fifteen minutes later, according to the hair-raising account Jake had related eventually to Doc Gilmour, it was like he couldn't breathe any air in. He looked at his gauge and it read zero.

He had no choice.

He had to surface or he was dead. His air tanks were empty.

Jake knew he had air in his lungs. He knew the air was compressed and would expand as he headed toward the surface. He also knew he couldn't beat his own bubbles up, or he'd get nitrogen narcosis and possibly end up dead anyway. He swam for the surface, looking at his gauge.

Fifty feet.

Forty feet.

Thirty feet.

He had been sure he was going to die.

He had finally hit the surface of the water, and by some miracle he had survived, but Jake Hollister had discovered something that day, according to his friend.

He'd discovered that he wanted to live.

And he had found that he wasn't ready to die.

Jason Gilmour swore to Jane that Jake had become a different man from that time on. Less self-destructive. More introspective. Definitely more philosophical.

Jake may not always have practiced what he preached, but he certainly did now, Jane discovered as he went through the procedure of checking depth gauges, breathing regulators, buoyancy compensators, air pressure gauges, air tanks, every darned piece of their equipment one final time.

Then Jake looked at her, gave her an encouraging smile and mouthed, "Ready?"

"Ready." Jane adjusted her face mask, gave him the thumbs-up sign, and followed him into Redemption.

It was another world.

It was an underwater paradise.

The sun shone down into the crystal-clear water, fracturing into a million shards and leaving the pool a sheer golden glimmer of light.

Redemption was filled with wondrous sights: exotic plants and brilliantly colored flowers that swayed to and fro with the gentle underwater currents.

Fish that knew no fear of them, never having encountered a human being before. They ate directly from Jane's hand and nibbled at her fingertips.

Tiny aquatic creatures that encircled their ankles and darted back and forth through their legs, as if playing a game of hide and seek, before dashing off to explore something else, somewhere else.

Yet Jane knew they weren't here to play; the air in their tanks was limited.

Jake gave her a minute or two to enjoy her newfound world, then he motioned that it was time for her to follow him. He headed toward the waterfall and the churning, foaming water that signaled the entrance to the cave. She swam along directly behind him, knowing that she must never let him out of her sight.

She kept calm.

She remembered Jake's warning of what lay ahead. There would be a few seconds of feeling tossed to and fro. It would be difficult, if not impossible, to see clearly. But it would pass as they swam through the waterfall and into the entrance of the cave.

Jake switched on his underwater light.

Jane followed suit.

They began to fight their way through the watery maelstrom. She knew a moment of panic. Then the water gradually grew calmer and she could see, straight ahead of them, the entrance to the cave.

With Jake in the lead, Jane swam into the unknown.

Only it wasn't really the unknown, of course, because Jake had made this dive several times before. He knew where they were going and what they would find when they got there.

He had even strung a guide wire from the entrance of the cave to the point at the rear where it narrowed to an impassable channel. That passageway was dangerously small, too small for the average human being to pass through. Even Jake, it turned out, had not been able to follow the cave all the way to its conclusion.

This was a different world, Jane realized.

This was a world of dark shapes and darker shadows. This was a world defined only by what little they could see, and there was so much more that they could not see.

It was intriguing and frightening and beautiful in its own way.

Something startled Jane as it bumped against her arm. Perhaps a fish or an animal that preferred the dark to the light.

Weren't there always places, things, creatures, even people, who embraced the dark? Perhaps it was especially true for those who preferred night to day.

Her body was healthy and her legs were strong, yet Jane was relieved when Jake finally signaled that it was time to leave the cave and head back to the outside pool.

She nodded and swam alongside him, glad that she wasn't alone, glad that Jake was beside her, glad to be swimming out of the darkness.

He gave her the thumbs-up, and they began the journey through the waterfall and into the golden light of Redemption.

"Congratulations! You passed with flying colors," Jake complimented her as soon as they resurfaced, exited the pool, and began to remove their scuba apparatus. "You did exactly as you were told, and it came off without a hitch."

"I tried to think of it as a dress rehearsal," Jane remarked as she wiggled out of her gear. "Remembering, of course, that every dive is real and there are no dress rehearsals."

Jake unzipped his wetsuit and began shrugging it off his shoulders. "You're a smart woman, Jane Bennett. You stay calm under pressure, and you don't panic easily. I'm damned proud to have you for my partner."

"Don't you mean for your 'buddy'?" she teased as she dropped her air tanks to the grass.

"Partner. Buddy. And anything else you'd care to be of mine," he said as he finished undressing.

There was one advantage, Jake realized, to scuba diving with the woman you were also sleeping with. They were both unself-conscious about seeing each other in the brief swimsuits they had donned under their wetsuits.

The woman he was sleeping with.

Jake gave a sigh.

Sleeping was about all he and Jane had managed since that wonderful night they had spent together in the hammock.

For the past week their time and energies had been invested in planning, discussing, debating, and plotting where they were going to search for the shipwreck of the *Bella Doña*. Their stamina had been eaten up by numerous practice dives and endless equipment checks.

It had taken over their lives.

Preparing for the dive of a lifetime, they had discovered, was exhausting business.

That wasn't the whole truth and nothing but the truth, however, Jake admitted as he watched Jane brush the tangles from her wet hair and slip into a terrycloth coverup.

There was another reason—a very good reason—why he hadn't tried to make love to her since that night.

He'd wanted to wait until it was the right time and the right place. He had wanted to find a special time and a special place, one preferably *not* under the watchful eye of the Mayfair sisters or anyone else on this island.

And that included their watchful if unnamed snoop.

That was why, Jake persuaded himself, he had waited until today. Something told him that this might well be the time and the place.

And this time he had come prepared.

He passed his tongue over his lips. "Hungry?" he inquired, striving for a certain nonchalance in his manner.

"I'm famished," Jane told him.

So was he, come to think of it.

"We should have something to drink right away too," he said. "It's easy to get dehydrated while diving and not even be aware of it."

"Let's have a picnic," Jane suggested as they unloaded the thermos and food from the back of the Jeep.

"Great idea," he agreed.

Jane took one of the blankets from their stack of supplies and stood surveying the grassy knoll beside the pool. "Where should I spread out the blanket?"

"Not out here," Jake replied, knowing exactly where he planned to take her.

"Then where?"

"No more questions," he told Jane. "Just bring your things and follow me."

The day was turning out to be quite warm and sunny. With a towel still draped around his neck from the dive, Jake picked up the thermos of juice, the blanket, the basket of food and took Jane by the hand.

He led her toward the waterfall.

Apparently her curiosity got the better of her. "Where in the world are we going?"

"I have a surprise for you," Jake declared.

Jane gave him a sideways glance and repeated with a hint of suspicion in her tone, "A surprise?"

"Trust me," he said. "You're going to love it."

chapter*Twenty*

*J*ane was in love with him.

She wasn't certain exactly when it had happened. But sometime between the night they had spent together in the hammock—could it have been only a week ago?—and this afternoon, she realized that she had fallen in love with Jake Hollister.

It was the damnedest thing.

It was also the last thing she would have expected looking back on her initial meeting with the tall, dark, intense, and *unshaven* stranger aboard the ferry from Charlotte Amalie to Paradise.

How could she be in love with a man that she had known for a total of nineteen days?

She wasn't sure. She simply was.

Perhaps Brilliant Chang was right.

Perhaps time was irrelevant.

The gentleman had once remarked to her—in fact, it was on the occasion of their first meeting at the Delilah bungalow as two of the island boys were digging the hole for a spirit house—that time was an illusion. There were those, Brilliant Chang had claimed, who believed that the past, the present, and the future were as one.

It was certainly true that she had no concept of time when Jake kissed her, when Jake touched her, when Jake caressed her. There was only Jake, then, and there was only the present.

She was in love with Jake, but whether they had a future together beyond this moment, beyond even this day, Jane didn't know. All they had was now.

Perhaps all anyone had was now.

"I've been saving something special to show you," Jake declared as he guided her past one end of the Veil of Mist, around the corner and behind the waterfall, itself.

It was another cave, but it was unlike any cave Jane had ever seen before: its appearance was more that of a private room. The front entrance was concealed by the curtain of mist created by the rushing waterfall. The sides of the "room" were huge stones covered with vines, lush and green and surprisingly dry.

The dirt floor was overlaid with a layer of soft vegetation, ferns, palm fronds, and exotic, fragrant flowers. The ceiling was a canopy created by centuries of huge, thick vines, fallen trees, and slabs of stone the size of a small house. In the center of the ceiling was a sizeable opening through which the light of the bright and brilliant Caribbean sun shone down on everything below.

"What a remarkable place," Jane exclaimed as they stepped into the concealed room.

"I call it Sanctuary," Jake told her.

"Is that its name?"

"I don't know." He set their supplies down on a stone block with roughly the dimensions of a banquet table. "I'm not sure it has an official name. There aren't any signs of someone having been here in years, maybe in centuries . . . except me."

"Except us." Jane took a turn around the naturally formed chamber. It was large and airy and sun-filled. It seemed the perfect spot for a picnic. "Let's have lunch in here," she suggested.

"That's what I had in mind," Jake said, spreading the blanket out on a pile of thick and relatively clean foliage.

They nibbled on sandwiches. They sipped fruit juice and iced tea. They shared slices of orange and papaya and sweet banana. Then they packed the remnants of their lunch away and stretched out drowsily on the blanket: the waterfall on one side, warm, dry grass where they lay, the sun and the sky above, and heaven below.

Jane turned her face toward Jake's and watched him through eyes that were half-closed.

Appearances were deceptive, she mused lazily, appreciatively, as she studied his muscular physique.

They had been wrong, of course.

They had lied to her.

Neither clothes nor money made the man. What made the man was what he was on the outside and especially what he was on the inside: what he was in his mind and body, heart, and soul.

Jane tried to visualize the men she had met in her lifetime, personally and professionally, young and old, and lined them up single file without a stitch of clothing on.

Tall and short.

Fat and thin and those somewhere in between.

Light. Dark. Tanned.

The hairless and the hairy.

Those who were muscular and those who were lean.

The strong. The athletic. The sedentary.

Those who were handsome of face. Those who were

ugly. The few who were beautiful, even angelic in appearance.

They all had the same features, more or less, the same basic equipment and appendages.

What would enable a woman to discern the differences between one man and the next if he were wearing no clothes and sporting none of the accoutrements of success or failure?

How could she tell a good man from a bad one?

Jake stared at her with a degree of inquisitiveness. "What are you thinking about?"

"Naked men," she replied without hesitation.

That got his undivided attention. "Naked men?"

Jane spelled it out for him. "Naked. Nude. Bare. *Au naturel.* Undressed. Unclothed. Disrobed. Exposed. In the altogether. In the buff. Without a stitch. In their birthday suits. Starkers." She put her nose in the air a fraction of an inch and sniffed with the merest suggestion of haughtiness. "Or as the French would say: *en l'ensemble.*"

Jake appeared to smother a smile. "Were you thinking about naked men in general?" His voice dropped half an octave. "Or were you thinking about a particular naked man?"

"Naked men in general," she confessed, turning onto her back and staring up at the natural canopy above their heads. "I have a theory, you see."

"I can't wait to hear more about this theory of yours," Jake confessed as he edged closer to her on the blanket.

"It's not earth-shattering." She felt it was only fair to warn him. "It's not complex. It's not intellectual or cerebral or abstract. It's not even original."

"What is it, then?"

"Mine," she stated.

"That's good enough for me," he said with enthusiasm.

Jane didn't dare look at Jake. She feared she would lose her courage altogether if she did.

She stared straight up at the stone and timber rafters overhead and said, "How can a woman tell the difference between a good man and a bad man?"

Was this one of those trick questions?

Jake knew he shouldn't take too long to respond. Jane might begin to wonder if he had the answer.

"I suppose it depends on what you mean by good and bad," he replied.

What the hell did she mean anyway?

"They used to say you could judge a man by his clothes, or the company he kept, or by the kind of car he drove, or even by the brand of aftershave he used," she said.

Jake groaned inwardly.

This conversation was beginning to show all the signs of becoming a long, drawn-out dialogue. Frankly he had hoped it would be short and sweet. He had other plans for this afternoon, and they didn't include a lengthy discourse on naked men.

Still, the topic under consideration was in the right ballpark. It might work to his advantage.

Patience, Hollister.

Patience. It was supposed to be a virtue, after all.

He had to say something. It was expected of him. "Well, I suppose a woman could start by asking herself if a man is good or bad at any number of things."

Jane made a quick voluntary movement with her hands. "For instance?"

Jake had to think fast. He said the first thing that occurred to him. "Golf? Football? Bowling?"

Jane made a face.

He paused for some seconds before he tried again. "All right. His job? His treatment of other people? His general moral character? His judgment? His taste?"

Jane fiddled with the tie at the waist of her short terry-cloth robe. "His taste in what?"

Jake drew a temporary blank. Then it started to come to him. "Food. Restaurants. Clothes. Movies. Hobbies. Books. Art. Furniture." He only hoped he was gaining credibility as well as momentum. "Friends. Children. Animals. Women." He stopped and blew out his breath. "Not necessarily in that order, of course."

"I should hope not," was her response.

Jake was on a roll now. "Of course, in order for a woman to determine if a man is good or bad at any—or all—of the above, it would require her to observe him closely, to watch him in action, to listen to him, and to speak with him. In short, she would need to spend some real quality time with the guy."

Her tone was neutral. "Don't you believe actions speak louder than words?"

"Yes, I do." He paused for a quick count of three. "But words can be important too."

Her next comment came out of left field. It took Jake a moment to catch her drift.

"A woman must use her head when it comes to a man," Jane stated unequivocally.

Jake swallowed hard. He had a feeling he was skating on thin ice. "Of course she does. But a woman has to follow her feminine intuition"—he'd been about to say her gut instincts and thought better of it—"and her heart, as well."

"Anything else?"

She'd asked.

So he would answer.

"Well, sooner or later, a woman will need to find out for herself if a man is good or bad in bed."

There was a moment of total silence.

"Would you care to expound on that subject?" Jane inquired in a perfectly normal tone of voice, proving herself more than equal to the occasion.

He'd brought it up. No pun intended. Jake didn't feel that he had any choice but to expound.

"I don't mean simply whether a man is good or bad at the physical act of performing sexually," he said.

He seemed to be digging a rather nice hole for himself, Jake noticed, and getting himself in deeper and deeper.

Again, no pun intended.

He definitely had Jane Bennett's undivided attention, however. She had turned her head and was watching him intently.

"Go on," she urged.

"I believe a demonstration is in order," he said in a deceptively mild manner.

"A demonstration of what?"

"Good and bad, naturally." Jake knew it was a challenge that she wouldn't be able to resist.

Jane raised her eyebrows in a questioning arch. "Exactly how will this demonstration be conducted?"

"I'll begin by performing one simple act and you will respond by judging whether it was good or bad," Jake explained. "I can continue to demonstrate and you can continue to judge, or we can take turns, if you like."

"Sounds simple enough."

"Oh, it is," Jake assured her.

She dug her teeth into her bottom lip. "And when the demonstration is completed?"

"Why, then you'll have your answer," came his cheerful reply.

She blinked rapidly. "I'll have my answer to what?"

"To the question of whether a man is good or bad in bed."

Jane's eyes took on a definite spark of amusement. "Are you referring to men in general, Jake Hollister? Or are you speaking about a particular man?"

Touché.

Jake cleared his throat and announced, "I think we should begin with a simple kiss."

"A simple kiss is a reasonable place to start," Jane agreed.

Jake moved closer to her on the blanket, trying to ignore, for the time being, that she was dressed in a minuscule swimsuit and a scrap of terrycloth material that covered up very little, in his opinion.

He brought his mouth to hers, softly, briefly, and in an undemanding fashion. He could detect the sweet aftertaste of fruit on her lips and lingered for a few moments to savor the flavors of orange, papaya, banana, and Jane.

He drew back and inquired, "Good or bad?"

Her eyes told him the answer before she confirmed, "Good."

Jake carefully considered his next move. It was a little like a game of chess. Strategy was the key, and he had to be thinking several moves ahead of his opponent at all times. He didn't want to make the mistake of bringing out his king too soon or putting the lady in checkmate before she was good and truly ready.

"Perhaps another kiss," he advised. "This time more

complex, more demanding, requiring more skill if done correctly and if concluded with the proper results.''

He gathered Jane in his arms. Her hands went instinctively to his shoulders. He trailed his lips along her hand and halfway down her arm. He felt the resulting quiver that told him she was far from indifferent to his caress.

It was a game, after all, and they both realized that they were going to come out the winners.

There would be no losers.

His mouth covered hers. He tasted her lips with the arrowed tip of his tongue. He delved deeper into the inner recesses of her mouth and remained longer. She came to meet him halfway, to sample a taste of him, to perform the mating ritual that man and woman have been performing with their tongues since the beginning of time. Then he plunged between her lips and past her teeth in that simulation of the intimate act they knew would soon follow.

They were both out of breath when Jake retreated and rested his forehead against hers.

He didn't bother to ask.

Jane barely managed a breathless: ''Good.'' Then she pushed on his bare chest and forced him down on the blanket. ''I believe it's my turn,'' she growled softly, her eyes turning the tawny golden color of a wild tigress.

Jake found himself flat on his back. Jane sat up straight, her shoulders posture-perfect, and proceeded to swing one long, lovely leg across his lower torso. She straddled him as if he were a horse and she the rider. Being on top apparently gave Jane the impression that she was in control, Jake realized.

Perhaps it was time to move his pawn into position.

Jake was wearing only a pair of abbreviated swim trunks. They fit him like a second skin. They concealed nothing. His genitals were clearly outlined against the spandex material.

The lovely creature above him, hovering over his body, had to be fully aware that he was positioned directly between her legs and that his erection was pushing against that sensitive female aperture where it so longed to be allowed to enter.

Jane's hair fell forward around her face. Her lips were already swollen from his kisses. Her complexion was a rosy shade of pink, whether from pleasure, or anticipation, or embarrassment—perhaps a little of all three.

She leaned over Jake and began to rain a succession of kisses upon him from his forehead to his nose, from his nose to his mouth, from his mouth to his chin, from his chin to the hollow at the base of his throat, from his throat to his chest to his belly: teasing kisses, cruel kisses, wondrous kisses.

She gradually slid down his body, taking her remarkable kisses with her. Kisses that trailed across his abdomen, along his waist, to his leg and hipbone, burning his flesh wherever her lips touched him. Kisses that lingered at his navel, a tongue that dipped into the tiny indentation. Kisses that barely avoided the center of his arousal and went first to one thigh and then the other.

Jake groaned out loud.

"Is that good or bad?" Jane inquired huskily, without bothering to raise her head.

Jake found he couldn't speak. There was no longer any good or bad. There was only want, need, feeling, desire.

"Good or bad?" was repeated more insistently.

He finally managed in a raspy voice, "Good."

Jane separated his legs several inches and placed her mouth on his inner thigh, nipping at his sensitized flesh, tugging on the random smattering of manly hair, caressing the bone and muscle so near to his sex that he felt himself swell in reaction.

So near and yet so far!

"Good or bad?" she queried again as her teeth took tiny nibbles of him.

"Goddamned great," Jake swore, knowing he couldn't take another moment of this sweet torture.

Enough was enough.

"My turn, I believe," he proclaimed as he pulled Jane up his body, until he had gained easy access to the belt of her short terrycloth swimming robe.

It was dispensed with in record time.

Then, eyes wild, eyes dark, eyes wide with desire, Jake tugged on the top of Jane's swimming suit until it was in a roll down around her waist. He urged her toward his waiting mouth and touched the tip of each bared breast with his tongue.

"Good or bad?" he muttered.

Turnaround was fair play, after all.

Jane threw her head back and moaned, "Good."

Jake raised his shoulders off the blanket and attached his mouth to first one nipple and then the other. He licked with his tongue. He tugged with his lips. He nipped with his teeth and suckled like a man and not at all like a manchild.

Jane could not stop chanting: "Good. Oh, so good. Jake, please, so good."

In no time, Jake had dispensed with her swimming suit altogether and had tossed his on the blanket alongside hers. He raised her up for a moment and held her there suspended above his body. His arms, strong as they were, trembled with the effort as he slowly, oh-so-slowly, lowered her onto him.

She took just a little of him at first, the very tip and perhaps only an inch or two.

"Good or bad?" Jake asked as the sweat broke out on his skin.

Jane's eyes closed and then opened again. She stared straight down into his and whispered feelingly, "Good."

Gradually she was impaled on his hard flesh. She managed, in the end, to take every last bit of him into her. They paused and savored the sensation of his body buried deeply inside her. Then they began to move together, slowly at first, carefully, seeking to discover what pleased and what pleasured.

"God, honey, you feel so damned good," Jake exclaimed as he finally rolled over, staying inside her all the while, and found himself gazing down into eyes that were as deep as the sea itself.

"There is no good. There is no bad. There is only you, Jake," she whispered fervently as he began to thrust inside her again and again.

There was no past.

There was no present.

There was no future.

There was only now.

Jake Hollister didn't do anything by halves. And that included making love, Jane decided.

He put everything of himself into it, into her.

There was an intensity about the man that translated into an all-consuming, all-powerful experience. Suddenly no place else existed; no one else existed but the two of them. She was the only woman, and he was the only man.

It was earth-shattering.

It was soul-changing.

Somehow Jane knew that she would never be quite the same woman again.

He had come prepared this time and they both knew it was the right time, the right place, the right man and the right woman. They made love again and again until they stopped counting the times they sought each other out, there in that private haven, that sanctuary from the rest of the world, the place that would always be theirs and no one else's.

The moment came when there was no time, no place, no one, nothing but Jake and the way he made her feel.

"How do you feel?" Jake finally asked a long time later as they lay curled up in each other's arms.

"Good," she admitted, laughing in the back of her throat. "Very good. Great." She gazed up into the face of the man she loved. "How do you feel?"

"Better than good. Better than great. Better than I have ever felt in my entire thirty-seven years," Jake said as he looked down at her. "I feel free." There was a new and wondrous tone in his voice. "That's it. I feel free for the first time in my life."

" 'The truth shall make us free,' " she murmured, remembering the words that she had toasted with her first night on Paradise.

The truth she had discovered was that she loved this man with all of her mind and body, heart and soul.

But Jane couldn't help but wonder.

What was the truth that had finally set Jake Hollister free?

chapter *Twenty-one*

"We have received an invitation to dine at the Hacienda," Jane announced to Jake as she opened the envelope and scanned the writing inside.

The paper was thick cream-colored vellum of the highest quality. There was an elaborate crest embossed both at the top of the page and on the back flap of the envelope.

"How did it arrive?" he asked.

"It was hand-delivered by a messenger." By one of the islanders she assumed was employed by Don Carlos.

"I doubt if the invitation was meant to include both of us," Jake said, glancing up from the map he had been studying intently for the past ten minutes. "It must be for you."

She held the envelope up and waved it back and forth in front of his face. "It's clearly addressed to Miss Jane Bennett *and* Mr. Jake Hollister."

"Don't you find that a trifle odd?" Jake observed, his attention reverting to the map.

Now that he had mentioned it. Yes, she did find it a trifle odd, Jane realized.

The usual, proper, and socially correct procedure would have been for each of them to receive a separate invitation to dinner. After all, she and Jake were hardly considered a "couple" here on Paradise.

In fact, as far as Jane knew, no one was aware of the personal relationship between them. They had decided that discretion was definitely the best policy on an island as small as this one. Besides, they had no wish to offend the sensibilities of their landladies.

And last, but far from least, it was nobody else's business where she and Jake went, what they did once they got there, or how they felt about each other.

That was privileged information.

So privileged, Jane reflected with some bemusement, that not even she knew it.

Oh, she knew how she felt about Jake. She just wasn't sure how Jake felt about her.

Of course, she had never actually said the words out loud. She had never spoken of love. She had never told him how she felt. She'd kept her feelings to herself. But only a fool wouldn't have figured out by now that she was in love with him.

And Jake Hollister was nobody's fool.

But he did have other things on his mind. Things like the shipwreck of the *Bella Doña* and exactly where to begin searching for it.

As far as the faux pas concerning the dinner invitation . . . well, this was a remote island in the Caribbean, after all. It wasn't London or New York, Jane reminded herself.

"Do you want to go?" Jake pinched the bridge of his nose between thumb and forefinger.

"Headache?"

"No."

"Tired?"

"Yes. So are you, no doubt." He leaned back in the desk chair, balanced his hands on the sidearms and allowed the front legs to teeter off the floor by an inch or two. "That's why I was asking if you really want to go to this dinner party."

Jane hesitated. "I believe I do. Out of curiosity, if for no other reason. I've heard a lot about the Hacienda. I'd like to see the house. And I would enjoy meeting Don Carlos, as well." She made up her mind. "Yes, I'd like to go."

Jake didn't seem to have any problem with her decision. "Then let's RSVP that we'll be happy to dine with the island's premiere host. When is the invitation for?"

Jane glanced down at the piece of paper in her hand. "Tomorrow evening. Cocktails at seven. Dinner to follow at eight."

Jake paused and considered, then shook his head slowly. "Seems kind of spur of the moment to me."

It did to Jane as well.

"They appear pretty confident that we won't have any prior social engagements, don't they?" He was obviously amused rather than offended by the situation.

Jane tapped a fingernail against her bottom lip. "I wonder who else is invited."

"Hard to say," Jake mumbled. He wasn't exactly proving himself to be a fount of information.

Nevertheless, Jane persisted with her inquiry. "Who does Don Carlos usually invite to these affairs?"

"Don Carlos doesn't."

"I beg your pardon," she said, flopping down into the chair beside his. "Would you care to explain that last remark?"

"Do I have any choice?"

"No."

Jake combed his fingers through his hair. "That's what I've been trying to tell you, sweetheart. Don Carlos wouldn't."

"Wouldn't what?"

"Wouldn't issue a last minute dinner invitation, for one thing," he spelled out for her.

"How do you know?"

His reply was deliberately evasive. "Let's just say that I'm acquainted with Don Carlos."

The man never ceased to amaze her, Jane realized. "And . . . ?"

"I happen to know that he is a gracious and thoughtful host, but that he rarely if ever entertains here on Paradise."

"And . . . ?" She suspected there was more to all of this than he was telling her.

"I also happen to know that Don Carlos left the island this morning via his private helicopter."

"Via his private *what*?"

"You heard me correctly. By means of his private helicopter. He had business to attend to elsewhere."

She was still doubtful. "Where elsewhere?"

"If you must know"—Jake's tone implied that it was none of her business, which it wasn't, of course, but she wanted an answer anyway—"Buenos Aires."

Jane sank back in her chair, threw both hands up in a gesture of utter surprise and exclaimed, "Well, I'll be!"

Jake refrained from adding a well-deserved: *And you are!*

"Then who . . . ?"

"I assume the dinner invitation has come at the behest of that charming brother and sister duo, Tony and Megs St. Cyr."

"Oh no," she groaned. "Then let's not go."

Jake had the opposite reaction to hers. "All the more reason to go." He bounced to his feet with a grin that made her uneasy. "It's always wise to know what your enemy is up to."

"Enemy?" Jane tossed the invitation down on the desk. "Are the St. Cyrs the enemy?"

"They could be."

"Why?"

His eyes narrowed. "I don't like them."

"You don't know them," she pointed out logically.

"I don't like what I know *about* them, then."

"Which is?"

Jake seemed to be in possession of a list at least a mile long. "They are overbearing. They are pretentious. They are rude. They are moochers. And they are demanding and thoughtless of the people who try to graciously serve them at the Hacienda."

"Ah-ha!" Jane exclaimed, pointing a finger. "You have your spies too, don't you?"

Jake shrugged his khaki-covered shoulders. "Everyone has spies."

"I don't have spies."

"Perhaps you should. They come in handy every now and then," he informed her.

This conversation was taking on a definite surreal quality. "Do you actually have spies?"

"No. Not spies."

"What are they, then?"

"More like informants. Okay, I got my information from a friend of a friend of Rosey's who works as a housemaid at the Hacienda."

"Gossip," Jane snorted.

"Gossip can be quite useful," Jake said to her as he

sat down again and went back to his maps.

Jane picked up the book on Caribbean history that she had been studying before the knock at the front door of the Delilah bungalow had interrupted her. A paragraph on the subject of record-setting weather caught her eye.

She mentioned to Jake, "Did you know that modern meteorologists now believe there was both a hurricane of legendary force gales and a major volcanic eruption in the region of Paradise in the summer of 1692?"

"Fascinating," he murmured, obviously not paying any attention to what she was saying.

Something began to niggle at Jane.

"What's the name of the place where you believe we should head next week?"

Jake glanced up at her. "I can't pronounce the name in its native language, an obscure now-extinct dialect anyway, but someone on Paradise told me that the translation is 'The Place from Which Nothing Returns.' "

"I don't think I care for the sound of that," she confessed with a degree of anxiousness. She had to ask, of course. "Why does nothing return?"

"Apparently because there is a great sea monster that swallows up everything in its path. At least according to local legend." He tried to reassure her. "Don't worry, honey. It's all mumbo jumbo, anyway."

Jane snorted in a most unladylike fashion. "That's what Megs and Tony St. Cyr claimed about the fortune-teller and her predictions on the ferry that first day."

"So . . . ?"

"So, she hasn't been wrong yet."

"*Who* hasn't been wrong yet?"

"Nui, of course."

Of course, Nui had also issued a warning about the

dragon and its wrath—which had, so far, remained a total mystery.

Just then something rang a tiny bell in Jane Bennett's head.

Something she should remember. Some connection she should make and wasn't. Some clue that was staring her straight in the face, and she wasn't seeing it.

It had been there right on the tip of her tongue . . . and, blast, now it was gone!

Jane gave a dramatic sigh. "Back to the dinner invitation. Do you honestly think we should attend?"

"I think it would be very wise for us to go and keep our eyes, our ears, our—"

"Noses?"

"Even our noses open to whatever we might see or hear or—"

"Smell?"

"About what might be going on."

"Then I'll send our acceptance, but I'm not going to like it," Jane promised him.

Jake gave her one of his best smiles. "Hey, how bad can it be?"

It was even worse than Jane had imagined.

"We hear that you two adventurous types have been out traipsing around the countryside," Megs offered along with a plate of hors d'oeuvres that most closely resembled small hot dogs wrapped in cheese and soaked in thick barbecue sauce.

Jane wondered if Megs St. Cyr honestly believed that it was an American-style culinary treat that her American guests would enjoy . . . or if she was deliberately being cruel.

Jane took the smallest bite possible and tried to swallow. She ended up washing the hot dog down with a sip of sangria, apparently the beverage of choice this evening.

"Mr. Hollister is a wonderful and informative tour guide," she said, willing to extol his virtues for the sake of a good cause. "He's been showing me around the island in his Jeep. Why, we've been to all kinds of exotic places, haven't we, Jake?"

Jake crossed one blue-jeaned leg over the other, popped a barbecue-soaked hot dog into his mouth, chewed several times, swallowed audibly, and then responded, "Yup."

"How did you learn so much about the island, Hollister?" Tony St. Cyr inquired with just the proper amount of ennui in his voice.

Or it would have been the proper amount if Tony had been in Paris or Rome or Madrid. Or if he'd been on a yacht anchored somewhere off the Riviera, trying to impress some insignificant little count who only understood half of what he was saying anyway.

On Paradise, where that kind of uppity attitude was frowned upon and where rudeness was considered a genuine insult, it simply didn't cut the mustard.

Something flickered behind Jake Hollister's hazel eyes. "Well, you see, St. Cyr, when I landed on the island over a year ago, I wasn't in the best shape of my life."

"You certainly look very fit to me now," Megs purred with feminine appreciation.

"I'm not talking about physical fitness, Miss St. Cyr."

"Please, call me Megs," the blonde entreated her male guest. Jake immediately complied with her wishes. "I'm talking about mental fitness, Megs."

His statement brought a blank stare from both brother and sister.

Jake went on. "I'd been drinking."

Megs looked down her perfectly made-up nose. "You were a drunkard?"

"Let's just say that I had a thing or two I was trying to forget, and a few shots of alcohol every now and then seemed to help."

"You obviously gave it up," Megs said, indicating the glass of fruit juice in Jake's hand.

"Yes, I did. Except for a sip or two of champagne one night several weeks ago." With that he gave Jane a pointed look that neither their host or hostess missed.

"Anyway, the point to this whole story is I won the Mangy Moose during a card game. When I sobered up and took stock of what I'd inherited, so to speak, I discovered a pile of old maps and books in the back room of the bar. It seems the previous owner had been something of a treasure hunter."

"A treasure hunter, imagine that?"

Megs St. Cyr wasn't much of an actress, in Jane's opinion. It was clear to her that the St. Cyr woman knew every detail of the story before Jake told her.

"I'm always out there looking for treasure." Jake laughed. "Never found any, of course. But that's probably true for ninety-nine percent of those who try to get something for nothing. Wouldn't you agree, Megs?"

"I'm sure I wouldn't know, Mr. Hollister."

"Please. Call me Jake."

"I wouldn't know, Jake."

"Anyway, there isn't a lot to do on Paradise, in case you two hadn't noticed that yet."

Tony spoke up. "You can say that again, Hollister. I was under the impression that Don Carlos had polo ponies and that we might get a few good chukkers in while we visited the island. It turns out there aren't any horses, there certainly isn't any polo, and there's precious little else.'' The handsome blond man surveyed the room in which they were sitting. ''Even the Hacienda appears to be dilapidated and falling down around the old man.''

Jane decided *not* to mention the magnificent and priceless collection of Santos she had noticed upon entering the main room of the Hacienda. Nor the beautiful, primitive furniture and antique rugs.

Whatever else Don Carlos may have deleted from his island retreat, the house was a virtual treasure trove of South American and early Spanish antiquities.

Jane assumed the gentleman had kept publicity about his collections at a minimum for security reasons, but her estimate was that there were several million pounds of rare antiques in the house.

The good news, she supposed, was that Megs and Tony St. Cyr apparently didn't have a clue about the value of the artifacts surrounding them at every turn.

Jane tuned back into the conversation just as Jake was saying to their hosts, ''Why, a coral reef can be hundreds of feet thick and many miles long. Did you know that living coral only grows at the rate of one-half inch per year?''

''No, I didn't know,'' Tony confessed, finishing off his glass of sangria and pouring himself another without offering to refill either Jane or Meg's glass.

''You go down twenty feet and it's the time of Columbus,'' Jake related with genuine enthusiasm. ''You dive down eighty-five feet and it's the time of Christ. Once, with special equipment, I dove down nearly one hundred and eighty feet. To think that the coral had been there at the time of the pyramids! It was mind-boggling, I'll tell you.''

Jane was enthralled.

Tony St. Cyr tried to appear interested.

Megs didn't even bother to pretend she wasn't bored. She covered her mouth with her hand and yawned.

chapter *Twenty-two*

"*I* don't know who they think they're kidding," Megs snickered as she watched the couple drive away in the beat-up Jeep Wrangler. "He's no more her tour guide around this island than you're mine."

"What's that supposed to mean?" Tony quizzed, sipping a snifter of his absent host's excellent cognac.

Frankly Tony had been a little surprised, pleasantly surprised, as he had informed Megs earlier that evening, to discover that Don Carlos had an enviable supply of first-class brandy in his wine cellar.

"What it means," Megs said, failing to keep the impatience out of her tone—there were times when she got sick and tired of having to explain every blessed thing to Tony—"is that Jake Hollister and Jane Bennett are lovers."

"Lovers?"

"Yes, lovers."

Her husband could be so dense.

Megs permitted herself a small self-pitying sigh. She teetered precariously on her high-heeled sandals and tugged at the uncomfortably snug bodice of her haute couture gown.

The fact that the gown had been purchased at one of those discreet, elegant, yet definitely secondhand designer clothing shops in London was beside the point.

She had dressed for this evening with a very specific purpose in mind, and it hadn't done her a blessed bit of good. So much for her idea of posing as Tony's sister for this sojourn on Paradise.

Megs supposed the masquerade had had its occasional and titillating moments, but it had served no practical purpose in the end, and it hadn't lead to a single useful seduction. Even Jake Hollister had barely looked at her all evening.

"No doubt she finds him exciting."

Tony's expression was one of bafflement. *"She?"*

"Jane Bennett."

"No doubt Jane Bennett finds *who* exciting?"

"Jake Hollister."

"Ah . . ." Tony took another swig from his glass of brandy. "Can't say I understand the attraction myself."

Megs could.

"It's because the man is so intense," she said, measuring out her words. "Because he's a bit uncivilized and because he is a little rough around the edges."

"A little rough around the edges!" Tony hooted with liquor-ladened breath. "Did you watch him this evening?" He snorted, his nostrils flaring. "Of course you did. You couldn't take your eyes off him." Her husband took another swallow of expensive cognac. "What is it with women and the primitive male?"

Megs didn't answer his question. Her focus was still on their recently departed guests. "I'll bet my last pound that he's nothing like the lily-livered men she's used to dating in London.''

Tony tittered. ''Did you notice the way Hollister was dressed? I almost asked him, as a joke, to give my compliments to his tailor. He had the audacity to attend a formal dinner in jeans, a faded denim shirt and a sport coat that looked like he'd borrowed it from someone who was about twice his size, at least around the middle.''

''He did mention that the sport coat belonged to Dr. Gilmour,'' Megs reminded him.

Tony's handsome face took on an expression of ridicule. ''Now, there's a man who knows his way around—sartorially speaking. Jason Gilmour always looks like he's slept in his clothes.''

Megs kicked off her high heels one at a time and sent them flying across the *sala*. Then she proceeded to pad around the living room in her bare feet. She enjoyed—in fact, she relished—the sensual contrast between the thick, woven area rugs and the hard, cool Spanish tiles on the floor.

She wet her lips with the tip of her tongue. ''They say clothes don't make the man.''

In Jake Hollister's case, it was true. For a half-pence she would have invited him for a casual stroll through the Hacienda grounds, perhaps to the *placita*, and shared a few private moments with him.

But it was obvious that the ''tour guide'' was already getting plenty of whatever he wanted or needed from his lady customer. Megs wondered if Jane Bennett was paying him for his services . . . or if she was simply a big tipper.

Tony swaggered toward an overstuffed leather chair and plopped himself down into its forgiving cushions. ''Hollister is a bloody fool,'' he announced.

Megs didn't agree. "I don't think so."

"What is he, then?"

"Clever." She gave the matter further thought. "And perhaps not quite the actor he assumes he is."

"I know that look, Megs. And that tone of voice. You're planning something," Tony proclaimed, pointing one finger in her direction as he held the brandy snifter up to his lips. "You've got something up your sleeve . . ." He paused and laughed bawdily. ". . . or up your *whatever*. What is it, Megs, my dear?"

"Small potatoes."

Tony appeared stumped. "Small potatoes?"

"Whatever Don Carlos or Jane Bennett have in terms of financial resources must be small potatoes compared to the treasure that could be found on a seventeenth-century Spanish galleon that sank with tons of gold aboard."

The subject of money always grabbed Tony's attention. "How much would something like that be worth today?"

Megs shrugged her satin and brocade shoulders. "Millions. Maybe more. Maybe a billion."

"Holy shit."

Megs sashayed toward him and plucked the brandy snifter from his fingers. "I need a drink. I'll have some of your cognac." She took a sip, followed it with a second and then a third. She made an expressive face. "I can't believe our guests actually drank that cheap sangria you served them."

"She did. He didn't." Tony added as an afterthought, "I don't think Ms. Bennett drank that much of it either. I told you we should have chosen something else."

Megs made a negative sound. "And have Don Carlos come back from God knows where he's gone off to and suspect that we've been in his wine cellar.''

''But we have been in his wine cellar.''

Megs perched on the arm of his chair, leaned over—her ample cleavage nearly spilling from the front of her dress—and allowed her partner to refill the brandy snifter before cooing in their own private version of babytalk: ''What did Tonykins say to Megsy when he discovered the key to our host's private cache?''

'' 'While the cat's away, the mice will play,' '' Tony repeated with a sly grin.

''Very good,'' Megs praised, patting his cheek. That was exactly what he'd said to her as he had helped himself to a bottle of brandy earlier that evening. ''Since only the two of us know we 'borrowed' a bottle of cognac, we can always deny any knowledge of its disappearance and blame it on the servants.''

''Don Carlos is hardly the kind of man to accuse his guests of thievery,'' Tony stated.

''Let's take the bottle and our glasses and go for a stroll,'' Megs suggested.

He glanced down at her feet. ''Barefoot?''

''Why not?''

Tony grabbed a second snifter from the bar and followed her out into the balmy Caribbean evening. He seemed perfectly willing—one might even say eager, Megs thought—to go along with whatever suggestions she made tonight.

Perhaps ''Tonykins'' had his own plans for later. Perhaps those plans included a dalliance with one of the housemaids.

Well, she'd have to see about that.

It had been a long time, too long, since she'd had a man. She was tired of taking care of her own needs. It was all right in an emergency. Or in addition to having

a good man between her legs. But a regular diet of anything got boring after a while.

Whatever Tony had in the offing would just have to
wait. Megs had her own plans for him.

They paused on the grassy pathway and Tony poured
her another splash of cognac.

Megs took a healthy gulp.

"Sip it, darling," he advised her. "Hold it against the
roof of your mouth for a moment and inhale the flavor
before you swallow. This is some of the finest brandy
ever distilled. It costs a fortune. It's meant to be savored."

Megs laughed lewdly and motioned rather recklessly
in his direction with the bowl of her crystal glass. "Remember those words later, the dishonorable Tony St. Cyr.
'Hold it against the roof of your mouth and inhale the
flavor.'" She laughed again. "'It's supposed to be
sipped.' 'It's meant to be savored.'"

"You're drunk," he scoffed.

"No. Just a little high."

"Well, you're certainly in a rare mood tonight," he
observed as they wandered along the pathway that lead
down to the sea on the right or in the direction of the
parking garage on the left.

"Something's fishy," Megs said, sniffing.

Tony raised his nose a notch in the air. "I do believe
you're right, Megs, old thing."

"Of course I'm right." She took a swing at him and
missed. "And don't call me 'old thing.'"

"Sorry."

"I'm not talking about the sea air. I'm talking about
Jane Bennett and Jake Hollister."

"Not them again."

"Yes, them again. Tonight was a performance that

they were putting on strictly for our benefit,'' she stated.

"I didn't notice anything out of the ordinary, except the man was a bloody awful bore about all that diving stuff. Then she started in on the incredible natural wonders that he's been showing her, and that's when I nearly nodded off.''

Megs made a noise somewhere between a giggle and a groan as she reached out to grab at Tony's crotch. "I can just imagine what kind of natural wonders Jake Hollister has been showing our Ms. Bennett, can't you?''

"As a matter of fact, I can,'' he agreed, grasping her hand, holding it captive, flattening her palm against him, allowing—no, insisting—that she feel the physical changes in his body as they swiftly took place. "Let's do it right here!'' he urged, panting, backing her up against the wall of the garage.

"No. Not here.'' She threw her head to one side as an indicator. "Inside.''

Tony frowned. "Inside what? The garage?''

"Not just inside the garage. Inside the Rolls Royce.'' Megs laughed, half-intoxicated, and confessed to him: "I've always wanted to do it in a Rolls Royce.''

The brandy snifters were dispensed with behind a pile of rubble, but the bottle of expensive cognac went with them. They climbed into the back seat of the Rolls and sat there for a moment.

"It even smells different,'' Megs observed, breathing in the imposing air of the vintage aristocratic automobile. "It feels different too,'' she claimed, caressing the buttery soft leather seats.

"Whatever you say, sweetheart,'' Tony agreed, taking a swig of brandy directly from the bottle before he set it to one side and clumsily reached for her.

The zipper on the back of the designer gown quickly

and easily slid down past the indentation at the base of her spine, displaying her round and fleshy cheeks. The dress dropped below Meg's waist, revealing that she was wearing nothing underneath.

Not a stitch.

Tony mocked her mercilessly. He made a disapproving and clicking sound with his teeth and tongue. "No brassiere, my dear. No panties. No stockings."

Megs pouted her pretty red lips. "I thought they would just get in the way."

"Get in whose way?" Tony smiled and showed all his teeth, but it was not from amusement.

"Get in your way, of course," she declared.

Apparently he decided to believe her. Perhaps because it suited his own purposes to do so.

"Is the gem real?" Tony inquired as he rolled his tongue around the large green stone that hung from a chain around Meg's neck and dangled between her bare breasts.

It wasn't the first time he'd asked her that question about a piece of her jewelry. It wouldn't be the last.

Her breath was coming in short, little bursts of anticipation. "Of course."

"What is it? An emerald?"

"Yes. An emerald."

Tony licked the precious gemstone, wetting it thoroughly with his tongue. Then he wrapped his lips around the emerald, sucked it into his mouth and tugged on the chain.

"Be careful, darling," Megs implored with a calculated laugh. "You wouldn't want to break anything and swallow it whole."

"No, I wouldn't."

Tony reached for the bottle of cognac. He took a sip

and held it in his mouth for an instant. Then he went after the emerald again.

"Hey, what about me?" Megs complained, but not too loudly nor for too long.

Without missing a beat, or swallowing a drop of the expensive brandy, Tony St. Cyr opened his mouth and added one of her nipples to the erotic mixture.

Megs could feel the hard, green stone, the heady liquor and her aroused nipple all rolling around in his mouth simultaneously. "Oh my God, Tony!"

Tony swallowed the brandy, spit out the emerald and released her breast.

But only for an instant.

He repeated the process with another sip of cognac, another mouthful of emerald, and her other aroused nipple.

"Like that, do you?" he inquired at last.

"Yes." Megs couldn't catch her breath and she didn't even care. "Oh yes."

He did it again and again. The strange, erotic abrasion of gemstone and nipple, Tony's teeth and tongue and lips drove her wild, drove her mad, drove her over the edge.

She felt herself starting to come.

Tony also felt the climax that sent a stunning shudder through her from head to toe.

He laughed and sat back, releasing her for a moment. He reached out and clasped the green stone in his hand. "How much would you say this would be worth if it were real?"

He hadn't been fooled, she realized.

Megs smiled. "An emerald of this size and clarity: probably a million dollars, anyway."

"One million dollars." Tony chortled. "I always said you had a million-dollar body, old thing."

This time she didn't scold him for calling her "old thing."

Tony had that light in his Nordic blue eyes that Megs knew only too well. "Let's see what else you've got for a million."

There wasn't much she hadn't tried in her thirty-four years, but before it was all said and done that night, Megs St. Cyr had learned a new thing or two.

"You were very bad tonight, Tony," she murmured, utterly exhausted and depleted.

"But you know how good I am when I'm bad," he reminded her with a vulgar laugh.

chapter *Twenty-three*

*P*eople assumed that she had been born with a silver spoon in her mouth because of her family's name, her family's wealth, and her family's social position.

Perhaps it was true.

But a silver spoon had never been enough to guarantee success in this world, and it never would be.

Cordelia Jane Bennett liked to believe that she had been born with a pretty good brain inside her head, as well. Perhaps that was the reason she had lain awake half the night thinking and rethinking the pieces of the puzzle.

The past was a puzzle.

It was a puzzle that she needed to solve—indeed, she must solve—if she hoped to have a future.

Charlie Bennett.

The *Bella Doña.*

"You seek something. No. You seek some*one.* A man. You will find him, *senorita,* but there is danger."

Danger. She should have seen it coming. She didn't.

All is not what it seems to be.

"You must be careful what you seek on Paradise, Miss Bennett. You may well find it."

"Today shalt thou be with me in Paradise."

How easy is it to buy a piece of paradise?

Some questions have no answers.

Treasure ships.

"Dearest Cordelia: Paradise Regained. I have, indeed, seen the Beautiful Lady."

No tengo mas que darte.

Hurricanes.

Volcanos.

Sea monsters.

For it is said: "Come not between the dragon and its wrath."

"Time is an illusion. There are those who believe the past, the present, the future are as one."

"Nothing endures but change."

The Place from Which Nothing Returns.

"The truth shall make us free."

"Why in the hell would a grown man dream about a butterfly?"

Jake was dreaming again.

Only this time there was a hammering in his brain as well. It wouldn't stop. It went on and on. A tremendous pounding. He came half awake—not even that really, more like a quarter awake—and pulled the covers over his head.

The pounding wasn't as loud as before, but it didn't stop either.

Then it slowly, finally, dawned on Jake that the noise wasn't in his head.

Someone was knocking on a door somewhere.

"Go away," he muttered groggily, more asleep than awake and not wanting to be awake at all. He took the extra pillow from his bed and heaved it toward the closed door of his bedroom.

The bedroom door opened.

He could distinctly hear the telltale creak and scrape of the unoiled hinges as they moved.

That quickly he was wide awake.

Damn! Someone was sneaking into his bedroom. He could hear the trespasser's breathing. He could sense someone was there. He could almost *feel* the intruder approaching the bed.

A series of vivid pictures formed in Jake's mind: the glint of moonlight reflecting off the razor-sharp blade of a knife; a heavy bludgeon raised to strike a single, deadly blow; a small, yet lethal pistol aimed directly at his heart.

Jake tried not to give himself away.

He tried not to let his assailant know that he was awake. It was the breathing that gave you away if you weren't careful. He deliberately slowed his down and kept the rhythm of his chest movement regular. It took an enormous amount of willpower and discipline on his part.

A floorboard squeaked.

The intruder must be only a foot, maybe two, from the end of the bed.

Jake prepared himself to spring into action.

That's when he heard a new sound. A new and completely unexpected sound. A sound that sent a chill tiptoeing down every vertebrae of his spine, one by one.

"Jake . . . !"

The old line popped into his head: "That's my name; don't wear it out."

"Jake, wake up!" came an insistent whisper.

Jake rolled over and reached for the light switch beside the bed. He didn't give a tinker's damn—or any other kind, for that matter—that he was lying there without a stitch of clothing on as the bedroom was flooded with light.

"What in the . . . ?"

Jane stood poised at the foot of his bed. Her hands, white-knuckled, were clutching the wrought-iron frame. She was dressed in her nightgown. No robe. No slippers. No shawl hastily thrown around her bare arms despite the chill in the night air.

Her hair was a wild, uncombed, unbrushed tangle hanging down around her shoulders. Her eyes were huge and dark. And there was the most extraordinary expression on her face.

"What is it?" Jake shot up, swung his legs off the bed and was standing beside her in a matter of a second, maybe two at the most. He was afraid to touch her. Rage began to fill him and his eyes blazed. "Has someone been in your bungalow again?" he asked.

Jane shook her head.

He let go of the rage and tried the next possibility that occurred to him. "Are you ill?"

She shook her head repeatedly.

His brow creased. "Did you have a nightmare?"

"No," finally came from her lips.

"What is it, then, honey?" Jake glanced at the clock on the bedside table. It was three-fifteen. Hardly the time for a social visit. Hardly the time for anything but sleep.

Maybe she was sleepwalking.

Although she seemed alert. Her eyes were wide open, and there was something different yet normal about them.

"Jane, what is it?"

She was obviously struggling to get the words out. She finally managed to say them in a hoarse whisper. "I know where it is."

He would be indulgent just this once. It wasn't her habit, after all, to rouse him in the middle of the night. "You know where what is, sweetheart?"

"The *Bella Doña*," was all she said.

"I know you think I'm crazy for waking you up in the middle of the night," Jane said in preamble as she helped herself to one of the denim shirts in his closet. She slipped it on over her nightgown. She hadn't realized how cool the air was until now. "But trust me, you won't be sorry."

"I'm already sorry," Jake muttered, rubbing the stubble on his chin and looking, admittedly, like he could use another four or five hours of uninterrupted sleep.

"Put on a pair of pants and join me in the kitchen," she said, starting to issue orders right and left. "I'll make us a pot of strong black coffee. We're going to need it." She paused at the door of his bedroom and glanced back over her shoulder at him. "Oh, and bring that old map book in Spanish."

"Yessir!" he snapped under his breath.

"I believe the correct address is 'yes, ma'am,' but I'll let it pass this time," Jane teased and barely made it out of his bedroom before a pillow came flying in her direction.

She poured Jake a cup of coffee and one for herself before she sat down at the small kitchen table. The decor of Samson was identical to that of Delilah, she noted, except for one minor detail: the color scheme. Delilah was painted a shocking shade of pink, while Samson was a bright pumpkin orange.

There were more important matters to consider, however, especially at this hour.

Where to begin?

That was the question. Jane knew she was right. But she needed to have her facts straight and her logic in order if she was going to convince the skeptical man sitting across from her.

Jake gulped down one cup of coffee—how he managed not to burn the inside of his mouth and his tongue was beyond her—helped himself to a second, leaned his elbows on the kitchen table, stared at her intently and commanded in a no-nonsense tone, "Start talking."

She obeyed. "Your pet theory has always been that the *Bella Doña* was swept into a cave or a cavern during the legendary hurricane of 1692, correct?"

"Correct."

"And the cave is either somewhere along the coast of Paradise or on a nearby island."

"That's what I believe," he said.

Jane gave him a genuine smile of encouragement. "Well, I think that you're right."

Jake didn't appear to be overcome by her vote of confidence. "You're the only one who does, then."

"I not only think you're right, Jake." She put her cup down on the table, reached out, took his hand in hers and squeezed it tightly. "I *know* that you're right."

He shook his head disconsolately. "Honey, I have searched every nook and cranny on this island that could even remotely contain the remnants of a shipwreck. And so far *nada*."

"That's because you forgot one thing," she declared, the excitement in her voice showing.

"What did I forget?"

"The dragon."

His brows rose quizzically. "The dragon?" He was plainly cynical. "This isn't that game of twenty questions, is it?"

"No."

But she had taken most of the night to work the problem through to its only logical conclusion. The least he could do was give her five minutes of his precious time and a nominal amount of his patience.

And she told him so.

"You're the only one I'd do this for," Jake stated, his voice heavy with fatigue.

"The same goes for me," Jane shot back. She'd doubtlessly had even less sleep than he'd had that night. "You see," she said, beginning her explanation, "Nui was right again."

Jake rubbed his hand back and forth along his jawline. "And who is Nui?"

"Nui was the fortune-teller on the ferry."

He gave her a condescending look. "Ah, c'mon, we're not back to that mumbo jumbo, are we?"

"Bear with me, Jake," she instructed, suddenly very serious. "You won't regret it."

"All right."

"Nui said to me that first afternoon: 'Beware the dragon and its wrath.' "

He sighed. "I remember."

"It didn't make any sense to me at the time."

"It still doesn't make any sense to me," he confessed in a dry tone of voice.

Jane refused to allow his attitude to dissuade her. "What does a dragon do?"

"I don't know. I haven't run into any dragons lately," he muttered in a surly manner. "Why don't you tell me? What does a dragon do?"

"A dragon breathes fire."

"You're right. I should have guessed."

"What if you were a Caribe Indian who lived more

than three hundred years ago and your world was ruled by unforgiving gods, fierce demons, and terrifying monsters. How would you describe an erupting volcano that was spewing forth smoke and ash, fire and destruction down on every living thing in its path?''

Jake inhaled a deep breath and held it for a count of five. Then he exhaled and said expressively: ''An angry, fire-breathing dragon. A monster taking its wrath out on all the inhabitants of the world below, whether plant or animal or human.''

'' 'Beware the dragon and its wrath,' '' Jane repeated softly.

Jake pushed his coffee aside and reached for the old book of maps written in Spanish. ''So, like Doc Gilmour, you think I've been looking in all the wrong places too.''

''Not at all,'' she quickly assured him. ''You've probably been so close several times that it's amazing you didn't stumble right over the wreck of the *Bella Doña*.''

Jake opened the yellowed pages of the book and scanned one map after another. Then he stopped and pointed, thumping the page again and again with his finger. ''It was right there in front of me and I didn't even see it.''

Jane waited.

''It was there all the time.'' Jake glanced up at her. His eyes were ablaze with discovery. ''That's got to be it.''

''What has to be it?'' she asked.

He turned the book around and indicated a point on one of the maps. *''Montaña de Fuego.''*

''Literal translation meaning mountain of fire,'' she said with her limited command of Spanish.

''Fire Mountain,'' Jake stated.

Jane tried to decipher the archaic drawing. "It appears to be on the other side of the island."

"It is."

"Then the mountain we're seeking is on the dark side of Paradise," she said, tasting the words.

"Yup."

There was the faintest hint of concern—perhaps even of apprehension—in her tone. "Brilliant Chang mentioned the opposite side of the island to me one day. He said there were volcanic mountains and beaches with black sand, strange rocks with knife-sharp edges fashioned by the wind, and the cavern the native Caribes once called 'the place from which nothing returns.' "

"Don't forget the legendary sea monster," he added.

"And the legendary sea monster that swallows up everything in its path."

"It's all proof positive that we're headed in the right direction," Jake stated. His mind was racing ahead. She could almost hear the wheels turning. "We'll need extra fuel for the Jeep, camping gear, food, water, diving equipment, extra air tanks." He grabbed a pen and pad and began to jot down notes.

"When will we get started?" Jane wanted to know.

"First thing in the morning."

She gazed out the kitchen window at the faint pink light of dawn as it washed across the Caribbean sky. "It's already first thing in the morning," she pointed out to him.

"Then we'd better get a move on," Jake announced, jumping to his feet. "I want to be on our way by midday."

chapter *Twenty-four*

"*W*here's the *X*?" Jane asked him as the Jeep trundled over the road that cut through the rolling green hills and thickening forest toward the other side of Paradise.

"The *X*?"

"Doesn't *X* always mark the spot?" she said, holding up the modern map in her hand.

Jake knew the copyright date in the bottom right-hand corner was 1947, so the term "modern" was relative.

Jane was functioning in the role of navigator on this trip since he was the only who could control the temperamental and aging four-wheel drive vehicle.

He kept his eyes straight ahead. He didn't dare take his attention off the road for an instant, or they might find themselves careening down a steep ravine or getting stuck in a ditch. And on Paradise there were no tow trucks to call if you suddenly found yourself in trouble.

Yup, Jake reflected as he concentrated on his driving, tow trucks were few and far between on the island. There weren't any telephones on Paradise either.

Communication between islands was accomplished primarily by ham radio operators. On Paradise itself, the

good, old-fashioned human being, usually on foot, sometimes by bicycle or donkey, delivered whatever messages
needed to be conveyed.

It wasn't the most efficient method of operating a social system, Jake had to acknowledge, but then sometimes efficiency wasn't all it was cracked up to be.

There were currently only three vehicles on the island:
his own ancient Jeep, Doc Gilmour's almost-as-ancient
station wagon—Jake had a hunch it had once been a
hearse, judging by the elaborate shape of the automobile
and the color: funereal black—and, of course, Don Carlos' vintage Rolls Royce, twenty years old, if it was a
day.

Since the true *el patron* of Paradise was rarely on the
island, Jake didn't count the gentleman's helicopter.

Infrastructure on most remote Caribbean islands was
non-existent. Paradise was no exception. They were two
hours out of Purgatory and had managed to cover almost
twenty miles.

Almost.

At this rate it would be late afternoon before they traveled the relatively short distance, as the crow flies, to
Montaña de Fuego, or Fire Mountain.

Jake figured they would arrive with just about enough
daylight remaining to pitch a tent, fix themselves a bite
to eat, and roll out their sleeping bags. Any exploration
of the area would have to wait until the next morning.

''There's a pen in the glove compartment if you want
to place an *X* on the map,'' Jake finally answered.

Jane sighed and tugged on the billed khaki cap covering her head. ''I guess we don't really need an *X* when
Montaña de Fuego is the highest point, geographically
speaking, on the island.''

''It was probably even taller before it blew,'' Jake

mentioned to her, resting his left arm on the cranked-down window of the driver's side of the Jeep.

"That's right, it no doubt was. How much did Mount Saint Helen's lose when she erupted?"

Jake racked his brain. He had just started working in California back in 1980, so the dramatic events surrounding Mount Saint Helen's had been major headlines on every radio station, television network and newspaper up and down the Pacific coast. "At least some 1,300 feet of the mountaintop were blown away in the eruption." Something else occurred to him. "Did you know that the original name of Mount Saint Helen's was *Tah-one-lat-clah*?"

Jane shook her head. "Which translated means?"

"In the language of the Klickitat Indians of that region: 'Fire Mountain.' "

"Sometimes it seems like a very small world to me," Jane said quietly, thoughtfully.

"Sometimes it is," he agreed.

They drove for quite a while in silence. As they approached the far side of the island, the differences in the land formations became more pronounced. The coastline, occasionally glimpsed between the trees, was darker, rockier, more rugged.

The trees were entirely different species, as well. They were no longer the tropical date palms and coconut palms that waved along the pristine white beaches of the bay below the Four Sisters Inn. These were the lush, dark, and dense trees of the rainforest. "There it is," Jake announced, hitting the brakes for a moment and pointing off to the west. *"Montaña de Fuego."*

"It almost appears as though the mountain is actually on fire," Jane observed.

"It's the way the sunlight is hitting its slopes," Jake explained. "Maybe there's a fiery coloration lent by a particular kind of vegetation. Or there could be a native tree or bush with reddish leaves or flowers," he speculated.

"There doesn't seem to be any sign of human beings," Jane said, looking around.

"No doubt this region is uninhabited."

She glanced down at her lap. "The map shows the mountain and that's about it. The rest appears to be uninhabited *and* uncharted."

Jake leaned forward for a moment and stared out at the lush wilderness and the fiery mountain in the distance. " 'Here be dragons,' " he murmured.

" 'Here be dragons?' " Jane repeated.

"That's what they used to write on uncharted areas of a map back a few hundred years ago." He took his foot off the brake and started down the deserted road.

It was another hour before they located a natural clearing at the base of the mountain. It appeared to be the perfect spot to make camp for the night.

"We'll stay here," Jake announced. Then he added, "Don't worry, honey, I know how to survive in the jungle."

Jane gave an indignant little sniff. "So do I," she informed him. "I've lived in New York for years."

They went about the business of preparing their campsite. Once that was completed, they discovered that neither of them were particularly hungry, but they were curious.

Since there was more daylight remaining than Jake had figured on, Jane spread the map out on the hood of the Jeep and began to study it in detail.

"How in the blue blazes are we going to find the entrance to the cavern?'' she muttered under her breath, speaking more to herself than to Jake.

He scratched his head. That was going to be the tough part, of course. They knew they were in the right vicinity. But that wasn't the same thing as knowing where the cave was or even if there was a means of gaining access.

''I won't allow us to have come this far and fail now,'' Jane stated with absolute determination and utter tenacity.

It was one of the things Jake liked about the woman: she didn't give up. Period.

''We won't,'' he assured her.

''How can you be so certain?''

''Obstacles are meant to be overcome.''

She smiled briefly. ''And I suppose that challenges are intended to be met.''

''Something will present itself,'' Jake announced with a bright countenance. ''It always does.''

Jane looked at him askance. ''When did you become the great optimist, Jake Hollister?''

He turned, glanced down at her for a moment, and proclaimed, ''The day I met you.'' Then he dropped a kiss on her mouth and suggested, ''Let's do a bit of exploring. We've got an extra hour of daylight that I hadn't counted on.''

She followed him as he took off across the foothills.

''What if . . . ?'' Jane commenced.

Jake noticed that she often did her best thinking in a kind of stream of consciousness.

''What if . . . ?'' he encouraged.

Jane paused, put her head back, and gazed up at the mountain that loomed before them. It wasn't a mountain by the standards set by the Colorado Rockies or even the Adirondacks of her native New York State, but it was a mountain by Paradise standards.

She began to think out loud. "What if the *Bella Doña* was caught up in the great hurricane of the summer of 1692? What if the ship was tossed to and fro against the rocky coastline in this region?"

Jake noted that there was a rising sense of excitement in her tone of voice, and she was gesturing animatedly with both hands.

"Or what if," Jane went on, "the ship sailed safely— or what she thought was safely—into the haven of a protected cove or a great cavern? And then, between the ravaging winds of the hurricane and the eruption of the volcano that must have occurred soon after, the *Bella Doña* was buried beneath it all?"

Jake's mouth dropped open. "You think the *Bella Doña*—or what's left of her—is buried *inside* the mountain?"

She immediately became apologetic. "It sounds ridiculous, doesn't it?"

"No."

"Stupid, then?"

"I think it's brilliant!" he nearly shouted.

Jane's entire face lit up. "You do?"

"I do." Jake put his head back. "*Montaña de Fuego*. Fire Mountain. An ancient volcano perhaps once described by native Caribe Indians as a fire-breathing mountain or a great monster swallowing up everything in its path or as a wrathful—"

"—dragon," she finished.

" 'Here be dragons.' " Jake's heart was pounding. "It is the mountain."

Jane's frustration was readily apparent. "But how do we find a way to get inside?"

"We look for an entrance."

The woman beside him gave Jake one of those looks. "As opposed to an 'exit.' "

"I mean, we literally circle the base of the mountain and look for a crevice, a hole, a fissure, a crack, anything that looks like it might be an opening. We brought enough food and water with us for a week. We keep looking. If we haven't found anything in five or six days, then we'll pack up and head back to civilization."

Jane seemed to approve of his plan. "It's a deal, partner," she said, and she actually shook his hand.

Jake knew this was just as important to her—maybe more so—than it was to him.

"C'mon, let's take a look around while we still have some daylight left," Jane urged, grabbing his hand and tugging him in the direction of the mountain.

"I wish there really was an *X* to mark the spot," Jane said wistfully as they wandered around the face of *Montaña de Fuego* that fronted their campsite.

So far they had found nothing but rocks and more rocks, dense underbrush, a few clusters of small bushes, and some trees.

"We need to head back to camp in a few minutes," Jake informed her. "We'll lose the daylight quickly and we don't want to be out here wandering around in the dark."

"We have our flashlights with us."

That brought a raised eyebrow from the man beside her. "There will always be tomorrow."

Jane stopped dead in her tracks. She planted her hands on her hips, the blue jeans purchased at Maxwell's were still two sizes too large, and she was well aware that she appeared a little ridiculous in them, but frankly she no longer cared.

She announced in her most determined voice, "There must be a clue around here somewhere."

"I'm sure there is," Jake said placatingly.

She turned her head and told him, "I'm considered something of a first-class detective in the world where I work, even a miracle worker at times, if you must know. You would think that I could come up with something, even out here in the middle of this godforsaken country, that would be of some help to us."

Jake's mouth fell open.

Jane felt her face turn a fiery red. "I'm sorry about the tirade. I hope it didn't shock you."

He appeared to be shocked. In fact, he seemed flabbergasted, even speechless. He didn't say a word. He simply stood there, his mouth agape, his eyes wide open, utter astonishment written all over his handsome features.

"Jake, I'm sorry."

He snapped his mouth shut. "About what?"

"About the tirade. It obviously took you by surprise."

"What tirade?"

"Are we having the same conversation?" she inquired.

"Not entirely," he said.

That was a relief. Jane was beginning to wonder if one of them was losing their grip on reality.

"Then would you mind explaining—"

Jake cut her off. "You are a genius, Jane Bennett."

She was flattered naturally. "Thank you, but—"

"Don't you see?" he said, turning in a slow circle.

Her gaze followed his to a large cluster of bushes on the ground at the base of the mountain; they were a mere five to ten feet from where they were standing.

The bushes ranged from eighteen inches to perhaps three feet in height. Their leaves were oval-shaped and pointed, somewhere between three to six inches in length and reddish in color. In fact, in the fading light of day, some of the leaves almost appeared to be purple. And there were shiny blackberries everywhere.

"Don't you see?" Jake repeated.

"Don't I see what?"

"Can't you smell it?"

Jane put her nose in the air. "I do smell something now that you mention it. It's rather a disagreeable odor."

"It would *taste* even worse."

She made a distasteful face. "What is it?" Her nostrils twitched. "Some kind of herb?"

"You might say that," Jake reported to her. "The bush is definitely in the herb family."

"Do you know the name of it?"

"It has a number of common names." And Jake began to list them: "Banewort, dwale, naked lady lily, lirio, Barbados lily, English nightshade and deadly nightshade."

"Deadly nightshade," Jane repeated and swallowed. "But that's . . . deadly."

He nodded his head vigorously. "Its best-known name, however, is belladonna."

"Belladonna," she echoed. Then half a minute later, Jane said, "Can it be a coincidence?"

"If it is, it's a hell of a one," Jake swore as his eyes began to scan the mountainside beyond the group of plants. "I don't believe in coincidences myself."

"What are you looking for?"

"The entrance to the cave. It has to be around here somewhere."

He was right, of course. He had to be. It was too much of a coincidence.

"It must be here," Jane agreed, giving wide berth to

the patch of poisonous herbs and heading closer to *Montaña de Fuego*.

She hooked her flashlight over the belt of her jeans and began to feel along the base of a strange outcropping of rock. Jake did the same. There were still a few minutes of daylight left, and they intended to make use of every single minute.

"Jane."

She knew simply by the way Jake said her name that he had found something.

"What is it?" she asked.

"An opening in the rock behind these vines."

She went straight to his side. Together, they began to pull at the creeping vines with their bare hands, ripping them away from the face of the rock.

"It is an opening," Jane exclaimed.

There was a breach between two rock formations at the foot of the mountain. The gap was just large enough for two people to walk through abreast.

Her heart was pounding. She knew Jake's must be too. He switched on his flashlight and held it up in front of them.

"There's a passageway." He took a step forward but held her back with his free hand. "I can make out the beginning of something. A path, I think. I'm pretty sure that it turns to the left about ten or twelve feet past this entrance," he said to her.

Reason told Jane that it would be wiser if they waited until morning before going in.

Jake had to know it as well.

She watched him lick his lips.

"You stay here, Jane," he finally ordered.

"What do you mean, you stay here, Jane? Where are you going?"

"I'm going in."

He was hoping and praying the same thing she was, of course: That this was the entrance to the cavern.

"I'm only going to explore as far as the turn, the first ten or fifteen feet," Jake stated emphatically. "Five minutes, that's all, and I'll be back. I promise."

"And you always keep your promises," she repeated in a slightly sardonic tone.

"Yes, I do."

"Well, I'm not staying out here where it's nice and safe while the man I love goes in alone," she declared, and she wasn't about to budge on this issue.

Jake Hollister stopped in his tracks, turned and stared at her. "What did you say?"

Jane repeated her statement. "I'm not about to stay out here while you go in alone."

"That's not what you said."

"Yes, it is."

"Not verbatim."

"Well, I can't remember the exact words."

"I can. You said: 'I'm not staying out here where it's nice and safe while the man I love goes in alone.' "

"Hollister, this is no time to bring up the word love."

"I didn't bring it up. You did."

"Well, it was a mistake."

"You don't love me."

"Of course I love you. The mistake was letting it slip out now when there must be a thousand better times and places to discuss the topic," she said.

He stood his ground. "This time and this place is just fine."

"No, it isn't. We only have a limited amount of daylight left. Maybe fifteen minutes. Maybe twenty. And we'd better make the most of them. Love can always be discussed in the dark.''

He actually laughed with delight. "You've got a point there, Ms. Bennett."

"The main point right now is that I'm going in with you because we're partners." She could be bullheaded too. "It's either both of us or neither of us."

"You are one stubborn woman."

"Yes, I am."

Jake nodded. "This opening could lead nowhere."

"In which case, we'll be back out in no time flat, return to our base camp, have something to eat, get a good night's sleep, and try again in the morning."

Flashlights shining in front of them, and gentleman first in this instance, Jake and Jane entered the passageway. It was approximately four feet in width and slightly more than six feet in height initially; the ceiling was just above Jake's head.

Fifteen feet into the entrance, the trail took a sharp turn to the left. To the right was a dead end.

They turned to the left and followed along the passage. It appeared to enlarge in both width and height as they progressed along its length. They could tell they were hiking deeper and deeper into the very heart of *Montaña de Fuego* itself. Yet neither of them suggested that they turn back.

Straight ahead.

They heard the sound of water.

No.

The resonance of . . . rain.

There was the smell of moisture in the air and the scent of salt and the heavy odor of a place long enclosed away from the world. They could feel a slight breeze coming from somewhere just ahead of them. Together they both held up their flashlights and attempted to give themselves the broadest range of vision.

They stopped simultaneously. They could feel, they could sense, even if they couldn't see the large cavern directly in front of them.

They were standing at the doorway to another world.

Raised flashlights illuminated only a small portion of the immense cave before them.

It was huge and dark.

The floor underfoot was black sand and black stone and black lava. Further out into the center of the vast chamber, they could make out the merest glimmer of black water.

There were stalactites and stalagmites growing from both above and below around the fringes of the cavern. Some were a mere six inches in length. Some were closer to six feet long. They were like a field of wondrous icicles.

And, everywhere—from the dark, concealed ceiling of the cavern above, from the stalactites closer by, to the rocks overhead—there was water dripping like rain.

Jake stopped for the first time since he had instructed her to stay directly behind him and match her every step to his.

There was something in his voice when he spoke that Jane had never heard before. Something akin to awe. "This is the legendary Raining Room," he said reverently.

"Yes," Jane said softly.

The same Raining Room that Brilliant Chang had mentioned to her that first day at her bungalow.

All of a sudden Jake grabbed her arm.

"What is it?" she asked in a frenetic whisper.

"There! To the right."

Jane immediately turned to her right.

"Hold your flashlight at a forty-five-degree angle and hold it steady, if you can," he told her.

She did as she was instructed. Jake added his light to hers and they peered into the barely illuminated darkness just beyond their range.

There was something sticking up out of the black water. There was something rising into the black air of the cavern. It was large. It was old. It was unmistakable.

There was a gasp from one, perhaps both, of them.

It was the mast of a ship.

chapter *Twenty-five*

"*T*here are two rules," Jake stated as they finished dressing for their initial dive into the cold, black, forbidding waters of the Raining Room. "The first rule is: Don't do anything stupid."

Jane zipped up the front of her wetsuit and adjusted the wrist cuffs. She noticed her hands were shaking. "And the second?"

"Don't do anything stupid," he repeated, but she noticed Jake wasn't smiling.

They had spent several hours already that morning lugging equipment and lights from their campsite into the gargantuan underground cavern. It had been physically demanding work, but Jane had been determined to do her fair share.

Of course, they didn't have enough floodlights with them. What they had for the project was barely adequate; twice the number would have been better.

It had taken them another hour to decide where to place the lights to their best advantage: the primary concern was illuminating the area into which they would be diving.

There was an immense region—an almost unimaginable amount—of the huge cavern that was still a complete mystery to them. Beyond the range of their spotlights, they could see nothing but dark shapes and darker shadows.

Their final trip into the Raining Room had consisted primarily of hauling in their extra air tanks and backup equipment. This was strategically placed by the passageway into the cavern where they had first entered the previous evening.

Jake was all business.

This wasn't child's play, and they both knew it. Still, Jake was obviously taking no chances. He spelled it out for her syllable by syllable, word by word.

"This time we are both diving into the unknown. We are diving into complete and utter darkness. There have been no practice dives. There has been no wire prestrung to guide us in or to get us back out again," he said, not mincing words.

Jane tried to swallow. She had no saliva. Her mouth was as dry as the desert.

"We don't know where we are going, and we don't know what we will find once we get there. This won't be like diving into the crystal-clear water of the pool at Redemption. The water here is dark and murky. We may not be able to see more than a few inches in front of our faces even with headlights. This is diving at its most challenging," he said, refusing to pull any punches.

"I know." It didn't sound like her voice.

"You're scared."

"Yes."

"You should be."

"Are you?"

"A little," he admitted.

"But you're mostly excited, aren't you?" It was evident in the anticipatory way he moved his body, in the look in his eyes, even in the undertone of excitement in his voice.

"Yeah. I'm mostly excited. There is an incredible rush just realizing that you're going where you have never been before, that you're going where no man may ever have been before."

Jane took a deep breath and tried to calm her nerves.

Jake continued with his lecture. "There will be no heroics. There will be no risk-taking. We are not the same Jane and Jake when we dive as we are when we're on land. We aren't lovers. We aren't in love as long as we're down there. In the water we're buddies and only buddies. If I tell you to get the hell out, that's exactly what you do." He gave a decisive nod of his head. "Understood?"

"Understood."

"If something unforeseen happens, God forbid, and I can't get out for some reason, for any reason. You don't stay. You leave."

"You expect me to leave you down there?"

"Yes." There was no compromise in his voice, in his stance, in his attitude.

Tears suddenly burned at the back of her eyes. Jane's throat started to close on her. "Jake, how could I?"

"I know it seems difficult—"

"It doesn't seem difficult. It seems impossible."

"It isn't impossible. If necessary, Jane Bennett, you must think of yourself and only of yourself. You must think survival and you must get out."

Jane knew she wouldn't be able to do it.

Would he? If she were in a life-and-death situation, and there was nothing he could do to help her, would Jake be able to leave her there to die alone?

Jane didn't believe it for a moment.

That night, when someone had been in her bungalow, this man had promised that he would never allow anything to happen to her, and Jake Hollister always kept his promises.

He wouldn't leave her.

And whether he knew it or not—whether he liked it or not—she would never leave him.

What a strange time, Jane reflected as she finished preparing for the dive, to realize that she loved this man, completely, utterly, irrefutably, and forever.

Jake was talking again. "I will repeat: we are diving into the unknown. We have no idea what we'll find. Hell, we may find nothing. We don't know what's down there. Even if it is a ship, we don't know that she's the *Bella Doña.*"

It was all true.

"Our preliminary foray into shallow water has told us that there are some underwater currents. Therefore, at some point, this pool connects with the sea outside. Also, this is salt water, not fresh water. That's another indication."

Jane shivered. She also knew it meant several other things. If there was a shipwreck below the surface, then they were unlikely to encounter any human remains. They would have been consumed or washed out into the sea a long time ago.

Thank God.

"We discussed this last night, Jane. We're going in for two reasons only. First: To find out if there is anything that will prove or disprove whether the wreck is that of the *Bella Doña.*"

"And two," she said, "if it is the *Bella Doña*, is there any evidence that Charlie was actually here. That he had indeed discovered the shipwreck before his disappearance.''

''Otherwise, we don't have the equipment or the manpower to do any kind of salvage. That will be left to the experts if we decide to reveal the whereabouts of the site. Agreed?''

''Agreed.''

''We don't touch or disturb anything at the site.''

Jane understood and agreed with the logic for leaving the site as uncontaminated as they found it. If there was something special, something worthwhile, even in a purely historical sense, in these dark waters, then it would be up to the experts to excavate the shipwreck and salvage its contents.

Not a couple of amateurs like Jake and herself.

''I've got the special underwater Polaroid camera and I'll try to take as many photographs as I can,'' he said to her. ''We've got thirty minutes. Let's go.''

With that, they stepped into the dark, cold, dimly lit waters of the cavern and swam toward the ghostly remains of whatever was out there.

Jane was never more than a foot or two from Jake the entire dive.

It was cold.

It was dark.

It was frightening.

It was the most exhilarating experience of her life. Indeed, there was only one other experience that even came close to comparing with it, Jane reflected momentarily, amazed that she could be thinking of sex at a time like this.

The first items they spotted within the range of their lights were rotting timbers lying on the bottom of the cavern. Nearby were mounds—small anthill-like shapes—

of scrap metal corroded together by time and water and salt into solid lumps and masses.

A little further on Jake pointed out to her what appeared to be dozens of earthen jars and vessels, many still intact, half-buried in the muck on the floor of the pool.

There was a metal lockbox. A traveler's trunk, perhaps that of the captain or one of the wealthier passengers. Jake paused long enough to take a few photographs for posterity.

Then he stopped suddenly in the water and simply stared down at whatever had apparently caught his eye. Jane turned her light toward the spot where she saw his.

And there it was.

Strewn across the sea floor like so much jetsam and flotsam, still as untarnished, still as pure and yellow and magnificent as the day it had sunk into this unforeseen grave: Gold.

Piles of gold coins.

Long bars of gold.

Smaller gold ingots spilling from half-open metal boxes.

Heavy, thick chains of gold.

Gold everywhere.

Jake pointed again. They swam closer and he raised the camera and began to take a number of photographs. For they had their proof of one mystery solved: the markings on the ingots matched those in the manifest of the *Bella Doña*.

This was what remained of the great Spanish galleon.

On the one hand, Jane was thrilled. Jake had his proof. Jake had accomplished what no one had managed to do in over three hundred years.

On the other, she felt a sense of disappointment. There

had been not a single indication, not a single sign that anyone had been here before them, and that included her father.

Charlie Bennett had not realized his dream.

Jane checked her gauges. It would soon be time to surface. Jake motioned to her, and she started toward the surface of the water. She failed to notice that Jake paused and took several more photographs on his way up.

Jane took one last look back.

This is—this was—the *Bella Doña.*

"I took several photographs at the conclusion of the dive that I'll want to show you as soon as we get out of our gear, into some clothes, and get back to the campsite," Jake told her as he pulled off his face mask.

"What are they?"

"Patience, Ms. Bennett," he admonished. "It's too dark to see much in here anyway."

He also needed time to think about what he should say to her when he showed her the photographs. It wasn't going to be easy. But it was going to answer some questions for the daughter of Charlie Bennett.

Jane stared at the first photograph. "What is it?"

"A gold ingot."

"We saw piles of gold ingots down there. What is so special about this one that you felt you had to take a close-up of it?"

"It's a little hard to make out," Jake admitted. "But if you look closely you can see that something has been crudely chiseled into the surface."

"It almost looks like someone's initials."

"Yes, it does."

Jane held the photograph up for a better look and there

it was, clear as could be, crudely carved but perfectly legible nevertheless: the initials C.A.B.

Her hand flew to her mouth. "Ohmigod." Then she turned and stared at Jake. "Do you honestly think the initials stand for Charles Avery Bennett?"

"Yes, I do."

Tears sprang to her eyes. "Then he did find the *Bella Doña*. He did realize his dream."

Jake nodded. "Charlie must have carved his initials into the ingot to claim his find. I suspect he did it on the first of several dives he no doubt made down to the *Bella Doña*."

There was more. Jane could tell from the way he was behaving.

"What is it?" she asked.

"There is one more photograph I need to show you," he said and it was obviously with great reluctance that he was doing so.

Her hand was trembling as she accepted the second picture. "It's a Polaroid of air tanks," she observed. "Are they . . ." She stopped and took a deep breath before she could continue. ". . . Charlie's?"

"Yes."

"No mistake about it."

"No mistake. His name is still legible on the tanks."

Jane walked off some small distance and gazed out to the sea. She had no more tears for Charlie, which surprised her. Apparently she had cried them all a long time ago.

"I'm sorry, Jane."

She looked out across the blue Caribbean. "Charlie Bennett loved the thrill of it all: the hunt for treasure, the search for untold riches, the quest for the unknown."

She felt Jake come up and stand beside her.

"Nothing was ever enough to keep Charlie at home with his wife and children. So you see, Jake, at least his last wish came true. He found the *Bella Doña*, probably the greatest treasure in the history of Spanish shipping. He lived and he died exactly the way he would have chosen." Jane wrapped her arms around herself. "My father always wanted to be buried at sea. Now I believe with all my heart that he is."

"How do you feel about being buried at sea yourself, Ms. Bennett?"

Jane and Jake spun around.

Megs and Tony St. Cyr were standing not ten feet from them.

Pointed directly at Jane's heart—the safety off, her finger on the trigger—was the deadly revolver Megs was expertly clutching in her hand.

chapter *Twenty-six*

"What are you going to do, Megs, shoot both of us at once?" Jake inquired casually as he slowly turned to face the blond couple standing behind them.

"I was thinking more of disposing of you one at a time," Megs St. Cyr responded with characteristic aplomb.

Something wasn't right here. Indeed, something was very wrong. Jane found that she was more perplexed than frightened by the situation in which she presently found herself.

It was Jake.

He was acting as if the threat weren't real. As far as she could tell it was very real. How could the man be so damned blasé, so nonchalant, so cavalier in his attitude, when there was a large, black, deadly revolver pointing directly at them?

"I must warn you, Mr. Hollister." Megs straightened her back, relaxed her shoulders, spread her stance an inch or two—as though making certain her balance was perfect—and licked her ruby-red mouth in anticipation. "I was considered a crack shot at the public school I attended back home in England.''

''And I must warn you, Mrs. St. Cyr,'' Jake said in a voice filled with indifference, ''that I don't really give a damn what kind of shot you were then or what kind of shot you are now.''

Megs laughed out loud. She was apparently highly amused. ''So you guessed.''

Jake's smile was more than faintly predatory. ''I didn't have to guess. I knew.''

''Do you mind if I ask how you knew?''

''From the beginning, there was something about you and Tony here that didn't ring true. I have a few contacts. I asked a few questions. It didn't take long to discover that you aren't siblings.'' Jake added in a sardonic tone, ''By the way, congratulations. I understand you two recently celebrated your third wedding anniversary.''

Jane was stunned.

''They're not brother and sister?'' She finally managed to get the question out.

''Nope.''

She stared at Jake and ignored the other couple. ''They're married? They're husband and wife?''

''That's right.''

Jane looked from one to the other until she had glared equally at all three of them.

''I don't like being left out,'' she stated. ''I don't appreciate being the only one who doesn't know these things. In the future, please be advised that I expect to be kept informed.''

Megs St. Cyr gave a short, humorless laugh and glanced at Jake for confirmation. ''Is she for real?''

''Yes. She is.''

The blonde shook her head slightly. ''I can't believe

this conversation." She hesitated only briefly, however, before adding, "But in case you two hadn't noticed, I have a loaded revolver pointed at you and I am a very good shot."

"Why would you want to shoot us?" Jane blurted out without thinking.

Megs and Tony St. Cyr laughed simultaneously.

It was Tony who answered her question. "To get rid of you, naturally."

She still didn't understand. "Why, pray tell, would you want to get rid of us?"

Jake almost seemed to be enjoying her exchange with the couple, Jane noticed. But she also noted that he was very slyly and cleverly inching his way closer to where the St. Cyrs were standing.

Once again, Tony responded for the two of them. "So we can have all that lovely treasure for ourselves."

"That is the most ridiculous, asinine, moronic thing I have ever heard," Jane shot back at him.

Tony seemed quite taken aback. "I beg your pardon."

"That is the dumbest idea I've ever heard, and, believe me, I have heard some pretty dumb ideas in my time."

Tony took it personally. "I don't care to have my ideas labeled as dumb, Ms. Bennett."

Jane decided it was better if she asked the questions. It might give Jake the time and the opportunity to figure out how to get them out of this predicament.

"Are either of you experienced divers? Do you have any notion what to do if you encounter a shark, for instance?"

There was no answer from the St. Cyrs.

"Well, you had better know what you're doing because I'm quite certain I spotted several tiger sharks swimming around the shipwreck," she concocted.

"Not to mention the octopus wrapped around the anchor," Jake chimed in. "I didn't want to startle you at the time, darling, but I would have put the creature's length at a good ten or twelve feet."

Jane made a face. "I don't like octopuses."

"I know you don't, sweetheart. That's why I decided not to bring up the subject until now."

Jane shook off her displeasure. She fired her next question at Megs and Tony. "Are either of you scuba-certified?"

"Scuba-certified?" Tony repeated, suddenly looking like he wished he had a drink.

"The shipwreck we have discovered is in a very dark and very wet cave under thirty or forty feet of very cold water. How do you propose to go down and bring up the so-called treasure if you can't dive down and get it?"

It took a minute, but a solution to the problem seemed to present itself to Megs. "We won't kill you two right off the bat. We'll make you bring up the treasure first. Then we'll dispose of you."

Jane shook her head from side to side and even risked a glance at Jake who seemed to be standing there, hands casually stuffed into the pockets of his jeans, listening to the entire exchange as though he didn't have a care in the world.

"Can you believe it?" she remarked to him.

Jake shook his head from side to side in what could only be interpreted as complete disbelief. "Nope."

"They don't have a clue, do they?"

He shook his head again. "Apparently not a single one."

Megs had evidently had enough. More than enough, in fact. "That's enough," she ordered, brandishing her weapon in their direction. "What in the hell are you two talking about?"

Jane spelled it out in plain and simple English. "The gold we saw at the site of the shipwreck must literally weigh tons."

"What did I tell you, Tony?" Megs gloated. "It will be worth a bloody fortune."

"I suppose it might be worth something someday," Jane answered blithely.

"What do you mean it might be worth something someday?" Ostensibly Tony St. Cyr hadn't cared for what he had just heard. "Why not a bloody lot today?"

"Because there is no possible way a human being can bring up the salvage from a ship like the *Bella Doña*, not even one single bar of gold," Jane exaggerated slightly. "The gold weighs far too much. And the silver coins and ingots are all corroded and clumped together into huge masses of debris."

"Well, crap!" was Tony St. Cyr's latest erudite addition to the conversation.

"It will take special and very expensive equipment, a team of expert divers, a contingent of historians and archaeologists and another of experienced salvers to go down and bring up what we saw today inside that cave. And it will take them several years."

Tony actually lost most of the color from his handsome, tanned face. "Several years?"

Jane couldn't resist adding, "Maybe longer."

The couple almost gave the appearance of physically wilting.

Jane had more to say, and she addressed her remarks to Megs.

"Frankly I didn't realize that you and Tony had the

financial resources for this kind of salvage, or the patience, or the interest.''

Megs and Tony exchanged pointed glances.

Jane looked from one to the other. "I thought you knew. Treasure hunting is bloody hard work."

"So, you may as well put the gun away, Mrs. St. Cyr," Jake suggested. "There's no reason for anyone to get hurt."

"I told you this was all a mistake," Tony blurted out, his face turning red.

"That's enough," Megs ordered.

He wasn't about to let his wife order him around now. "But oh no, you had to waggle an invitation out of Don Carlos and then drag us to this godforsaken island where there is nothing to do: no polo, no restaurants, no casinos, no nothing."

Megs St. Cyr turned and shrieked at her spouse. "Shut the fuck up, Tony!"

That was when Jake made his move.

It happened so quickly that it was over and done with practically before anyone realized what had occurred.

"I have the revolver now," Jake stated, pointing the weapon at their uninvited guests. "So I will call the shots, as they say."

"I must say, Hollister, you handled yourself like a real trooper," came the booming and appreciative voice of Jason Gilmour.

They turned around and there were Benjamin, Brilliant Chang, and Jason Gilmour.

"I see we've arrived too late to be of any assistance," the gentleman stated.

"Not at all," Jane countered. "I don't like guns. I'm sure Jake will be more than happy to give you his. And

I don't like the St. Cyrs either. Perhaps you would be willing to take them away with you.''

"Benjamin and I will escort the St. Cyrs to the proper authorities,'' Brilliant Chang stated.

"Which of you two thinks you can make us do anything?'' asked Tony with a final attempt at bravado and a glance at the Rolls Royce he and Megs had borrowed for the day.

"Since I am what you Westerners call a black belt in several forms of martial arts,'' Brilliant Chang spoke up, "and since Benjamin, son of Nui, is my best pupil, I would think either of us could manage.''

Benjamin gave Jane a shy smile, followed by a polite bow. "I knew who to tell, and I knew when to tell them. I sensed the moment you were in danger. I would not have allowed anything or anyone to harm you, Miss Bennett.''

She gave him a polite bow in return. "Thank you, Benjamin.''

"You are most welcome.''

Jane turned to Brilliant Chang. "Thank you again, kind gentleman.''

He gave her one of his inscrutable smiles: "We will meet again, Miss Bennett, on the bridge of Time.''

"Privately, I know an investor who might be willing to put up the money for this particular salvage operation,'' Jake was saying to her later as they packed their camping gear.

"So do I,'' she answered back.

Jake gave her his best and biggest smile. "Maybe we could form a partnership.''

"I thought we already had.''

Jake was momentarily distracted. "I wonder what Jason Gilmour is up to?'' he wondered aloud.

The good doctor was standing some distance away, studying the local vegetation and shaking his head.

''What is it, Doc?''

''I think I finally understand.''

Jane and Jake exchanged glances.

''Finally understand what?'' Jake inquired of his friend.

''I considered it odd at the time. I even remember thinking to myself how strange it was that she would mispronounce the name of a ship when that's all she and Charlie ever talked about.'' Jason Gilmour pulled on his sideburns. ''She wasn't speaking of the ship. She didn't mean the Spanish galleon, *Bella Doña*. She meant belladonna, of course.''

''The poison,'' Jake said.

The doctor continued thinking out loud. ''I've wondered about it for twenty years. Which poison did she use? Where could she have gotten it from?''

''Where could *who* have gotten *what* from?'' Jane inquired.

''Belladonna. Scientific name is *Atropa belladonna*, of course. It's also known as black nightshade, belladonna lily, and a host of other common names.''

''Yes, we know.''

''I didn't realize there was a patch of it growing here on the island. How symbolic that it should lead you to the discovery of the *Bella Doña*,'' Jason Gilmour commented.

''Very symbolic.''

Then he looked directly at Jane. ''I couldn't tell you before, of course, but I did know your father. Charles Bennett was a fascinating man. Something of a dreamer, but I suppose you already know that.''

Jane smiled a bit sadly. "Yes, my father was something of a dreamer."

"But he did find his fabulous treasure in the end, didn't he?"

"Yes, he did."

"I suppose that was what sealed his doom, poor Charlie."

Jane and Jake both looked at the doctor. "What do you mean that's what sealed his doom?"

"Why, Mary Magdalene, of course."

"Who is Mary Magdalene?" asked Jane.

"The fourth Mayfair sister." Jason Gilmour shook his head. "She's been gone nearly twenty years now too. But what happened—that's not for me to say."

"Who can say?"

"Rachel Mayfair. She may know the whole story. I certainly don't. I found her, but it was poor Rachel who was with her sister in the end." The doctor shook his head again. "*Bella Doña* and belladonna."

chapter *Twenty-seven*

"*I* understand that you are planning to leave us soon," Miss Rachel remarked as she and Jane sat together on the front porch swing.

It was an especially warm afternoon for early June, and there was precious little breeze off the Caribbean. They had deliberately chosen a shady spot, one out of the direct sunlight, in which to sit and enjoy a glass of iced tea.

"Yes, I will be leaving soon," Jane confirmed.

She followed Rachel's gaze as the older woman looked out over the expanse of green lawn toward the azure-blue bay below. "I hope you have enjoyed your stay with us."

Jane reached across the short distance between them and placed her hand over Rachel Mayfair's. "Coming here to this island, being here on this island, has changed my life in ways you will never know, Miss Rachel. I owe you so much beyond your warm hospitality." Jane started to take her hand away.

Rachel clung to it.

For a moment she seemed intent upon studying the marked contrast between the smooth, youthful skin on

ane's hand and the wrinkled, age-spotted flesh of her
own.

"It's not easy to admit when you've been wrong," she
began, her Southern accent suddenly more pronounced.
"Especially as you grow older. But I believe I have been
very wrong about you, Jane Bennett. And for that, I am
truly sorry."

"There's no need for you to apologize, Miss Rachel.
If anyone owes an apology, it's me."

Rachel Mayfair moved her head in a vigorous gesture
of denial. "I assumed you came here to make trouble,
young lady. I was afraid you were going to dig up the
past and cause only more pain for those who had already
suffered so much pain." She sighed. "I have a confession to make."

"Please, Miss Rachel—"

"No. They say confession is good for the soul. I won't
rest until I tell you that it was I who invaded your privacy
and tried to search your cottage." She gave another sigh.
"In the end, I couldn't go through with it and I left."
She patted Jane's hand affectionately. "So you see, I owe
you several apologies. You have put the past to rest at
last. You have brought relief from suffering. You, my
dearest girl, have made Paradise a better place because
you were here."

Jane suddenly discovered there were tears on her face.
"My father always used to say to me 'the truth shall
make us free.' " She reached up with her other hand and
wiped at her cheeks. "I came for the truth, Miss Rachel,
because I wanted, I needed, to be free of the past. Not
only am I now free from the past, but I believe I have a
future. A future I could never have imagined before."
She exhaled and gave a small laugh. "At least I hope I
do."

"You must mean young Mr. Hollister, our other *former* tenant," Miss Rachel ventured with a sly smile.

"You guessed?"

"I knew."

Jane felt a rush of color to her face. "Thank you for not telling anyone."

"You're welcome. I was young once myself, of course."

They laughed together.

"But I never had a beau. I never had the good or bad fortune to fall in love." She sighed, and it wasn't a sigh completely filled with regret. "How could I blame either you or poor Mary Magdalene?"

"Mary Magdalene?"

"Yes." Rachel Mayfair put her glass of iced tea down on the white wrought-iron table at her elbow and rose from the porch swing, keeping Jane's hand in hers all the while. "Shall we walk together for a time and talk?"

"Of course."

They started down the sweeping front steps of the Four Sisters Inn and across the lawn before Rachel said, "There's no reason for the others to know about the things we will speak of today."

"The others?"

"Naomi and Esther."

Naturally it was Rachel Mayfair's decision to make. Not hers, Jane recognized.

"My sisters have suffered so much already. First, because our parents were exiled to this island after Daddy broke every holy commandment a man can break. Then later, because of Mary Magdalene. There is no reason they should suffer any more now, after all these years."

Jane nodded her head, not fully understanding in her mind but certainly in her heart. "I agree."

"There were four of us, of course. Mary Magdalene was the youngest and the prettiest. Have you ever seen a picture of her when she was your age?"

Jane slowed her walk to match Rachel Mayfair's more leisurely pace. "No, I haven't."

"We don't keep a great many photographs on display around the house as you may have noticed, but there is one of Mary tucked away in my bureau drawer. I take it out every now and then and look at it. Remind me to show it to you."

Jane slipped her arm through the other woman's as they strolled. "I do the same with a photograph of my father. In fact, I never travel anywhere without it."

"Then you understand."

"I understand."

"Your father was Charles Bennett, wasn't he?"

"Yes." Jane sighed. "Can you forgive me for not telling you before now?"

"There's no need to ask for forgiveness, not between the two of us. Our pasts are intertwined in more ways than you can imagine. Did Jason Gilmour explain?"

Jane shook her head. "Dr. Gilmour said that it wasn't his story to tell. I think he made a promise to you—or perhaps he made one to himself—a long time ago. So, no, he didn't explain."

They walked a little farther.

Jane felt she had put part of the puzzle pieces together on her own. "Was Mary Magdalene in love with my father?"

"She thought she was."

"And was he in love with her?"

It was a moment before Rachel answered. "Charlie Bennett was handsome and charming and a bit spoiled when it came to women. Men too, for that matter. People were attracted to him.''

''Yes, they were.''

''Charlie was also living proof that our greatest strength is often our greatest weakness.''

Jane knew precisely what Rachel Mayfair was talking about. ''He was, indeed.''

''Your father was amusing. He told wonderful stories. He had apparently been everywhere and done everything and he knew absolutely everyone. He was all of the things that Mary wanted and could never have, never be, poor girl.''

''And he used her.''

''Possibly.''

''Charlie had a way of using people,'' Jane said dispassionately. ''His wife. His own children. His friends. Even complete strangers. I don't think he meant any harm. It was simply Charlie being Charlie.''

''He was certainly everything my sister thought she wanted in life. She just didn't understand she could never have him,'' Rachel said as they walked on.

''Because he was already married?''

There was a moment of well-intentioned hesitation. ''No.''

''Ah, I see. My father failed to mention to Mary Magdalene that he had a wife and three daughters back home.''

Somehow that knowledge didn't come as a complete surprise to Jane.

''He wouldn't have been the first man to do so, and he certainly won't be the last,'' Rachel said with surprising forbearance.

''It's deceitful, all the same,'' Jane said.

''I'm not sure he really meant to deceive Mary or any

of us. The mundane, everyday, family kind of life didn't fit the image Charlie had created of himself."

"The mundane, everyday, family kind of life wasn't exactly a priority with my father either."

"Some men simply aren't meant to be husbands or fathers."

Jane finally got her nerve up and asked the question that had been on her mind during their entire conversation. "What happened to Charlie and Mary?"

Rachel gave her hand a squeeze. "I don't think we will ever know for certain."

"There are some questions that have no answers," Jane murmured more to herself than to her companion.

"I see you've been speaking with our Mr. Chang. He is a very wise man, Brilliant Chang."

"Yes, he is."

It was a minute, perhaps longer, before Rachel Mayfair went on. "To answer your question the best way I know how. Charlie never returned from the last dive he made down to the *Bella Doña*."

It was what she had suspected. It was what she had known in her heart all along, Jane realized.

"Perhaps Mary realized that Charlie had found the shipwreck and fulfilled his dream of obtaining great riches—the reason that had brought him to Paradise in the first place, after all—and now he would leave the island and her."

Jane gave a sigh of understanding. "Charlie was always searching for that pot of gold at the end of the rainbow."

"Maybe my sister discovered that Charlie was married and had children."

Not an impossibility.

"Maybe what happened to him in the cave was truly

an accident. Or perhaps Mary drained part of the air from his tanks and never meant for him to return from that last dive. Maybe it was guilt. Maybe it was remorse. Maybe it was losing the only man she had ever loved. We will never know. We only knew she had done something wrong when his boat was found out at sea. That never made any sense to us. We assume it was Mary, as well."

Somehow Jane had known that this was a question without an answer.

Rachel finished her story. "By the time Dr. Gilmour found Mary Magdalene along the roadway, she was incoherent. She died soon after in my arms."

There was a period of silence.

Rachel finished. "Apparently she had eaten the deadly belladonna berry or plant, although we didn't know that until recently, of course."

"I am so very sorry."

Jane glanced up and realized that they had reached the perimeter of the lovely garden at the edge of the property.

"This is a lovely spot," she commented.

"This was Mary's garden originally. Not Esther's. Esther had no interest in flowers and such until after Mary was gone. Then it became her passion, her mission, her purpose in life: to create the most beautiful garden she could . . . in tribute."

"It is a fitting tribute."

Rachel raised one hand and pointed toward the far corner of the garden. "That was always her favorite spot. That's why we buried Mary there. Someday, when the time comes, the rest of the Mayfair sisters will join her."

> *Mary, Mary, quite contrary,*
> *How does your garden grow?*

With silver bells and cockleshells
And pretty maids all in a row.

"I only have one wish," Rachel was telling Jane later that same afternoon as they were strolling leisurely back toward the great Victorian house.

"What is that?"

"Perhaps I should explain that on one of his first dives down to the *Bella Doña*, Charlie brought a single artifact back with him. We didn't know it at the time, of course. It was only much later that I found the small cardboard box, marked with a B.D. and tied up with string, and with a name scribbled on the top in his handwriting."

"What was in the box?"

"I don't know. I have never opened it. I put it away in a drawer twenty years ago, and that is where it has remained to this day," she said to her companion.

"And what is your one wish?" Jane inquired.

Rachel heaved a wistful sigh. "I wish I knew who Cordelia was. Besides the only one of King Lear's three daughters who loved him, of course . . . at least according to Shakespeare's play."

Rachel Mayfair suddenly appeared to realize that her youthful friend had stopped and was standing there inert. "What is it?"

Jane couldn't speak for a moment.

"Are you ill?"

"No."

"What is it, then, my dear?"

"I'm Cordelia."

"You're Cordelia?" It was obvious the older woman didn't understand what she was being told.

And why should Rachel Mayfair understand?

"My full name," she finally said, her throat filled with tears, "is Cordelia Jane Bennett."

"Isn't that your young man coming across the lawn now?" Rachel said as they watched Jake's approach. "He seems to be shouting something. I can't quite make out the words. What is he saying?"

"He's saying: 'I've lost! I've lost!' " Jane was starting to move faster herself. "Isn't it wonderful?" she exclaimed, clapping her hands together. "He's lost, don't you see?"

"He's lost?" Miss Rachel laughed, not quite understanding, but understanding that it didn't matter at the moment if she didn't. She would in time.

"He's lost," Jane exclaimed, leaving the older woman and running toward the man. "But he's won!"

chapter Twenty-eight

"*I*'ve lost!" Jake exclaimed, pulling her into his arms and hugging her tightly to him.

"I know. How wonderful."

"I had no idea," he was fairly shouting with joy as he put his head back for a moment and smiled down at Jane, "how hard it is to lose at poker."

"Really?"

"I guess I've never tried to lose before." He was rambling on a bit, but Jane didn't care. "I've always been a gambler. Let me tell you, any successful businessman has to be one. But in the past I tried to win. I always did too. This is the first time I set out to deliberately lose anything in my life." Jake Hollister heaved a great sigh as if the weight of the world had been removed from his broad shoulders. "But I did it. I actually did it, Jane."

"Who won?"

Jake grinned from ear to ear. "Tommy Bahama is now the new and very proud owner of the Mangy Moose. He'll do just fine too. Rosey will be there to help out. She'll whip the place into shape. And Tommy right along with it no doubt."

Jane shook her head. It was a thought that hadn't occurred to her before now. "Tommy Bahama and Rosey?"

"Sure. Why not? There have been odder couples in this world who have met and fallen in love."

Jane thought of that first day on the ferry from Charlotte Amalie to Paradise. Anyone seeing her and Jake Hollister together that day would have found them an odd couple.

Jake took her by the hand and guided her toward the relative privacy of the canvas hammock between their bungalows. "We have something to discuss, Ms. Bennett."

"We do?" Her stomach was filling with butterflies.

Jake insisted that they sit side by side on the edge of the canvas contraption. "We do, and if I'm going to keep my mind on what I want to say I'd better sit up."

Implying, of course, that if they stretched out on the hammock together their conversation would take a different tone altogether.

That's when Jake noticed that she was holding a small box in her hands. "What's in the box?"

"I don't know."

He laughed. "What do you mean you don't know?"

Jane shrugged her shoulders. "Rachel Mayfair just gave it to me this afternoon."

"Odd that she didn't mention what was inside."

"She doesn't know either."

Jake appeared to be puzzled. "Perhaps you would care to explain to me."

"It was found among my father's possessions after he disappeared and Mary Magdalene died. Rachel put it away on the chance, I guess, that Cordelia would one day show up on Paradise."

"Cordelia?"

"My full legal name is Cordelia Jane Bennett," she explained. "The only person who ever called me Cordelia was my father."

"This is from Charlie to you," Jake said, immediately recognizing its significance. "It's something he meant for you to have twenty years ago."

Jane swallowed hard. "Apparently."

"Are you going to open it?"

Her hands were trembling. "I'm afraid to."

"Why?"

"I don't know."

"Fear of the unknown. Oh, my dear Jane, how many times have you faced it so bravely in the past? In the recent past? And how many times will you face it in the future? Don't you realize that you're a very brave woman?"

She shook her head. She reached for the end of the old string tied around the simple and now-yellowed-with-age cardboard box. She carefully placed the string to one side and removed the lid.

It was sitting there on a piece of crumpled tissue paper: an offering, a gift.

It was smaller than she'd expected, but the gold was still yellow and pure after three hundred years. She didn't dare touch it. She simply stared at the gold brooch in the cardboard box: it was a heart clasped by a hand. The inscription was clear and finely etched in Spanish: *No tengo mas que darte.*

Jake read it aloud: " 'I have nothing more to give thee.' "

Jane was moved beyond tears. "Charlie was thinking of me in the end, wasn't he?"

"Yes, he was."

"From one father to his daughter so many centuries ago. And now from another father to his daughter so many years later."

"Charlie loved you, Jane, in his own way. Maybe he just never knew how to tell you or how to show you."

It was some minutes later, as they still sat on their favorite hammock, that the subject was brought up again. "We still have something to discuss, Ms. Bennett."

Jane moistened her lips. "We do." It had been an emotional day. She wasn't certain she could handle much more. "What subject could that be?"

"Love."

That's what she was afraid Jake was going to say.

"We—you—brought up the subject just before we went into the cavern for the first time. I wanted to talk about it then, but you insisted that we only had a few minutes of daylight left and we had to make the most of them. You said that love could always be discussed in the dark." Jake never took his eyes from her. "We still haven't gotten back to discussing it."

"Gosh, I wonder why," Jane pointed out, swinging her legs self-consciously. "We've only been a little busy uncovering a three-hundred-year-old shipwreck."

"And a king's ransom in gold and silver, emeralds, and heaven knows what else," he said.

She held up two fingers. "Two kings' ransoms."

"Then, of course, there were always the gun-toting villains. Although I thought Megs and Tony St. Cyr gave up rather easily myself," Jake said facetiously.

"I would, too, Jake Hollister, if you were the opponent I had to face. You are a very formidable man."

"Thank you, my dear." He frowned. "I think."

"You're welcome."

"Of course, we mustn't forget to mention the fact that there were three other gentlemen who showed up at a most opportune moment to help out. We have to give credit where credit's due: to Benjamin and Doc Gilmour and certainly Brilliant Chang."

"We've also been busy solving a twenty-year-old mystery about my father and Mary Magdalene."

He scowled. "I still don't understand all of their story."

"I'll explain it to you one day, perhaps."

He seemed to understand that this wasn't the time and place to ask. "Then I had the difficult and challenging task of unloading my ownership of the only bar on the island."

"And don't forget that we've both been a little busy putting the past behind us."

"And bringing the truth to light. And setting ourselves free. We are both free at last," he proclaimed. "Other than that we haven't been up to a thing."

Jane arched one eyebrow.

"No pun intended, of course," Jake said without cracking a smile.

She didn't believe him this time.

Jake was suddenly serious. "I don't want to end up all alone like Doc Gilmour."

"He's not alone," she pointed out. "He has all the people on this island who depend on him, and he has China."

"That's what I mean. I don't want to end up alone."

"There are worse things than being alone, Jake." She smoothed the skirt of her sundress. "Being with the wrong person for the wrong reasons, for instance."

"What about the right person for the right reasons," he said in a soft voice.

"That's always a gamble because you never know ahead of time if they're right or wrong for you."

"I am finally free, Jane."

She wanted to ask: Free from what? Free to do what? Instead, she waited for him to go on.

"I'm finally free from the past that has haunted me. I'm finally free to go wherever I want. I'm free to do whatever I want to do. I'm free to love and free to be loved in return." He took a deep breath and finally said the words: "I love you, Jane Bennett."

"My father said he loved me. I was never enough to keep my father from leaving."

"You are all I'll ever need to stay. You once told me that all you had to do to get a piece of paradise was ask." Jake's voice actually broke. "Well, I'm asking."

"What are you asking, Jake?"

"Do you love me?"

"Yes, I do."

He went to gather her toward him.

Jane stopped him. "Falling in love is the easy part they say. Being in love is the hard part."

"No pun intended, huh?"

She blushed right down to her hairline.

"We're going to be very busy, you know," he informed her.

"We are?"

"First I'd like to go back home to Indiana. There are some people there I would like you to meet. And I want them to meet you. I need to spend some time in my hometown with my folks. Would you mind?"

"Not in the least. I've never been to Indiana, you know."

"Then we have to hire ourselves a first-class crew of divers and archaeologists and historians and photographers and scientists to see to the incredible undertaking of excavating the *Bella Doña*. Discreetly, of course. We don't want every two-bit recreational diver ruining the natural beauty of this island.''

''No, we don't.''

Jake paused and seemed to be thinking about something. ''I wonder if the Mayfair sisters have considered making their huge segment of the island into a nature preserve of some sort after they're gone. I'm certain something can be done about it legally. I'll look into it when we get back to civilization.''

''You do that,'' she said, patting his leg.

''Then we need to find a priest, of course.''

''A priest?'' She was confounded. ''Of course. A priest. To bless the site of the *Bella Doña*, of course.''

''To marry us.''

''Marry us?''

''I'm asking you to marry me, Jane Bennett.'' He slipped off the hammock and went on his knees in front of her. He clasped her hands in his and he said all the right words. ''I promise to love, honor, and cherish you every day for the rest of our lives and for whatever comes after. And I always keep my promises.''

And he did. . . .

Epilogue

From an announcement in the *International Museum News*:

The Charles Avery Bennett Maritime Museum opened its doors today to great interest and acclaim. The dedication of the museum was attended by dignitaries and scholars from around the globe, as well as family members, including the late Mr. Bennett's eldest daughter, Cordelia Jane Bennett Hollister.

After more than two decades, Charles Avery Bennett has been officially credited in the history books for having discovered the wreckage of the great Spanish galleon, *Bella Doña*, which sank in a hurricane off the coast of a small Caribbean island in 1692.

The treasure recovered from the *Bella Doña*, and now on display at the Buffalo-based museum, includes a vast collection of gold and silver coins and ingots, priceless jewelry and gemstones, and nu-

covered in 1967. The inscription was on a gold ring, however, which would have suggested that it was a parting gift of a lady to her lover.

But that is another story for another time. . . .

No Ordinary Man

*"Breathes there a man, with soul so dead,
Who never to himself hath said,
This is my own, my native land."*

—Sir Walter Scott

*"But to see her was to love her,
love but her, and love forever..."*

—Robert Burns

chapter*One*

*H*e'd made a mistake.

A big mistake.

Mitchell Storm stood at the bottom of the marble staircase and, like the four hundred guests crowded into the Great Hall below, gazed up at the young woman in the shimmering evening gown.

Even from this distance he could see that she was tall and slender and fine-boned in that way French women had of being fine-boned, although he knew she wasn't French.

Her neck was long and swanlike. Her shoulders were narrow—but not too narrow—and straight. Her posture was perfect. Her figure was exquisite: that was clearly evident despite the fact she was dressed in the fashion of the Victorian era.

Her features were delicate, yet defined: high cheekbones, a small, aristocrat nose, a chin that was neither too pointed nor too rounded, and an altogether lovely mouth.

Her skin was flawless: it was the color and texture of fine porcelain. Her hair was upswept in the style of the period with a few tasteful wisps left free to frame her face.

She held her gloved hands in front of her: a silk fan clasped in the right, a small jeweled evening bag dangling from the left. The gemstones glittering at her ears and throat were huge, blood-red and, from all accounts, priceless.

Mitchell had been circulating among the guests for the past quarter hour, eavesdropping on their conversations. In the process he had learned that Storm Point had been built for Andrew Storm more than a century ago by Richard Morris Hunt, *the* architect of the famed Newport, Rhode Island, "cottages."

That the cost of the mansion had been an astronomical $12 million: $4 million for its construction, and the balance going toward interior decoration.

That so much marble had been used in building the estate—yellow Siena and black-veined Brescia from Italy, pink-veined Numidian from western Algeria, and white stone for the facade from rural New York—that a private wharf and warehouse had been needed to unload and store the materials.

That the ceiling of the Great Hall—the very hall in which they now stood—Rubenesque cherubs, gilded cornices, magnificent rococo relief work and all, soared fifty feet overhead.

That Dickens, the butler, was left over from the "previous administration."

And that Victoria Storm—Torey, as her closest friends called her—was one of the richest women in the United States.

But he had known that before he'd left Scotland.

Mitchell swore softly under his breath. He'd made a mistake all right. A huge mistake. He had pinned his hopes for the future—and the hopes of three villages, several dozen sheep farms, and some eight hundred people—on a young woman of rare privilege and even rarer wealth who had obviously never had to worry about where her next designer ball gown was coming from, let alone her next meal.

"Doesn't Victoria look sensational?" came a sibilant whisper from nearby.

The imposing matron in front of Mitchell, elaborate hairdo and ample bosom dramatically draped with a king's ransom in diamonds, leaned slightly to one side, waggled her head, and mouthed to her acquaintance, "Yes, she does."

Her response was apparently seen by the second female as a signal to continue the conversation. "I understand the inspiration for her costume was a nineteenth-century ball gown designed by Charles Worth, the founding father of haute couture."

"Indeed." The richly attired matron managed to look down her nose even as she gazed up at the subject under their collective scrutiny. "I must confess that I've always been puzzled by the proclivity of redheads to wear pink." There was a particular emphasis on the word pink, as if it were something contagious.

The other woman studied the engraved card clasped in her hand. "The description in the program states that Victoria's gown is magnolia satin embroidered with thousands of tiny multicolored beads that give the material a rosy, iridescent tint. Her evening slippers are covered with magnolia satin as well, and her shoe buckles are fashioned of rubies and diamonds."

Leaning closer still, bosom and diamonds quivering in

the wake of her sudden movement, the bejeweled doy-
enne announced in a stage whisper that carried halfway
across the Great Hall, "I see Victoria is also wearing the
Storm rubies tonight."

Her companion appeared to be momentarily taken
aback. "They aren't being auctioned off as well, are
they?"

"Of course they aren't, Lola." The glare Lola received
said she had clearly taken leave of her senses if she
thought that was true. "Victoria Storm sell her great-
great-grandmother's jewels?" There was an incredulous
sniff. "Not in a thousand years. Not in a million years.
Not even for charity." She adjusted the corsage on her
costume before adding, "Why, I'll wager those rubies
haven't been out of the bank vault since Marilyn Storm
died."

The second woman took in a deep breath and released
it on a sigh. "Poor Victoria." She gave her head a shake
and heaved another sigh. "And poor Marilyn."

"Poor?" Another perfectly executed ladylike sniff that
managed to convey a wealth of implication. "I scarcely
think so."

The more timid of the two women became flustered.
"I only meant because Victoria lost both of her parents
... because Marilyn died so young..." She became
even more flustered and began to fan herself with the
evening's program. After a brief period, in which she
apparently managed to collect her wits, she spoke up in
a hopeful voice: "Perhaps we'll get a good look at the
rubies."

"Of course we will." There seemed to be no doubt
about it in the matron's mind. "Victoria understands her
responsibilities as the charity ball's hostess. She'll make
sure everyone has a look-see. After all, we each made a

sizeable donation to her pet projects for the privilege of being in attendance tonight."

"It's for a good cause," her companion volunteered. "Several good causes."

"I suppose so," the woman allowed, somewhat belatedly, before she finally fell silent.

The young woman at the center of their attention reached the bottom of the Grand Staircase, accepted the arm of the handsome, middle-aged man waiting there for her, turned and then glided into the adjoining crystal-chandeliered ballroom, passing within several feet of Mitchell.

He blew out his breath expressively.

Victoria Storm was beautiful.

He'd give her that.

And she was Scottish through and through. The red hair, the blue-green eyes, and the fair skin with the slightest smattering of freckles fairly shouted her heritage.

Unfortunately he just knew in his gut that she was going to be one of those supercilious young women with an annoying laugh, a well-bred nose perpetually raised in the air, and feet perpetually several inches off the ground; an essentially brainless creature who knew a great deal about art and literature and a wide variety of esoteric subjects, and absolutely nothing about real life.

Beautiful but brainless.

"This is bloody ridiculous," came an indignant whisper from somewhere behind his right shoulder.

Mitchell swung around. It was Iain MacClumpha, a serving platter of large, pink, plump shrimp grasped in his beefy hands and a furious expression on his forty-five-year-old face.

Without moving his lips, Mitchell said, "Keep your voice down and follow me."

He wended his way through the stragglers at the back of the crowd, checking every now and then to make sure the red-faced and red-haired giant was behind him.

There was a table beside a row of French doors. Mitchell took the platter of seafood from his companion and right-hand man, plunked it down on the table, and stepped out into the night.

"This is sheer madness, laddie," Iain MacClumpha gritted through his front teeth, his soft Scottish burr all the more pronounced for his indignation.

"Yes. It is," he agreed.

But no more so than a number of things he'd done in the past year, Mitchell reminded himself.

For a minute or two, the only sound was the scuff of their ghillie brogues on the crushed seashell path as they put a discreet distance between themselves and the house.

The man beside him asked in a sharp tone: "Did you see she was wearing the plaid and the *suaicheantas*?"

Mitchell had.

Although he'd caught only a brief glimpse of the silk evening sash and the silver clan-badge pinned at her shoulder as Victoria had made her way down the Grand Staircase.

"Crist," his companion swore, thumping his muscular thigh with the palm of his broad hand, "I canna believe the local constables thought we were a couple of gussied-up waiters hired for the fancy party the lass is throwing."

Mitchell almost laughed.

Earlier that evening, *not* local constables but uniformed security guards had mistaken the two of them for members of the catering staff. He and Iain had been summarily dispatched to the service entrance of the mansion and put to work.

Frankly they hadn't argued the point. After all, he and the MacClumpha weren't exactly guests either. Mitchell had decided on the spot not to try to explain the situation to a hired guard or anyone outside of the woman it concerned.

Hell, it was going to be tough enough explaining it to Victoria Storm when the time came.

"And that bloody Englishman in charge."

He knew Iain meant the butler, Dickens.

"It's the kilts," Mitchell explained.

It had seemed like a good idea: both of them dressing in traditional Scottish kilts to make a lasting first impression on their American relation. The MacClumpha rarely wore trousers, of course, but it was a fairly new experience for Mitchell.

They'd had no way of knowing the staff was going to be dressed in kilts. Or, for that matter, that they were arriving on the eve of Victoria Storm's annual costume ball.

The other man failed to see the humor in the situation. That much was apparent.

"Obviously I need to take a different approach to confronting—" Mitchell immediately corrected himself. "—to meeting with my cousin." He made another quick correction. "With *our* cousin."

Iain MacClumpha's branch of the family had descended through an illegimate son of the third earl. Even though generations had passed, everyone knew who were legitimate septs of Clan Storm—and who were not.

The big man's voice had the timbre of a bass drum. "I lay no claim to the lass."

Mitchell would've liked to be able to say the same,

but he couldn't. Victoria Storm was his fourth cousin, and he had traveled to the United States specifically to meet her.

Actually he was here on a mission; a mission that he was a far cry from accomplishing. He would just have to put up with a snub or two or a case of mistaken identity, if that's what it took.

Beggars couldn't be choosers.

"Maybe this wasn't my best idea," Mitchell conceded, rubbing a hand across his tired eyes as he finished the thought out loud.

Iain MacClumpha shook his head. "Hell of a time to start second guessing yourself, if you don't mind my saying so. Not that your side of the family ever did lay claim to having the *Da-Shealladh*."

The Gaelic word rolled awkwardly off Mitchell's tongue. "The *Da-Shealladh*?"

"The Second Sight."

He made an interested sound. "You mean the ability to predict events?"

"I do. The vision may come in any place and at any time of the day or night, and it comes unbidden. Too bad there was none on your side of the blanket with the gift. It'd come in handy about now." An additional bit of philosophy was tacked on. "'Course some say the Sight isn't a gift at all but a terrible burden."

His burden was of another kind altogether, Mitchell acknowledged, picturing the crumbling castle, the great, brooding mountains, and the wild, windswept island an ocean away.

In the past few months he'd come to rely on Iain MacClumpha's brusque opinion. The man was outspoken and too big for anyone, except perhaps Mitchell, to argue with.

Uneasiness and weariness—he hadn't slept since leaving Glasgow yesterday—made Mitchell shift his stance. "So far it hasn't exactly gone according to our plans, has it, my friend?"

His traveling companion seemed to recover a portion of his sense of humor. He raised his arm and slapped Mitchell between the shoulder blades. "Burns had somethin' to say on the subject."

"Did he?"

Iain MacClumpha was fond of quoting Scotland's favorite son and poet, Robert Burns, who had had something to say on just about every subject.

The MacClumpha bobbed his shaggy head up and down. "Rabbie Burns wrote that they tend to 'gang aft a-gley.' "

"Who does?"

"Not who, laddie. What."

Mitchell was willing to play along for a minute. "What tends to go 'aft a-gley'?"

The Scotsman smiled, and his face was transformed. "Why, 'the best laid schemes o' mice and men.' "

Both men laughed.

"Now, do you mind telling me again what we're doin' here?" Iain inquired in better humor.

Mitchell answered the question, without really answering it. "We're here to see the lady."

The Scotsman tugged on the sleeve of his evening jacket—a Prince Charlie Coatee with matching vest—and made a sound halfway between a chuckle and a snort. "This is MacClumpha you're talkin' to, *my lord*, lest you've forgotten." Iain only referred to Mitchell formally when he was trying to make a very particular point.

Mitchell reconsidered his answer. " 'Know thy enemy,' " he finally said tersely.

Thick, reddish-blond eyebrows drew into a frown. "Did you learn that lesson at your grandfather's knee?"

Mitchell indicated otherwise as he walked on some small distance. "The London School of Economics by way of Jakarta and the University of Texas."

The seashell path curved around a large flagstone terrace that extended past the stately home and onto an expanse of rolling, green lawn. The impressive row of French doors—glass panes sparkling like faceted diamonds, brass knobs and fittings gleaming like burnished gold—had been thrown open to the summer night. Light poured from every window and door of the house, and the melodious strains of an orchestra playing a waltz could be heard somewhere in the background.

Mitchell Storm raised his face to the night air. He could make out the distinctive tang of salt and sea. The ocean must be very close by. Then he heard the solitary screech of a gull and the sound of waves pounding rhythmically against the shoreline.

He closed his eyes for a moment. He could almost imagine himself back on the Isle of Storm. Scotland seemed so near . . . and yet so far away.

"Is she the enemy?"

He came out of his reverie. "Is who the enemy?"

"The lass."

"Everyone is an enemy until they prove themselves to be a friend," he stated pragmatically.

Iain MacClumpha appeared to be biting his tongue. "Sounds like somethin' a Clansman might have said two hundred and fifty years ago during the Rising."

"I suppose we picked the wrong side back then too."

"We tried not to pick sides. We tried to stay neutral. The story goes that your great-great-great-great-great-grandfather entertained, in turn, both Bonnie Prince Charlie and the 'Butcher' Cumberland just before the Battle of Culloden.''

He needed to bone up on his Scottish history. "The 'Butcher' Cumberland?''

"The Duke of Cumberland. He led the English forces—recorded to be nine thousand strong—against half that number of Highlanders. The battle lasted an hour, but the slaughter continued through that bleak day and into the next, and for weeks to come. The moor at Culloden was stained with the best blood of Scotland.''

"How fortunate that we remained neutral then,'' Mitchell said sardonically.

"A man does what a man has to do.''

He arched an eyebrow in the MacClumpha's direction. "Burns again?''

The burly man shook his head. "My dad.'' The Scotsman wasn't above giving a small history lesson every chance he got. "We're neither Highlanders nor Lowlanders when it comes to that, laddie. The Storms have always been a law unto themselves.''

"It's a pity all that neutrality and diplomacy hasn't paid the bills and shored up the crumbling walls.''

"These are hard times for the people of the Western Isles,'' he was informed.

And it was his responsibility to find a way to restore the family's fortunes, and, in the process, bring prosperity—or at least guarantee survival—to the people who depended on him, Mitchell had discovered with his grandfather's death.

But he was having second and third thoughts about approaching Victoria Storm for help. She somehow didn't seem like the type who would give a damn about the fate of the inhabitants of a small island an ocean away. Maybe this whole thing, including the long trip from Scotland, had been a mistake from beginning to end.

"Why not wait and call on your cousin tomorrow?" his friend suggested.

"The morning after a formal ball?" Mitchell shook his head. "I wouldn't call that an opportune moment. And I have no intention of waiting around until it's convenient for my dear cousin to grant me an audience."

Iain MacClumpha stepped back, folded his arms across his massive chest, planted his feet and gazed up at the imposing four-story stone edifice. "It's a bloody big house."

"It is."

He took another step backwards and replanted his feet. "I suppose they refer to it as a mansion in this country."

"I suppose they do."

"It must take a great walloping lot of money to keep up a place like this."

"I'm sure it does." Mitchell decided he might as well tell Iain what he knew. "Our cousin inherited not only this house but a luxury penthouse apartment in New York City, a villa on the Mediterranean, and a ski chalet in the Swiss Alps."

Breath whistled out between Iain MacClumpha's teeth. "By the blessed bones of St. Columba!"

He couldn't have said it better himself. "Victoria Storm has a great deal of money."

"Andrew did all right for himself."

"He certainly did." Mitchell could tell that the man beside him was duly impressed. "Do you know what men like Andrew Storm were called in this country during the last century?"

The MacClumpha gave a grimace. "Naw."

"Robber barons."

The MacClumpha grunted. "Seems appropriate."

"Yes, it does."

They turned and made their way back to the great house. Mitchell followed a kilted waiter through the service entrance and into the kitchen: it was all stainless steel and polished brass, what seemed like miles of marble countertops and walls of cupboards, huge ovens, and rows of cooking stoves, a bank of subzero refrigerators, and a walk-in freezer. There were chefs in their distinctive white hats, maids in neat, black, aproned uniforms and waiters in plaid.

Out of the corner of his mouth, Mitchell instructed, "Grab another tray of canapes and circulate."

He could tell Iain wasn't thrilled by the prospect of playing waiter again.

"Then what?" the man inquired with a scowl.

"Keep your eyes and ears open."

Iain MacClumpha picked up the first tray he came to. "What am I looking for?"

"Any of the Victorias. And keep in mind they could come in any form or shape or size, especially the marble one. The list I have only makes it clear there were at least a half dozen different Victorias disposed of at the 1879 auction."

"And if I find one?"

"Then I'll approach my dear cousin and offer her a deal she can't refuse."

"Do you think she'll go for it?"

"I'll make certain that she does," Mitchell said confidently as he hoisted an oversized serving tray ladened with mounds of black Beluga caviar and paper-thin slices of pink Scottish salmon.

"Not above using your charms on the lass, are you?"

"You said it yourself: 'A man does what a man has

to do.' " A short silence followed. "On second thought, why don't you start with the terrace and the gardens, then move inside to the Billiard Room and the Great Hall?" His suggestion would give the headstrong Scot additional time to cool off.

Iain gladly set his tray back down. "Where are you headed?"

"I'm going to follow our dear cousin around her own party for a while."

"Mind your P's and Q's, laddie."

"Believe me," Mitchell Storm assured him, putting his shoulder to the swinging door between kitchen and service hallway—a cacophony of music, laughter and voices from the formal reception rooms beyond washed over him—"I intend to."

He had to.

There was too damned much at stake not to.

merous historical artifacts, including the ship's anchor.

The Charles Avery Bennett Maritime Museum is open to the public. All proceeds from the museum go to support the Gilmour Foundation, which establishes and maintains medical clinics on remote Caribbean islands where health facilities are otherwise unavailable.

The day's celebrations ended on a surprising and joyous note when a magnificent painting was unveiled for the main entrance hall. Donated in his wife's name by philanthropist Jake Hollister, the painting is the betrothal portrait of the beautiful young lady, Bella Doña, for which the Spanish galleon was so long ago named.

Author's Note

The manifest of the *Bella Doña*—indeed, the *Bella Doña* herself—is of my own creation, but the ship and her cargo are based on fact, in particular, the *Nuestra Senora de Atocha*, whose unbelievable treasure was discovered by Mel Fisher in 1985, the *Nuestra Senora de la Concepcion*, the *Conde de Tolosa*, and the *Nuestra Senora de Guadalupe*, all galleons of the Spanish fleet, all ships lost long ago somewhere off the coast of Florida or in the region of the Caribbean.

The rare blooming flower, *tiare apetahi*, grows only on the holy mountain of Temehani in Polynesia. It is true that efforts to transplant the *tiare apetahi* to other locations have met with utter failure. Fiction can sometimes achieve what fact, indeed, cannot since the exotic plant grows successfully on the island of Paradise, the island of my imagination.

The brooch given to Bella Doña by her beloved father before she set sail for Spain and inscribed with the words *"No tengo mas que darte"*—I have nothing more to give thee—is part fact and part fiction. It was among the salvage of the *Girona*, a ship of the Spanish Armada, dis-

WIN A TRIP TO PARADISE ISLAND

~

The Paradise Man
Sweepstakes

~

ONE GRAND PRIZE: A trip for two to Paradise Island in the Bahamas, including round-trip airfare and one week (7 days/6 nights) accommodations on Paradise Island.

Prize provided courtesy of
McCord Travel Management

McCord is one of the largest travel management firms in the United States with more than 540 travel professionals at 58 locations nationwide.

- -

OFFICIAL ENTRY FORM

Mail to: THE PARADISE MAN SWEEPSTAKES
c/o St. Martin's Paperbacks
175 Fifth Avenue, Suite 1615
New York, NY 10010-7848

Name _____

Address _____

City/State/Zip _____

Phone (day) _____ Phone (night) _____

See next page for Official Rules. No purchase necessary. Void in the province of Quebec, Puerto Rico and wherever else prohibited by law. Ends October 1, 1997.

The Paradise Man Sweepstakes

No purchase necessary

OFFICIAL RULES

1. **To Enter:** Complete the Official Entry Form. Or you may enter by hand printing on a 3"x5" postcard your name, address (including zip code), daytime and evening phone numbers and the words, "THE PARADISE MAN." Mail entries to THE PARADISE MAN Sweepstakes, c/o St. Martin's Paperbacks, 175 Fifth Avenue Suite 1615, New York, NY 10010-7848. Entries must be received by October 1 1997. Limit one entry per person. No mechanically reproduced or illegible entries accepted. Not responsible for lost, misdirected, mutilated or late entries.

2. **Random Drawing.** Winner will be determined in a random drawing to be held on or about October 2, 1997 from all eligible entries received. Odds of winning depend on the number of eligible entries received. Potential winner will be notified by mail on or about October 31, 1997, and will be asked to execute and return an Affidavit of Eligibility/Release/Prize Acceptance Form within fourteen (14) days of attempted notification. Non-compliance within this time may result in disqualification and the selection of an alternate winner. Return of any prize/prize notification as undeliverable will result in disqualification and an alternate winner will be selected. Travel companion will also be required to execute a release.

3. **Prize and Approximate Retail Value:** Grand Prize winner will receive a seven (7) day, six (6) night trip for two (2) to Paradise Island, the Bahamas. Trip consists of round-trip economy class air transportation from any United States or Canadian international airport, to the Bahamas, six nights, double-occupancy hotel accommodation (approximate retail value $2,000). Winner is responsible for all other costs and expenses in connection with the trip. Trip is subject to availability certain blackout dates apply. Trip must be taken by November 1, 1998.

4. **Eligibility.** Open to U.S. and Canadian residents (excluding residents of the province of Quebec) who are 18 at the time of entry. Employees of St. Martin's its parent, affilliate and subsidiaries, its and their directors, officers and agents and their immediate families or those living in the same household, are ineligible to enter. Potential Canadian winners will be required to correctly answer a time limited arithmetic skill question by mail. Void in Puerto Rico and wherever else prohibited by law.

5. **General Conditions:** Winner is responsible for all federal, state and local taxes. No subsitution or cash redemption of prize permitted by winner. Prize i not transferable. Acceptance of prize constitutes permission to use winner's and travel companion's name, photograph and likeness, for purpose of advertising and promotion without additional compensation or permission, unless prohibited by law. Travel companion must be over the age of 18 on date prize is awarded

6. All entries become the property of sponsor, and will not be returned. Winner agrees that St. Martin's, its parent, subsidiaries and affiliates, and its and the officers, directors, employees, agents, and promotion agencies shall not be liable for injuries or losses of any kind resulting from the acceptance or use of prize By participating in this sweepstakes, entrants agree to be bound by these officia rules and the decision of the judges, which are final in all respects.

7. For the name of the winner, available after October 1, 1997, send by November 1, 1997 a stamped, self-addressed envelope to Winner's List, THE PARADISE MAN Sweepstakes, St. Martin's Paperbacks, 175 Fifth Avenue, Suite 1615 New York, NY 10010-7848.